When Z

D1489025

"Peggy Darty takes a look at what happens when nice people get mixed up in murder. *When Zeffie Got a Clue* is an easy-going mystery with a satisfying resolution. The Gulf Coast setting is vivid, and I'm dying to visit the heroine's resale shop!"

> —JOANNA CARL, author of the Chocoholic Mysteries,
> including *The Chocolate Jewel Case* and *The Chocolate
> Bridal Bash*

"Murder and mayhem on the crystal shores of Florida's Emerald Coast. It's a setting to die for, and somebody does. Peggy Darty does it again. I dare you to put this one down."

> —JOYCE HOLLAND, president, Emerald Coast Writers

"Peggy Darty has created a setting that is both rich and memorable. Summer Breeze feels like the small southern town just around the bend in the road. Christy Castleman is the perfect sleuth next door, a clever mystery writer with a tender heart and real life struggles."

> —SHARON DUNN, author of the Bargain Hunter
> mysteries, including *Death of a Six-Foot Teddy Bear*

When Zeffie

Got a Clue

A Cozy Mystery by
Peggy Darty

WATERBROOK
P R E S S

WHEN ZEFFIE GOT A CLUE
PUBLISHED BY WATERBROOK PRESS
12265 Oracle Boulevard, Suite 200
Colorado Springs, Colorado 80921
A division of Random House Inc.

The characters and events in this book are fictional, and any resemblance to actual persons or events is coincidental.

ISBN 978-1-4000-7333-7

Library of Congress Cataloging-in-Publication Data
Darty, Peggy.
    When Zeffie got a clue : a cozy mystery / Peggy Darty. — 1st ed.
       p. cm.
    ISBN 978-1-4000-7333-7
1. Murder—Investigation—Fiction. 2. Florida—Fiction. I. Title.
    PS3554.A79W48 2008
    813'.54—dc22

                              2007038231

Printed in the United States of America
2008—First Edition

10 9 8 7 6 5 4 3 2 1

*To all the wonderful staff at WaterBrook Press who have
encouraged, supported, and believed in me throughout this series.
Thanks and God bless!*

Friday, November 10, 2006

"Do you want to buy a jewelry box?"

A little girl stood in the open door of I Saw It First, the shop that Christy Castleman and her aunt Bobbie Bodine had recently opened. Sunlight bounced off the girl's long blond hair, forming a gauzy halo that lit her face and exaggerated the wisdom and sorrow in her green eyes. She wore jeans too short, shoes too scuffed, and a sweatshirt too big for her, the living definition of the word *waif.*

Gripping a small brown chest with slim hands, she glanced back at the sign in the calico-framed window that read "We buy, We sell, We trade."

"Come in," Christy called. A breeze rolled in from the Gulf to ruffle the vintage parasols decorating a cast-iron hall tree beside the door.

The little girl stepped in, then hesitated. Christy could imagine a budding beauty, but today she read only sadness and fear in the girl's small, delicate features. Her face looked too pale for a child who should be out riding a bike or playing at the beach.

"My name's Christy Castleman." She crossed the polished wood floor to close the door. "What's your name?"

"Zeffie Adams," the girl answered in a clear, firm voice despite the indecision on her face.

"I'm glad to meet you, Zeffie."

Christy looked at the scarred mahogany jewelry box Zeffie hugged. It appeared similar to others she had seen at discount stores, though less valuable because of a tiny dark stain on its lid.

"Does the jewelry box belong to you?" Christy asked.

"Yes ma'am. I need to sell it." She lifted the lid. "It plays music."

Christy recognized an old, melancholy love song and bent to examine the box. The top compartment was made of three small sections for earrings or broaches. The red suede lining smelled musty and old, and in one corner the fabric had been Scotch-taped together. Two narrow drawers completed the box.

"Nice," Christy said, looking more closely at the little girl. She thought she had seen her with a thin, gray-haired woman at the market, but she didn't recognize the name Adams. "May I see it?"

Zeffie studied Christy's blue eyes, then slowly extended the box. Christy smiled, took the box, and headed toward the counter.

"Come on over," she called, glancing back. Zeffie looked her up and down.

Christy's small frame would not be intimidating, but ever since she'd begun her association with her long-lost aunt, she wore more jewelry, dressed with flair, and arranged shell or antique combs in her long brown hair. Zeffie's eyes followed the swish of Christy's skirt, a frothy autumn print, matched with a gold camisole and a crimson cardigan.

"I'd rather be wearing my jeans and sweatshirt," she said, winking at Zeffie.

"But your clothes are so pretty," Zeffie blurted, dropping her guard. Her gaze swept the shop again. "I like pretty things."

"So do I. What we like to do here is rework something that's lost its purpose and make it pretty again. Most of the things you see here are castoffs, things other people no longer wanted or tossed aside as broken. My aunt repainted and repaired them. See that cupboard?" She pointed to the red, crackled-paint cupboard, its door open to display a collection of mismatched plates and saucers. "She found it at a garage sale. It was an ugly brown, all scratched up, but she turned it into this."

She swiveled and pointed at another object. "And this teacart was once a baby carriage that had lost its wheels. My aunt replaced the wheels and converted it into a teacart."

Zeffie admired the English tea sets displayed on the glass top.

"And over here," Christy said, moving to stand near a scuffed trunk, "this came out of a warehouse near the docks. She rescued it, cleaned it up, and covered it with a quilt she purchased from a ninety-year-old quilter up in the Smokies."

Zeffie looked at the crowded mix of ladder-back chairs, settees, armoires, and bistro sets. "What did you make?" she asked.

"Well," Christy sighed, "you see the mirror framed with seashells? Those are shells I collected over the years and kept in a crystal vase at home. My aunt taught me to superglue them to the plain frame of the mirror. Other than that, I just wait on customers and run errands."

Zeffie continued to stare at the contents of the shop, her mouth open in awe. Christy smiled.

"Come on, I'll show you where she creates the magic." She led Zeffie to the wide workroom in the back of the store that held a pegboard of tools, shelves of fabric and upholstery, and a bookcase overflowing with books and magazines covering every topic from crafts to flea markets to antiques. There were at least a dozen how-to books stacked on the top shelf.

"My aunt is great at refinishing furniture or upholstering chairs." Christy pointed to a child's rocking chair with a torn cushion centered on the long worktable. "She's going to remove the torn fabric and cover the cushion with something new and pretty."

"Maybe she could do that to the lining of my jewelry box." Zeffie looked hopeful.

Christy knew Bobbie would have little use for the jewelry box, but this little girl had a refreshing dignity about her, rare in one so young. If she was determined to sell her jewelry box, then Christy would buy it for more than its worth.

"I love crafts," Zeffie said, staring at one of the craft magazines. "I'd like to learn how to make jewelry."

"Maybe we could start a crafts class for kids."

"That would be wonderful!" The sadness in Zeffie's eyes when she first entered the shop disappeared, but then her smile faded. "You probably can't do much with my jewelry box."

Christy stared at her, unsure why the little girl and her words tugged at her heart. She fought an impulse to reach out, take Zeffie in her arms, and ask how she could make the sadness go away.

"I have an idea," Christy said, leading the way back to the front room. "See that dress?" She pointed out the beaded cocktail dress displayed on a French chair.

Zeffie nodded, clasping her hands tightly before her. Christy wondered if she was fighting an impulse to touch the beads and sequins, which is what Christy would have done at Zeffie's age.

"Well," Christy continued, walking back to the counter where the jewelry box sat. "Maybe we can fix up your box and display some vintage jewelry in it on a table beside the dress. Do you have any jewelry in the drawers?"

"No. I moved it to a shoe box."

Christy dropped her gaze, trying to conceal a rush of pity. "Would you mind telling me why you're selling this? We always ask our customers that question."

Zeffie hesitated, twisting a corner of her sweatshirt. She stared at Christy, her green eyes glittering like emeralds beneath the glow of a Tiffany lamp.

"Grandma is sick. She has lots of doctor's bills. And that"—she looked at the jewelry box—"belonged to my mother. She left it the last time she took off."

"Oh. Where is she now?" Christy knew she was overstepping polite boundaries, but the little girl fascinated her.

"She died years ago." Zeffie spoke as though discussing a stranger.

"What about your dad?" Christy asked softly, pretending to study the jewelry box.

Zeffie shrugged. "We don't know who he is."

Christy felt a flush of embarrassment and wished she had not forced such terrible truths out of this troubled child. "Tell you what. I'll take the jewelry box, if you're sure you want to sell it." She glanced across the counter at Zeffie.

"I'm sure."

"You didn't say how much you want for it."

"Is five dollars too much?" Zeffie asked. Her small hands bunched into fists at her side.

"You're cheating yourself," Christy replied, opening the box's drawers to find more tattered lining. "Not all jewelry boxes play music, so that makes it worth at least ten dollars."

She closed the drawers and picked up the jewelry box to examine the bottom. The scuffed wood appeared to be real mahogany, not a cheap imitation. She had been wrong about it on first glance; at one time, many years ago, this had probably been a very nice jewelry box.

"And because the grain of wood is good," she continued optimistically, "that's worth another ten dollars." She looked at Zeffie. "How does twenty dollars sound?" She'd buy it herself if no one else wanted it.

Zeffie's hands relaxed at her sides, and a smile curved her lips, showing off the tiny dimple in her chin. "That sounds fine. That'll pay for Grandma's medicine."

Christy frowned. "Doesn't your grandmother have insurance?"

Zeffie shook her head, the ends of her long blond hair swinging about her face. "All she has is Medicare and some help from welfare."

"How old are you?" Christy asked, struck by the intelligence behind Zeffie's words.

"I'm eight."

"Are you in third grade? Mrs. Ragland's class?"

Zeffie nodded. "She's nice."

Christy removed two ten dollar bills from the cash register. "How about I send you home with some ice cream from the shop down the street? Maybe that would make your grandmother feel better."

Zeffie backed away. "I can't take things from strangers."

Christy walked around the counter and pressed the bills in Zeffie's small hand. "Please don't think of me as a stranger. I'd like to be your friend. I'm not married, and I don't have any children. I don't even have a niece."

Her admission captured Zeffie's attention. "Do you have a brother or sister?"

"A brother, Seth, but he's away at Florida State and not married. So you see, I don't have any little friends, and I'd like one. I hope you'll come back to see me, Zeffie. Do you live near here?"

She nodded but volunteered nothing. "I'll come back," she said. Her face lit up, and Christy caught her breath. The glow in Zeffie's eyes and the bright smile transformed her into a beauty. "I like it here."

"What about you, Zeffie? Do you have brothers and sisters?"

"No," she said, turning toward the door.

"I might know your grandmother," Christy said, keeping her tone light. "What's her name?"

"Molly Adams."

Christy shook her head. "I guess I don't know her. Thanks for stopping by, Zeffie. I'm usually here on Mondays and Fridays. If you come in after school on one of those days, we could walk down and get an ice cream cone, and I could show you what I've done with your jewelry box." She looked at it perched on the counter by the cash register. "I imagine I'll clean it up and put some new lining inside. It'll be pretty, don't you think?"

Zeffie nodded, casting a final glance at the box before thrusting the bills into her jeans pocket. "Thank you."

"You're welcome. If you need anything or have anything else to sell, let me know. I work at home part of the week. I'm a writer. Do you like to read?"

The green eyes lit up again. "I love to read! What kind of books do you write?"

"I write mysteries about pirates and treasure chests and stories I've heard over the years about Shipwreck Island."

Zeffie looked as though she'd just met a celebrity.

"Anyway, my home phone number is listed in the telephone directory, and my name is Christy Castleman. Can you remember that? Oh!" Christy rolled her eyes. "What a silly question. Of course you'll remember."

"Yes, I'll remember it, Miss Christy." She opened the door and rushed out. Christy walked to the window and watched her hurry along the sidewalk, turn down Fourth Street, and disappear around the corner.

Christy mentally reviewed the street of middle-income homes.

She knew everyone on that street, but she'd never heard of a Molly Adams. Two blocks down, a side street held smaller, cheaper rentals. She had a hunch this was where Zeffie and her grandmother lived.

She turned away from the window and walked back to sit behind the counter. It had been a busy day, since the area was celebrating Veterans Day weekend. The Florida panhandle was heavily populated with veterans, especially around Bay County, home to active-duty air force, navy, and coast guard personnel and retirees.

The schools and some of the businesses had closed today to honor Saturday's holiday, but she and Bobbie had been asked to remain open. A group of veterans' wives were hosting a luncheon and a shopping spree, and they wanted to browse through I Saw It First. The annual Holly Fair was also this weekend, and Bobbie had taken several wreaths to display at their booth. She called earlier to say there were hundreds of shoppers at the boardwalk inspecting the Christmas-themed fair.

Her aunt loved those events, but while Christy enjoyed shopping, she didn't care for large crowds. Between Veterans Weekend activities and the Holly Fair, minding the shop had been the easiest alternative for her.

She glanced at the clock, suddenly aware that for the first time all day she was alone in the shop. She sighed, then picked up her cold cup of tea and took a sip, her eyes on the jewelry box perched on the counter.

As soon as she'd finished off her tea, she picked up the box and took it back to the workroom. She placed it on the worktable and picked up a lemon oilcloth. She began to rub the mahogany box, smiling to herself as the grain of the wood responded with a shine.

She laid the rag aside and studied the huge array of tools on the pegboard, most of which baffled her. Unlike her aunt, she was clumsy with tools and made herself useful by knowing everyone in the area and helping sell some of the unique items in their shop. She'd seen her aunt use an X-Acto knife to remove linings before, so she reached for one. She couldn't live with the soiled, musty-smelling fabric inside the drawers.

Lifting the lid, she positioned the knife at the edge of the lining and pried it away from the wood. It peeled away in chunks, but one tiny corner held stubbornly. Christy yanked harder, and the stained piece of cloth popped out. The top drawer was even tougher. But the lining in the bottom drawer came away easily, revealing a thin sheet of paper, yellow with age, lying flat against the wood. She picked up the worn paper, noting the name of a prominent jewelry store in Panama City stamped at the top, and realized it was a jewelry appraisal. On the first line she read the name *Annabell Strickland*.

Christy frowned at the familiar name, her heartbeat accelerating as her eyes moved to the next line. When she read the rural address in the community where her grandmother lived, she stared in shock.

Adjacent to Granny Castleman's farm was Deerfield, the Strickland estate. Mrs. Annabell Strickland, a collector of expensive jewelry, had died of a heart attack in 1998. Soon afterward, her son Kirby had been murdered during a robbery at the Strickland mansion. The criminal who took the jewelry and Kirby's life had never been caught.

The paper fluttered in Christy's shaking hand, and she dropped it on the table, her mind spinning.

Whenever she thought of Kirby Strickland, she recalled that hot July Fourth in 1987 when she and Seth had visited Granny. She was eleven years old and overconfident of her new skill as a swimmer after a few lessons in summer day camp. Granny had taken them to a community picnic at the lake where everyone was swimming. Eager to show off what she had learned, she dove into the cool water.

Her confidence abandoned her with the same speed as her ability to float, and she began to flounder. When she went under the second time, gulping water, arms flailing, she felt panic overwhelm her, as cold and terrifying as the dark water.

Then, in the next second, strong arms enveloped her, lifting her to the surface. She blinked through wet lashes and focused on the kind blue eyes of Kirby Strickland. He smiled at her as his dark hair dripped lake water onto his tan shoulders.

"Hey, Christy," he said. "Let's go to shore." With a protective arm around her shoulders, he steered her to safe ground. Having saved her life, he then salvaged her wounded pride by telling everyone she'd been doing okay and he'd just helped her a little.

Later, wrapped in a towel, her teeth chattering, Christy stared in adoration at seventeen-year-old Kirby, starting his senior year of high school. He grew taller in her mind's eye, settling into the role of a hero as she replayed over and over how he had saved her. From that day on, she'd had a huge crush on him. In dreamy moments during her adolescence, she imagined being a sophisticated senior, attending football games and parties with Kirby, riding beside him in his white convertible. She swore that someday she'd do something to repay him, but that day never came.

Until now.

Christy stared at the appraisal slip, swallowing a rush of tears. It was too late to save Kirby, but she could help find the monster who had robbed him, not just of heirloom jewels, but of his most precious gift—his life.

Tears blurred the small jewelry box as she turned to stare at it, struck dumb by the possibility of what she faced. Fresh horror flooded her senses, as cold and stark as the lake water so many years ago.

Whose blood-stained hands had touched this jewelry box? And how had it ended up in little Zeffie's arms?

2

Christy tried to decide what to do. First, she should verify the jewelry box came from the home of Zeffie's grandmother. After all, she didn't know the child, even though she had seemed convincing.

She hurried to the desk and picked up the new phone directory. Flipping pages with fingers clumsy from nerves, she found M. Adams listed. She hesitated for a moment, then decided to call.

The voice of an older woman answered. "Hello."

"Is this Molly Adams?" Christy inquired.

"Yes. Who's calling?" She sounded tired and weak.

"This is Christy Castleman at I Saw It First, a shop on—"

"I know. My granddaughter was just there."

Christy hesitated. "It's our policy at the shop to verify a sale when dealing with a minor. Does the jewelry box belong to you?"

A heavy sigh followed the question. "It belonged to my daughter April, who died four years ago. I think she bought it at a garage sale."

"I see," Christy replied. "Well, I'm sorry to have troubled you. Thanks for letting me know you approve of the sale."

"That old jewelry box is of little value to us. Zeffie was just trying to do something nice for me. And by the way, you were very generous."

"My pleasure," Christy replied. "Zeffie is a delightful little girl. And I certainly hope you feel better soon."

There was a momentary pause. "Thank you."

Christy said good-bye and hung up, wondering what to do next.

She picked up the phone and dialed her father's cell phone. "Hi. Where are you?" she asked as soon as he answered. A horn beeped in the background.

"Just left the church. Shame on you!"

"Excuse me?"

He laughed. "When I reached for my cell, I strayed over the yellow line and got too close to a truck with an impolite driver. I didn't appreciate the hand signal he gave me."

"Well, he obviously doesn't know you're the pastor of Community Church." Her heart was too heavy for jokes. "Dad, how many Annabell Stricklands have you known?"

He hesitated for a second. When he replied his tone had changed from lighthearted to grave. "Only one. She married my best friend Paul and died years ago, but you know that already. The tragedy with Kirby still bothers me."

Christy paced the shop, the handset pressed against her ear. "I remember when Seth and I spent the weekend with Granny as children, we'd often end up at the Strickland farm. There was always an ice cream supper or a game of tennis."

"It almost killed Annabell when Paul died of liver cancer at forty-nine." Grant sighed. "Ellen and Kirby were still in high school. Every time Kirby went on that football field, he'd look up at the sky before the game began. He always believed his dad was watching. Then it was January 1998, I think, when Annabell died of a massive heart attack. About two months later…well, you know what happened to Kirby. The tragedies in that family still torment me. But why are you asking?"

"A little girl brought a jewelry box into the shop this afternoon." She hesitated. If she told him everything, he would insist she call Bob Arnold, the deputy sheriff who ran Summer Breeze here in Bay County, and he'd pass everything on to the authorities in Washington County, where the murder took place. She wasn't ready for that.

"How does this connect to Annabell?" her father asked, interrupting her thoughts.

"I'm…not sure. What are you and Mom doing tonight?"

He paused. "I forget how quick you bounce from one subject to another. The way Tommy Hatfield's ball bounces from the yard to the street." She heard a screech of brakes and the distant words of her father. "Tommy, you need to be careful with your ball this time of day when folks are coming home."

She could picture his dark head stuck out the car window, a gentle smile on his face despite the calm warning.

"Uh, where were we?" he asked.

"What are you and Mom doing tonight?"

"I'm barbecuing chicken since your mom is working at the Holly Fair. She promised to be home by five thirty. Want to join us?"

Christy's pacing ended before the front window. The November afternoon was turning gray, and soon streetlights would halo the narrow street of shops. The days were growing shorter now, and her boyfriend, Dan Brockman, worked late on the subdivision he was developing.

"I'm waiting on Dan," she told her father. She buttoned her crimson cardigan, knowing they'd be grilling outside. "Mind if he joins us?"

"Not at all! We'd love to have you two for dinner. It'll just be chicken, bread, and a salad your mom will whip up when she gets home."

"Wow, I've lucked into a favorite meal." She tried to lighten her tone but already her mind, like her body, was turning toward the jewelry box in the back room. "Can I pick up anything at the grocery?"

"Nah, you know me and my barbecuing. I always cook extra. I'm turning into the driveway," he said, "so I'll get busy." She could hear the slam of his car door as he got out of his car.

"Love you," she said and hung up.

Christy placed her elbows on the counter and stared into space, thinking. She had been living in Colorado the year Kirby was killed, but she'd still been devastated when the news reached her. She'd kept up with Kirby over the years and knew he'd already begun to win awards for his commercial Web site designs.

Everyone loved kind and affable Kirby, but it was a Florida State cheerleader who captured his heart. Kirby asked Julie Clark to marry him and everyone from Panama City to Tallahassee had been caught up in the romantic whirlwind preceding their summer wedding. If one didn't attend one of the many celebratory parties, one read about them in the newspaper or heard the details over the back fence.

The front door flew open, jolting Christy back to reality.

Her aunt Bobbie blew in with the breeze, chandelier earrings dangling from her small ears, rhinestones twinkling in the eyes of the Santa Claus whose face centered her red sweatshirt. Another tiny Santa graced the back pocket of her jeans.

"Hey, sweetie." Bobbie wiggled her jeweled fingers in a little wave as she rushed across the shop. As usual, she tottered on three-inch heels—red pumps today—to increase her height of five feet.

"How'd it go at the fair?"

"Wonderful. I think I added some new clients to our list. I have to change clothes," she called over her shoulder as she grabbed an outfit from a closet and disappeared into the dressing room.

The front door opened, and Jack Watson sauntered in, wearing dress pants and a polo shirt.

Blue eyes framed by sun-crinkled skin and a muscular body typed Jack as ruggedly handsome. Before he met Bobbie, he'd been living like a hermit on the twenty acres he owned near Rainbow Bay. Life lost its luster for Jack after his wife died, followed by the death of his only son ten years later. He had found solace and an income from his favorite hobby—fishing.

Christy knew Jack hadn't expected to find love again, but when Bobbie Bodine descended on Summer Breeze like a rainbow after the rain, Jack had decided to come out and play.

"How's my favorite girl?" he asked, giving Christy a hug and a nice whiff of aftershave.

"Don't exclude me," Bobbie called, cracking the door of the dressing room.

"You're more than my favorite girl," he yelled back. "You're the woman I intend to marry."

Christy smiled, feeling her tense shoulders relax for the first time since she stumbled across the appraisal.

"So where are you headed?" she asked, as Bobbie emerged from the dressing room. Having changed to black slacks and a white satin blouse, her aunt fumbled under the counter for her black boots.

"We're going over to Baytown to check out that new blues club," Bobbie replied, thrusting her feet into the boots.

"But first we're stopping for fried catfish," Jack said, daring Christy with his eyes.

She had ceased teasing him about his fondness for fried foods and anything generally unhealthy, knowing she'd never convince him to give it up. Jack Watson had always done what he pleased, until he met Bobbie Bodine. He made concessions now.

"Bobbie, you won't be able to change his eating habits," Christy said, "but I have to give you credit for inspiring him to dress like a guy worthy of you."

"But am I worthy of him?" Bobbie asked in wide-eyed innocence, linking her arm through his.

"Hey, you want to join us?" Jack asked. "You can sit across from me and giggle while I pick the catfish bones out of my teeth."

"As tempting as that sounds, no, thank you. Dad's barbecuing, and I've already put mine and Dan's name on the guest list. Or on the grill."

Bobbie rushed up to give Christy a hug. "I'm so glad you two are together again."

"Me too." She and Dan had met in February of 2005, and love came quickly. Too quickly. They decided to slow down, to be sure of one another before they made a commitment. That decision proved to have been a good idea and took the mounting tension out of their relationship. She no longer anticipated a proposal from Dan each time they were together. Dan, on the other hand, seemed ready to offer that proposal.

"Yeah, kid. I think you two are more in love than ever," Jack teased.

Christy nodded. "We are."

"Okay, I'm ready," Bobbie called, grabbing her purse.

Christy remembered the jewelry box. "Jack," she called as he headed for the door. "Do you remember hearing about the Kirby Strickland murder?"

He stopped and turned toward her, the smile disappearing from his face. "Sure do. Didn't know Kirby, but a friend of mine, Willie Pitt, catered the party at Deerfield the day Kirby was killed. The investigators put him high on their suspect list in the beginning. When his alibi checked out, they quit hounding him, but the publicity killed his business. He moved to Mexico Beach and opened a café. I go down and eat with him couple of times a month." He frowned. "Why do you ask?"

Christy looked from him to Bobbie. "Let me show you something."

"Oops, look at the time." Bobbie pointed to the cuckoo clock. "Can it wait, Christy? Jack and I promised to pick up Mary and Phil five minutes ago."

Jack winked. "Gotta go. There must be an extra ten thousand people on the coast this weekend. We'll have a long wait at the restaurant if we don't hurry."

"Sure," Christy said. "You two go on."

"We'll talk later, Toots." Jack gave her his famous wink.

They bounded out the front door like teenagers off for a hot night on the town. Christy shook her head, amazed and grateful that two fifty-something people, survivors of trauma and heartbreak, had found the happiness they deserved. The discussion about the jewelry box could wait since neither knew the Stricklands, but she'd make sure to bring it up the next time she saw Jack. She wanted to hear more about Willie Pitt.

On her own again, Christy decided to call Ellen Strickland Brown and tell her about the box and the appraisal slip. She could describe the box and let Ellen decide whether or not to go to the police.

She flipped through the telephone directory until she found Ellen and Vince Brown's telephone number. She dialed, but after four rings, the answering machine picked up. She took a deep breath, waiting for the tone so she could leave a message.

"Hi, Ellen. This is Christy Castleman. I'm Elsa Castleman's granddaughter. I know it's been years, but something came up this afternoon I'd like to discuss with you." Maybe she shouldn't go into details over the phone. "I'm thinking of driving up to Granny's tomorrow. If you're going to be home, I'd like to drop by whenever it's convenient." She left her home phone number as well as the shop's. As she hung up, she heard the roar of Dan's new sports car.

She turned toward the front window, smiling as the sleek black car wheeled into the curb. After reaching for keys and purse, she began to turn out lights. She tucked the appraisal in the bottom drawer of the jewelry box and hugged it against her, as little Zeffie had done.

As Dan entered, Christy took in his broad shoulders and trim physique. He had changed from work clothes to casual wear, and when he looked her over, he whistled. "You look great."

"Thanks. So do you."

A warm kiss followed, and Dan lingered, his arms around her. "We don't have to be in a hurry," he teased.

She sighed, reluctantly stepping out of his embrace. "Actually, we do. I hope you don't mind, but I agreed to join my parents for a cookout. Dad's a stickler for being on time."

"Okay." His blue eyes centered on the small jewelry box. "Are you taking that home?"

"Yeah, but first I wanted to show it to Dad." An idea struck her. "Listen, do you want to drive up to Granny's with me in the morning?"

"I can't. I'm scheduled for lunch with a new client, and I don't want to cancel this late. He'll only be here for the weekend. His wife's an artist, and she's one of the vendors at the fair this weekend."

Christy nodded. "I understand. And I'm not sure I'm going, anyway. But tomorrow night—"

"Tomorrow night?" he teased, pulling her closer.

"Hey, we'd better get going," she said, stepping out of his arms.

Dan sighed. "Are we still watching the Alaska DVD at your place later?"

They were considering accompanying the church singles class on a summer cruise to Alaska and were both excited about the idea.

"Sure. But first we get to dine on some great barbecued chicken. I promise not to keep us there too long."

"I like your parents, but I like being alone with you even more."

3

Grant, what makes your barbecued chicken the best there is?" Dan asked as he and Christy approached her parents' back patio.

Grant Castleman sat in a deck chair, watching the charcoal turn gray in the black belly of the grill. "Don't know that mine is the best, but I can show you how I do it. Pull up a chair."

"Watch carefully, Dan," Christy said. "Dad doesn't have a recipe."

She smiled, her gaze moving from one man to the other. At fifty-two, her father remained fit and trim with a daily regimen of walking or golfing. Soft brown eyes and a quick smile reflected his joy for life.

She looked back at Dan, the epitome of tall, dark, and handsome. Intelligence, wit, and integrity radiated from him, and these traits, like a lighthouse on a foggy night, had been a beacon, drawing her in.

"Someone open the door," Beth Castleman called, balancing two mugs.

Christy rushed over to open the screen door for her mother.

"I left one for you on the counter," Beth said, as Christy peered into the mugs of hot cocoa topped with whipped cream. "Here guys! A reward for your hard work."

Christy's eyes lingered on her mother, more petite than Christy, with short, pale blond hair and small, even features. The years had added a few wrinkles to her brow, and smile lines creased her cheeks, but she had aged gracefully.

"So did you have a busy day?" Christy asked.

"Incredible." Beth shook her head. "I'm glad we planned on Grant barbecuing."

She handed her husband a mug, then turned to Dan, who stood to give her a hug before accepting his hot drink.

"You and Grant could take this show on the road," Dan said. "He wins first place for barbecued chicken, and you get the blue ribbon for hot cocoa."

Beth laughed. "I know it seems like an odd combination, but it's a perfect autumn night, and hot cocoa sounded better than my usual lemonade." She turned to Grant. "How soon should I put the potatoes in the microwave?"

Grant pursed his lips as he studied the large chicken halves. "Maybe an hour. That'll give you time to show Christy how to make your special salad dressing while I teach Dan how I barbecue chicken."

Dan glanced at the small jar of water and the covered container near the grill. "You have quite an operation here. Tell me how you do it."

"For starters, the fire has to be the right temperature—not too hot, because the chicken has to be cooked slowly. And I always buy the same size chicken breasts for even cooking." He picked up a stainless-steel grilling fork and speared a piece of chicken from the metal tray, placing it skin side down on the grill.

"What's that?" Dan asked, indicating the small pieces of dark wood Grant withdrew from the covered container and tossed onto the charcoal.

"Hickory chips soaked in water. Keeps the wood from burning too fast and produces a heavy smoke to accent the flavor in the chicken." He pulled down the lid of the grill to smother the heat, then leaned back in his chair.

Christy, who had fidgeted with her cocoa mug during her father's explanation, straightened in her chair. She wanted to get to the matter she had come to discuss.

"Dad, a little girl came into the shop to sell an old jewelry box. She looked like she needed money, and she mentioned her grandmother was sick—"

Dan reached for her hand. "And you're a soft touch."

Christy smiled. "Depends who's touching. And I have more to tell."

"Does it have anything to do with the jewelry box you shoved in the back seat of the car?" Dan asked.

"Would you get it, please?"

"I was just getting comfortable," he complained, but his pretense was obvious and she knew he didn't mind.

As Dan crossed the lawn, her father turned to face her.

"I can see you have something on your mind," he said. "I assume it involves Annabell Strickland, since you asked about her earlier."

"Maybe. What happened after Kirby was killed?" Christy asked.

Grant shook his head and stared at the smoke curling up from the grill. "A lot of investigation, a lot of false hope, and years of dead-end leads."

"So now it's a cold case," Christy summarized. "I've always felt indebted to Kirby for saving my life when I had more nerve than sense."

"We were all indebted to him."

"Yeah. Granny wanted me to set my sights on him when I was eighteen and he was graduating with his MBA." She grinned. "He was always yanking my ponytail and teasing me when Seth and I went to visit. He was such a nice guy." The grin faded, replaced by a feeling of sadness.

"I know. There's been a lot of heartache in that family, beginning with the death of Paul." Her dad shook his dark head. "I couldn't believe it when he was diagnosed with cancer at such a young age."

She glanced at the kitchen window that framed her mother's face as she hummed and rinsed lettuce leaves. Christy was glad her mother was inside, as she preferred not to involve her in this discussion. The Castlemans had finally settled back into their peaceful lives. Last month's trauma with Beth's sister Bobbie was difficult for everyone, but now the family had united again. The only member missing from the family circle was her younger brother, Seth, who seemed to be heading in the right direction, having returned to college with a definite purpose and a nice scholarship. Her parents' ruffled feathers were finally settling after Seth's years of rebellion.

"How has Ellen been? We went to her wedding…" She paused, thinking back. "Ten years ago?"

Grant nodded. "Something like that."

"What do you think of her husband? I only saw him the one time at the wedding."

"Seems like a nice guy. He comes from a good middle-class background, though Annabell hoped for an attorney or future governor for a son-in-law," Grant said, smiling so that Christy understood his statement was humorously factual rather than critical. "Vince was working in a bank in Panama City, and Ellen was teaching fifth- and sixth-grade math when Kirby was killed."

Christy fixed her eyes on her father as he leaned back, stretching his legs before him and crossing his feet at the ankles.

"Vince took over Strickland Timber and management of the farm," he continued. "They eventually moved to Deerfield to live in the house. They have two little boys now."

Christy placed her mug of cocoa on the patio table as Dan returned and handed her the jewelry box. She opened the bottom drawer. "As I said, a little girl brought this in today. Look what I found inside it."

As she withdrew the slip of paper from the bottom drawer, she told herself she would not be involved in…whatever this meant. She just wanted to show the appraisal slip to her dad before turning it over to the authorities.

While the spacious yard dissolved into pools of darkness, the floodlight at the corner of the house illuminated the patio, providing ample light for barbecuing. Or for reading a slip of paper that could thrust everyone into another mystery.

She laid the appraisal on the patio table, smoothing the edges as Dan and Grant peered over her shoulder. "I found this when I ripped out the old lining in the bottom drawer. Apparently, it had been tucked away for safekeeping."

As she waited for Dan and her father to read the appraisal slip, it seemed to Christy that once again a mysterious circumstance had been tossed in her lap. Her latest mystery novel would soon be published, but two murders in quiet Summer Breeze had rivaled any fiction she could dream up. In both cases, she became so involved in the investigation that she ended up catching the unlikely criminals herself.

Dan whistled. "The jewelry listed here totals close to fifty grand."

Grant frowned. "That's Annabell's address for sure, and she had a passion for expensive jewelry." He turned curious eyes to Christy. "What was that little girl doing with this box? Why did she bring it to you?"

"She brought it into the shop to see if we wanted to buy it. She told me she needed money to help her grandmother pay medical bills."

"Who's the grandmother?" Grant asked, glancing at the jewelry box that now shone and gave off the pleasing scent of lemon oil.

"Molly Adams. I called her on the excuse of needing to verify a sale from a minor. Everything Zeffie told me was true. The jewelry box belonged to her mother, who bought it at a yard sale. She died several years ago."

Grant stared at Christy. "What are you going to do with this? You're a good mystery writer, but I don't want you playing detective again. I mean it."

From his stern frown, she had no doubt he meant what he said. "I don't have to play detective, Dad, but I can assure you I'm going to help the family. I simply want Ellen to see the jewelry box and verify whether it belonged to her mother. She'll know if it was taken during the robbery. I owe them that much, and I certainly owe something to Kirby."

Christy turned to Dan, who looked confused by her statements. She explained how Kirby had saved her from drowning as a child, then turned back to her father.

"Okay," Grant conceded, "but then let the authorities handle it."

Christy hesitated. "Since I'm going to visit Granny in the morning, I thought I would take the jewelry box by Ellen's house."

Her dad looked suspicious. With all the interesting activities around the area and huge late-season sales everywhere, he could guess her real motive for heading up to Granny's house.

"Christy, I thought you wanted to help make the salad dressing," Beth called from the back door.

Christy returned the appraisal slip to the bottom drawer of the jewelry box and handed it to Dan, nodding toward the car. She hopped up from her chair. "I do want to help."

She had told her father all he needed to know.

❧

By the time she got home, Christy's father had told her mother enough about the jewelry box to warrant a quick phone call. "Christy, stay out of this. I'm going to die of a stroke if you don't keep yourself out of these dangerous investigations."

"Relax, Mom," Christy said. "I'm just trying to do the right thing. Look, I need to go. Dan and I are about to watch a DVD on Alaska."

She hung up the kitchen phone and turned to Dan, who was spooning coffee grounds into the coffee maker. "I'd better call Aunt Bobbie and tell her about the jewelry box," she said. "Otherwise, she'll hear it from Mom."

"Well, you'd better call her on her cell. You know she's with Jack."

Christy hesitated. "Maybe I should wait."

"I'd try her now," Dan advised, flipping the switch on the coffee maker.

Her fingers flew over the familiar numbers, and to her surprise, Bobbie answered on the second ring. "Got a minute?" Christy asked.

"Actually, I'm in the ladies' room, but yes, I have a minute. What's up?"

Christy went through the story of what she had found and what her father had told her. She noticed the message light on her answering machine blinking as she talked and figured Ellen had called her back.

"Wow!" Bobbie yelled in her ear. "This is going to get interesting."

"I just wanted you to know in case anyone appears at the shop asking questions. I'll check with you tomorrow. Have a good evening."

"I'll have a good evening with Jack, but I'm still concerned about what you just told me."

"You have nothing to worry about," Christy said, her voice assuming a more lighthearted tone than she felt when she thought about the appraisal slip ending up in her hands.

They said their good-byes, and she hung up.

"Come on." Dan reached for her hand. "Let's put that DVD in. You need to get your mind on something pleasant."

Just being with you is a pleasure, she thought, tucking her hand in his.

4

Saturday

Christy took extra care styling her long brown hair, draping some blond-brown strands around her face, then pulling the rest back at her nape to clip with a gold barrette. She rarely wore more than mascara and lip gloss, but today she applied a light coat of foundation, then slipped into a pair of black-striped pants and a white shirt with three-quarter sleeves, showing off the gold bangle Dan had given her for her birthday. Her outfit seemed right for a casual visit to see Ellen Brown at Deerfield, where casual had been the mode of dress throughout her lifetime of visiting Granny and her neighbors.

She lifted the jewelry box from the kitchen counter and thrust her arm through the strap of her shoulder bag, checking the side pocket for her car keys and cell phone. She turned the lock on the kitchen door, then crossed the screened-in porch and stepped out into the sunny morning. The small thermometer by the back door read 72 degrees.

Christy unlocked her SUV with the remote on her key chain. She'd recently traded in her convertible in an attempt to be practical, as she needed a larger, more spacious vehicle since going into business with her aunt. She rarely left a flea market or estate sale empty handed. Still, she missed her convertible on sunny days when she would have put the top down and enjoyed Florida's gift of sunshine and Gulf breezes.

Glancing over her shoulder as she backed out of the driveway, she recalled Ellen's message.

"Christy, the boys have soccer practice first thing, but I should be back around ten in the morning. Other than that, we'll be here all day. The Gators are playing South Carolina on TV, and since Vince and I are avid Gator fans, we'll be watching the game. Stop by anytime you wish."

Christy knew from her conversations with Granny that Ellen had met Vince at the University of Florida. Her invitation was friendly enough, but the reserve that had always been typical of Ellen remained in her tone.

It was only eight o' clock on Saturday morning, but the traffic was already picking up in anticipation of a busy day. Christy decided to take the road leading past the beach to enjoy the view before she hit the highway into Panama City.

Pristine white beaches paralleled the Gulf of Mexico, where sun sparkles winked like diamonds. She spotted several fishing boats in the emerald waters closer to shore, and out on the horizon, where the water changed from emerald to deep blue, a lone sailboat drifted. A great way to start the day, she thought, hoping her mission would leave her feeling as great as she now felt but unable to quell her doubts.

Then she thought of Kirby and knew why she was making this trip. In the big picture, what was really important? Finding his killer. She glanced at the innocent-looking jewelry box lying on the passenger seat. Maybe Zeffie had given her an important clue.

She drove on autopilot, as she often did, covering huge distances out of habit and then surprising herself when she reached her destination. She skirted the suburbs of Panama City, turning onto the highway that led north. Although she focused on the busy highway, her thoughts moved with her vehicle to the rural countryside where her grandparents had lived most of their lives on the land her grandfather inherited. They had loved farm life. After her grandfather died, Granny refused to sell the farm and move closer to her adult children, Grant and Aunt Dianna, who lived in Summer Breeze.

"This is my home," Granny argued, "and it will always be yours to come back to." She hadn't mentioned the word *inherit,* but this was part of her reason for keeping the farm. Granny thought her children and grandchildren needed the stability of a lifestyle that had changed little over the years. Everyone appreciated her reasoning, and Christy and Seth had loved going to the farm during summers and long weekends.

Part of their fun included the occasional visit to the adjoining thousand acres known as Deerfield. The huge estate was a plantation in the 1800s, and despite the Civil War and the Depression, the Strickland family had managed to hang on to the land, passing it from one generation to the next. In the last twenty years, some of the acreage had been leased out to small cotton farmers, but for two centuries, dogs and cats, deer and horses had roamed the fields and meadows, and half the county gathered there for special occasions.

Christy glanced at the speedometer, surprised she hadn't been given a ticket somewhere along the way, because she was making the trip in record time. She crossed the county line and passed the fields that once produced cotton but now held real estate signs, bowing to progress as prosperity stretched north. Country homes with wide front porches and rocking chairs still dominated the view, however, as the highway wound around curves, then straightened, and she spotted Seminole Road.

The turnoff to Deerfield was only a mile up Seminole Road, and now she was looking at the familiar white fences that enclosed the Deerfield land. She followed the road, winding past huge live oaks and a green pasture where half a dozen horses grazed. The long drive-way dipped and swayed, then opened up before the sprawling brick mansion that dominated the landscape.

It was a typical antebellum home, carefully preserved, with four round columns rising past the upper gallery and ending beneath an obviously new roof. The house had been renovated several times over the years, and Christy suspected the neat white columns and porch rails got an annual dose of paint. Parking in the circle drive directly in front of the house, she looked at the wide steps leading to the huge porch filled with white wicker chairs and a matching wicker love seat.

The smell of burning leaves drifted through the open window of her car, testimony to late fall, sweeping her memory back to football games and chili suppers and the fresh country air. Christy felt a sudden craving for a slice of Granny's fried apple pie.

As she got out of the car, she spotted Vince Brown in the side yard, raking leaves into a pile. A baseball cap sat on his large head, balancing his broad, six-foot-four frame. Seeing her car, he placed the rake against the trunk of an oak and removed his work gloves.

Christy glanced at the jewelry box and decided to leave it on the front seat for now. She hopped out of the car, hurrying across the smooth concrete driveway to the lush grass in the side yard.

"Don't let me interrupt a guy who actually does yard work on Saturday!" she called.

"Sounds crazy to some people, but I enjoy yard work," he responded. "It helps clear the cobwebs out of my brain."

Christy smiled at the big man dressed in old jeans and a T-shirt. Since she'd last seen him, he had gained about ten pounds, but he carried it well. His hair—dark red, but not dark enough to be called auburn—was close cropped beneath his cap. His broad cheeks held only a smattering of freckles, and the nose and lips were full, but his features suited his face. The clear gray eyes that looked her over held the no-nonsense expression that defined Vince Brown. Although she didn't know him well, her first impression remained the same. Solid. Reliable. Maybe a fraction too serious for her taste, but it was Ellen who had married him.

"Ellen and the boys should be home soon, though with that crew you never know." The humor faded from his face. "Ellen told me you wanted to talk to her about something."

Christy hesitated. She wanted to speak to Ellen and Vince at the same time, but since she didn't know how long Ellen would be, she decided to get Vince's reaction first. She gave him a brief version of buying the jewelry box and discovering the appraisal slip, keeping to the facts. She tried to approach people on their own terms, and he was a bottom-line guy.

"I wanted Ellen to examine the box and decide whether it belonged to her mother. Dad thinks I should call our deputy sheriff, but I felt I should talk with Ellen first."

Vince stared at her, obviously trying to absorb everything she had told him.

"I don't know a lot about the...tragedy," Christy continued. "I was in Colorado in 1998. It happened in March, right?"

Vince nodded, his eyes rising above her head, staring off into the past. "March seventh. A day none of us will ever forget. Kirby hosted a barbecue here that Saturday, a ten-year reunion of his high-school football team. They were in the state play-offs their senior year. That evening he planned to drive to Tallahassee for dinner with the Clarks." He looked at Christy. "He was engaged to Julie Clark at the time."

Christy nodded as she listened intently to his deep voice. The air around them seemed to grow still, broken only by the distant crackle of burning leaves. She felt as though the years were rolling backwards, taking her with them as Vince spoke.

"Kirby left the house at five that afternoon. He called Julie just before he left home. At 5:12 she called him on his cell phone and asked him to bring an invitation list she'd left here the week before when they were planning a party. Kirby told her he was only ten minutes from home and he'd go back for the list and call her along the way.

"He never called back. Julie called his cell phone at 5:45 and got his voice mail. She called him again at 6:00, and she tried the house a couple of times. No answer. Finally, when he was a couple of hours late without returning any of her phone calls, Julie called our apartment. Ellen was baby-sitting for a friend, but I offered to check on him.

"I called the sheriff to see if any accidents had been reported in the area, but there were none. I called the hospital, but Kirby wasn't there. He tended to be forgetful, and I suspected he'd failed to charge the battery on his cell and was just running later than planned. Still, I drove out here to check on things."

Vince closed his eyes, and his pale lashes fluttered, as though the memory hammered his brain. "His car was parked out front. The front door was half open, and the lights in the office and hallway were on. I found him lying in a pool of blood in the hall. The gun he kept in his desk drawer was on the floor beside him."

He swallowed hard, caught a breath, and continued. "I ran to the phone and called 911, then waited out in the yard. I couldn't bear to be in the house, and I didn't know how I could possibly tell Ellen—" He broke off, his eyes as hazy as the smoke curling from the dead leaves. "She still grieved her mother's death from a few months before."

He blinked and looked away. "The estate was to be settled that next week, so all of Annabell's jewelry was still in the house. Her dresser drawers and closet had been ransacked, and the jewelry box was gone. A vase lay smashed on the floor, so the intruder must have knocked it over in his haste to get out. The theory was that Kirby surprised the burglar when he came back for the list, and the burglar killed him and ran out the back door."

He shook his head. "Ellen's never been the same. Ever since it happened, she's been in overdrive, like if she stays busy every minute of every day, she won't feel the pain. I try to slow her down, but she cranks right back up, going in a frenzy until she makes herself sick."

He spoke with great effort, and Christy hated reminding him of the nightmare. He looked as though the memory had drained all the energy from his body, and he took a step back and leaned against the broad trunk of an oak.

A gray Mercedes appeared in the driveway and parked behind Christy's car.

"This is going to upset Ellen," Vince said, as he and Christy watched the car doors fly open and two boys tumble out.

As Ellen emerged from the car and pulled a sack of groceries from the trunk, Christy studied her carefully. While Vince had gained weight, Ellen's five-foot-eight frame seemed to have shrunk, and she was so thin that her cheeks looked gaunt, her nose sharp, her lips little more than a thin line. The blond hair she had always worn long had been cut short on the sides and back and spiked on top. In the past, her long billowing hair had softened her face, but this style added a severity to her lean features. She wore navy designer jeans and an oversized white shirt. Her long feet, clad in running shoes, moved quickly around the Mercedes as she slammed her door and called instructions to the boys. She rushed past Christy's car, giving it a backward glance as she set the bag of groceries on the porch.

"Hi, Ellen," Christy called, stepping forward to greet her.

"Christy Castleman! It's been ages. I enjoy your books, and I see your grandmother often. Boys!" She whirled. "Come over here for a minute. This is Luke and Parker," she said to Christy, indicating the two young redheads, who looked close in age.

"Hi, guys," Christy said, fascinated by their shiny red hair, one a shade darker than the other. They greeted Christy politely, then turned to their mother, waiting to be dismissed.

"Okay, you can get to the video games now," Ellen said. They shot up the broad front steps and disappeared into the house. Ellen smiled at Vince as he walked up to stand beside her.

"Cute boys," Christy said. Remembering the equestrian shows and barrel races that had once been a major part of Ellen's life, she asked, "Do you still work with horses?"

Ellen shook her head, thrusting her hands in the back pockets of her jeans. She turned and looked toward the empty green meadow paralleling the house. "I sold most of my horses. We keep a few to ride for enjoyment, but with the boys, I don't have the time…"

Her voice trailed off, and she turned back to face Christy, obviously wondering what she wanted to discuss. Christy began to frame the words in her mind, but Vince spared her the awkward opening.

"Honey, Christy has something important to tell us concerning the jewelry box taken the night of the robbery."

Ellen gasped and stared at Christy, who repeated the story she had just told Vince.

"An appraisal slip with Mother's name on it?" Ellen's normally high-pitched voice rose to a screech, and Christy tried not to wince.

She walked to her SUV and opened the door on the passenger side to retrieve the jewelry box. She held it out to Ellen, whose tanned face looked pale. The slim nose twitched, and her thin lips tightened as she grabbed the jewelry box, staring at its lid.

"The stain—the grape-juice stain." She glanced at Vince. "Mother spilled her grape juice on the top of the jewelry box one morning." Her fingers trembled as she gently lifted the lid and the love song began to play, slow and mellow. Tears welled in Ellen's eyes and rolled down her cheeks. "Daddy gave this to her the year he died."

Vince wrapped an arm around her shoulders and pulled her close to his broad chest. "Calm down, honey."

His voice deepened, and he now appeared a tower of strength, which was exactly what Ellen needed. His laid-back style balanced Ellen's highly charged nature. She had always reminded Christy of one of the Deerfield thoroughbreds, sleek and beautiful but high-strung, requiring careful maintenance and constant care. Vince appeared willing to provide that for her.

"Come inside, Christy," Ellen said. "We have to talk."

Hugging the jewelry box, Ellen stepped out of Vince's embrace and walked up the front steps. Christy followed silently while Vince stooped to pick up the forgotten bag of groceries on the corner of the porch.

Christy entered the foyer. A huge crystal bowl of spiced Oriental potpourri sat on a Duncan Phyfe sideboard. The hardwood floor gleamed. Through open doors on either side, Christy could see high-ceilinged rooms where sunlight shimmered like rainbow prisms through long windows.

"Hey, guys," Vince yelled, striding to a back room where shouts competed with the high volume of the television. "Go up to your bedrooms. You can watch TV up there or play a video game. Just keep the noise down. I don't want to say that again."

Two red heads flashed past Christy, one boy shoving at the other, as they raced up the winding stairwell. The ceiling reverberated with heavy steps and a slammed door.

Vince turned into another back room, and Christy heard drawers and cabinets opening and closing, the familiar sound of groceries being put away.

Ellen said nothing as she walked into the formal living room on the left. Christy followed her, glancing around the huge space furnished with expensive pieces chosen to blend, rather than match. On a cherry desk, a polished amber paperweight and matching accessories would leave Aunt Bobbie speechless—until she began clamoring to buy it. But there wasn't enough money in their personal or business accounts to obtain anything in this room.

Ellen sank onto a Queen Anne sofa, her eyes fixed on the jewelry box as though it were a lost child that had just returned home after a painful and frightening absence. Christy sat on a love seat and watched Ellen use one slim finger to trace the edge of the box as the melody played, sounding old and slow, overpowered by the steady tick of the Big Ben. Tenderly, Ellen touched the wood of each drawer, and Christy felt like an intruder on a private moment. Then Ellen picked up the appraisal slip and studied it carefully.

"As I said, I removed the lining," Christy explained, feeling a need to apologize for damaging an object Ellen revered. "I'm sorry."

"But if you hadn't, you wouldn't have found the appraisal slip," Ellen replied, swiping at the tears flowing down her cheeks with the sleeve of her white blouse. She spoke in a raspy whisper, and her dark blue eyes glistened as she looked at Christy. "What do you think? The person who sold this to you—you said it was a child?"

"Her name is Zeffie Adams," Christy replied, scooting back on the love seat and folding her hands in her lap. "Her grandmother is Molly Adams. She said she wanted to sell it to help her grandmother with medical bills."

"Grandmother? What about the little girl's mother?" Ellen tensed, her words flying like darts. "She must have been involved."

"I looked up her grandmother in the telephone directory and called her," Christy said. "I didn't tell her about the appraisal slip; I just said I was calling because Zeffie was a minor. She sounded old and sick, and said the box belonged to her daughter, April, who was killed years ago in a car accident. She thinks April got the jewelry box at a yard sale. She sounded convincing." Christy looked at her hands, focusing on the gold bangle on her wrist. "Zeffie said she never knew her father."

"That's it! This...this April didn't buy it at a yard sale. I'll bet she and the mysterious father are the ones who—" Ellen's eyes darted toward the foyer, as though she could see the criminals standing there.

Christy feared Ellen was building false hope too quickly, but she didn't know how to stop her. She had debated asking Ellen a few questions, but it now seemed like a good idea. Ellen needed to focus on the known facts, harsh as they were.

"Would it be too difficult for you to tell me about the barbecue—I mean, the people who were here at the house that day? It seems to me they would be the obvious suspects."

Ellen shook her head. "No. They were all Kirby's friends. Whenever I came home from college on the weekends, he'd always be hosting a group of his friends, guys and girls. They all seemed nice. Mother would never have let them in the house otherwise." She paused for a moment, glancing at the portrait over the mantel.

Christy followed her gaze to the portrait of Annabell Strickland, a stunning blond woman who wore her hair in a French twist and whose large blue eyes were only a shade lighter than Ellen's. She wore a light blue dress, simple yet elegant, accessorized with a diamond necklace and matching earrings. Her features were small, softer than those of her daughter, and Christy recalled how everyone had raved over the woman's beauty and elegance.

"I still miss her," Ellen said, her eyes bleak as she turned back to Christy. "Then Kirby..." She wiped the tears from her cheeks. "It was hard for me to come back after the tragedy, but I was born and raised here, and I wanted to come home. So we painted the rooms, renovated the house. I converted Mother's bedroom to a den. I locked Kirby's bedroom upstairs and left everything just as it was for a while, in the hope that something among his possessions would help the investigators. When the case stalled, Vince convinced me to convert it to a storage room. I rarely go in there."

Her face turned toward the foyer, and her eyes held a savage pain. "But there's no closing off the area where Kirby was shot."

Christy pressed her lips together, sorry she had brought all this heartache back to the surface. She wanted to help and, despite inflicting fresh pain, maybe the jewelry box would lead to the murderer. She tried to divert the subject back to the barbecue.

"Did you and your husband attend the barbecue that day?"

"We stopped by for an hour or so," Ellen said. "We didn't stay long because I'd agreed to be at a friend's house by four. I was supposed to baby-sit her toddler Saturday night and Sunday so Jennie and her husband could have a weekend together at the beach.

"When we got here, there was a crowd in the house and out on the patio. I later learned that twenty-four people were here—most of the guys on the team and their wives or girlfriends."

She took a deep breath, and her thin body quivered beneath the white shirt. She placed the jewelry box on the sofa and went to a marble-topped washstand to open a drawer that appeared to contain keepsakes.

"Here's a brochure that Kirby printed up for the ten-year re-union, with pictures of the players and news clippings from their winning games."

Christy glanced from the brochure to an enlarged eight-by-ten photograph of the group on the end table. She studied the faces carefully.

Ellen found a yearbook and flipped through its pages. "Here are more pictures," she said, finding another photograph of the team. She pointed to the players who had been at the house that day. They looked happy, innocent. Ellen handed Christy the yearbook, her knuckles white, and her slim fingers touched the face of each man on the team, all wearing their uniforms.

"Kirby was the quarterback. This guy, Frank, was the center. I don't know where he is now. And this one, Wayne Crocker, was a running back. Wayne got a football scholarship to Florida State, but he quit after the first year. I'm not sure if he didn't make his grades or if he just didn't like playing college football. When we stopped by that day, these guys were gathered out at the picnic table, telling stories and laughing and having such a good time." She looked wistful as she studied the picture.

Christy looked at the framed eight by ten, where each face was clear. "May I look at that picture?" she asked.

"Of course! I always do things the hard way. I was just trying to put them in context this way."

Christy picked up the picture from a grouping on the table and rejoined Ellen. She glanced from the brochure to the enlargement, studying each guy, and had to agree with Ellen. None looked capable of killing Kirby. Christy tried not to stare at Kirby's smiling face. She couldn't recall ever seeing him without that pleasant smile.

"FDLE sent out their crime scene unit, and they went over the house and grounds. At first, the detectives suspected someone at the party. All the guests were questioned, and DNA and fingerprints were taken, but so many people were in and out of the house that day…" She shook her head. "Fingerprints and DNA were all over the place. That complicated the investigation."

Christy studied the faces in the enlargement, the brochure, and the yearbook, committing them to the memory for details on which she prided herself. Then she handed everything back to Ellen.

Ellen shook her head. "There was no DNA around Kirby or in Mother's room to incriminate anyone."

Christy stared at Ellen, feeling a wave of disappointment. Vince appeared in the doorway, glancing from Ellen to Christy and back. He strode over to the sofa and sat beside Ellen, wrapping her in his strong arms.

"I was explaining to Christy that fingerprints and DNA were taken from everyone who was in the house that day," she said. "Even the caterers. No luck."

Vince stared at the jewelry box as though willing it to give up a name, then blinked and looked at Christy. "It was well known that the Stricklands had money, but everyone in the area loved them. They were very generous to the community and donated wherever there was a need." He pulled Ellen closer. "The detectives finally decided that the killer or killers kept an eye on the house, watching and waiting for Kirby to leave. Maybe they'd even heard he was going to Tallahassee."

"What about an alarm system and house keys?" Christy asked.

Ellen shook her head. "Kirby hated alarm systems and had the one Mother installed turned off. He'd either set it off himself or forget to turn it on. He said it was more trouble than it was worth. As for keys, we had ours, and Kirby's keys were still in his pocket. The front and back door were unlocked, and the laundry room window was open. We don't know if he forgot to lock up or if he locked the front door and left the back door open."

"There were only a few keys to the house in a drawer in the kitchen," Vince said. "None were missing. The window in the laundry room was dusted for fingerprints, but nothing came of it." He sighed. "However they got in, the thieves thought they had a smart plan, but when Kirby returned for the wedding list, the person or persons panicked."

"Or perhaps they were hardened criminals who thought nothing of taking lives," Ellen added, her voice rasping through her throat. She turned her face up to Vince, as though looking to him for comfort.

Not wanting to impose further, Christy stood. "My grandmother is expecting me, so I should go."

Ellen leaped to her feet, placing the box on the sofa and reaching out to envelop Christy in her thin arms. "Thank you so much for bringing this to me."

Vince's gratitude softened his features as he looked down at Ellen. "I'll call the detectives right away. At least now we have a wedge for reopening the case."

Christy hesitated. "Did either of you ever have a feeling…about a suspect?"

The two exchanged glances. Vince spoke first.

"It's no secret that Kirby had an enemy in R. J. Wentworth. Julie—Kirby's fiancée—dated Wentworth throughout high school in Tallahassee, and he enrolled at FSU with her. When Kirby returned to Florida State for an alumni event and attended a football game, he fell in love with Julie the moment she came onto the field."

"She was a cheerleader," Ellen interjected. "Kirby arranged to meet her that weekend, and Julie broke up with R.J. the next week. He stalked them until Julie threatened him with a restraining order. Everyone who knew R.J. said he was obsessed with Julie. Once when she came here for the weekend, she said it amazed her how he seemed to know everywhere she went, everything she did. I remember her asking Kirby about a device that picked up calls on cell phones. She was certain R.J. had some way of knowing about every call she made. But then…" She fidgeted and looked to Vince to complete her statement.

"We liked Julie until she went back to R.J. a year after Kirby's death. The next year they got married."

Christy caught her breath. "That must have been a surprise."

Ellen shrugged. "Julie was brokenhearted over Kirby. Her father told me he feared she was suicidal and that he planned to get her in therapy. R.J. wormed his way back into her life when she was vulnerable, and he just never let up. She finally gave in."

"There's someone else I'd like to mention, since you asked our opinion on a suspect," Vince said. He gestured to the room opposite the living room. "The office was locked during the party. Kirby didn't want anyone in there. But the crime-scene investigators found the fingerprints of the caterer, Willie Pitt, on the back of a chair in the office and on a corner of the desk. And there was dirt around the desk."

"That's right," Ellen agreed. "Pitt told the police that after the guests left and he and his crew cleaned up, he went in the office with Kirby to be paid for catering the barbecue. He said that's why his fingerprints were in the office. And like R.J., he had an alibi for that night."

Vince rolled his eyes. "Supposedly Pitt and his wife had guests at their home after the barbecue. A minister and his wife from their church. It's one of those off-brand churches," he added with unmistakable cynicism.

Christy stared at him, bothered by two things: How did one consider a church *off-brand*? And wasn't Willie Pitt the friend Jack had mentioned?

Christy shook herself out of her speculations as they walked toward the front door. "Well, I do hope the detectives can use this lead to solve the case. If I can help in any way, let me know." She reached into her purse and handed Ellen a business card. "My home phone and the shop."

"Thanks." Ellen studied the card. "I'll stop by. I'd love to see your shop."

"The detectives will want to know about the people who sold you the jewelry box," Vince said from behind Ellen.

Christy nodded. "Tell them to call or come by."

A ruckus broke out upstairs, and one of the boys began to wail. Vince whirled and headed for the stairs while Ellen glanced nervously after him, then back at Christy as she followed her onto the front porch.

"We'll be in touch," Ellen said, hugging her arms against her torso, her hands rubbing her elbows. "The grief of losing Mother, then Kirby, has been the worst possible nightmare, but what haunts me day and night is the fact that whoever killed Kirby is still out there. I'll never have peace until the monster is caught."

The words sounded like bullets fired into the stillness around them, and Ellen's face looked carved in stone. Despite her fierce expression, Christy could see her trembling. She couldn't begin to imagine what this poor woman had endured.

"I'm so sorry. I'll be praying that justice is served. Soon."

Ellen merely nodded, looking doubtful, and Christy got in her car and started the engine. Ellen hurried back inside as Christy wound around the circle driveway.

Glancing at the clock on the dash, Christy realized she'd been at Deerfield for almost an hour. In that time, no one had smiled—not even before she'd delivered her news. Even the boys, Luke and Parker, had looked grim as they tumbled from the car and respectfully acknowledged her.

As she looked from the beautiful mansion to the lush meadows and white fences, she marveled that so much tension and sadness could dominate Deerfield, which for years had been the gathering place for fun and laughter.

5

C hristy turned back onto the highway and drove half a mile to the turnoff to Granny's farm, silently praying for Ellen and Vince. She desperately hoped the jewelry box would be the key to unlocking the mystery that had become a cold case.

As she drove toward Granny's house, casting a glance toward Cypress Lake and then the peach and pear trees lining the road, good memories began to overtake the sadness. When she passed the pear trees, she smiled to herself, recalling the fat, juicy fruit she and Seth had devoured until their stomachs ached.

She pulled up before the farmhouse, a simple contrast to the mansion she had just left. Despite the death of her grandfather, happiness seemed to flow from the rafters of the two-story, white frame house where her father and aunt had grown up. She knew the source of joy was the tall, gray-haired woman stepping onto the porch.

Granny's eyes, bright blue and sparkling with life, offset the wrinkles in her face, and a deeply spiritual lifetime had kept her young at heart. As usual, she wore a large apron over her pants and blouse.

Christy cut the engine and hopped out, meeting her grandmother on the steps and relishing the warm hug that wrapped her in delicious aromas. It seemed Granny spent most of her time cooking, even though she lived alone. For her, cooking was a joy.

"No overnight bag?" Granny asked, looking disappointed.

"Afraid not. We'll just have to talk as fast as we can."

"Does that mean you aren't even going to have lunch or stay for dinner?" Granny looked horrified at the prospect.

"I'm not foolish enough to come to your door on a full stomach. Of course I'll have lunch with you, but I have to get back for dinner with Dan."

Granny's eyes twinkled as she opened the front door for Christy and they entered the house. "How is Dan? And why didn't you bring him with you?"

"He had plans. Besides, I thought it'd be cozy for just you and me to have a chat."

Granny laughed, looking pleased. Judging by the scents drifting from the kitchen, she had veered from her usual fried chicken to something Christy couldn't identify but that smelled divine.

The table was already set with Granny's best dishes, and huge crystal glasses filled with iced tea rested on coasters. Granny hurried to the oven, thrust her large hands into mitts, and pulled out an oblong pan of roast beef with all the trimmings.

"Yum," Christy said. She spotted Lobo's big face peering through the glass pane of the back door. She walked over to open it and reached down to stroke the soft fur of the brown and white German shepherd. "Lobo, you rascal. Are you behaving yourself?"

"No, he's not!" Granny was quick to respond. "He's spending way too much time over at the McCoy farm."

Lobo wagged his tail, as though he understood every word.

"And what's at the McCoy farm that interests you?" Christy asked him, watching his dark eyes glaze over as she scratched behind his ears in the spot she knew he enjoyed.

"A new golden retriever," Granny answered for him. "A female." She spoke the words with a note of disgust, which was unusual coming from the woman who rarely spoke ill of people or pets.

Christy glanced over her shoulder. "Isn't Lobo getting a little old to be chasing females?"

"He's not as old as Grits McCoy, who's decided to act like a young rooster rather than a seventy-three-year-old widower. He told me the dog was a gift from a friend. I knew he wanted me to ask who gave it to him, but I wouldn't give him the satisfaction. Besides, I'd already heard he'd met some woman over at the bingo hall."

Christy laughed. Grits McCoy was as funny as his nickname and had tried on occasion to court Granny, but she'd never been interested. Now, however, Christy thought she detected a little resentment—or was it jealousy?—in Granny's tone.

"I haven't seen him in years, Granny. How does he look?"

"Same big belly, same white hair, only a bit thinner, and he still talks a mile a minute telling stories we've heard for years. Here, have a seat." She indicated a chair at the table, which held enough food for half a dozen people. Granny had never learned to cook in small portions, nor did she try. She enjoyed delivering food to her neighbors or whoever she thought looked hungry.

Christy slipped into the ladder-back chair, blissfully inhaling the aroma of cinnamon and cloves from the sweet potato casserole. She looked at her grandmother.

"Maybe Grits has given up on you and decided to find some lonely lady in town."

"Maybe he's hit his second childhood. Anyway, I'd rather discuss what you've been doing. But first let's say the blessing."

"Go ahead," Christy prompted.

Granny offered a brief prayer and then picked up her white linen napkin. Christy, a big fan of paper towels, realized Granny made everyone who sat at her table feel special with her nice dishes and sparkling silverware. She never minded washing linen napkins or taking the time to set a lovely table.

"When you called to say you were driving up here, you mentioned stopping at Deerfield," Granny said, handing her a platter of roast beef.

Christy nodded, forking a slice of meat onto her plate. "I had a very unusual experience this week." For the third time in the past couple of hours, she retold the story of the jewelry box, as Granny put down her fork and stared at her with wide blue eyes.

"That's amazing. Christy, God has put this right in your lap so that something can be done for that poor family!"

"Well, other than deliver the jewelry box and appraisal slip, I can't do much else. Of course Dad doesn't want me to get involved, but…" She paused, searching her grandmother's face. "I'll never forget that day at the lake when Kirby saved my life."

"Nor will I." Granny frowned. "But you're already involved." She was quiet for a moment as she spooned food onto her plate. Then she looked at Christy.

"Well, in case you're interested, I have a theory about what happened. When I left my driveway going to the grocery the day Kirby was killed, a red sports car zipped by headed toward Deerfield. I knew Kirby was having a barbecue, so I didn't think anything about it. Then when I came back home and stopped at the mailbox on the road, the same car flew by again. Turned out, the car belonged to Julie Clark's ex-boyfriend, R. J. Wentworth." She spoke slowly as she sliced the roast beef on her plate.

"Really?" Christy asked, her fork poised in midair.

"He was a leading suspect in the beginning since he wasn't invited to the party, didn't live in this area, and had no business driving up and down this road."

"Ellen mentioned him. She said he practically stalked Julie after she broke up with him."

Granny shook her head, a familiar look of regret settling over her face. "They could never prove anything with Wentworth, and he had an air-tight alibi, or so they said."

Christy sighed. "It always bothers me when I hear someone has an 'air-tight alibi.' Just a quirk of mine." And, she recalled, Willie Pitt also had an air-tight alibi, according to Vince. "I was really surprised to hear that Julie later married Wentworth."

Granny nodded. "I know, but the detectives took my statement, and I was never questioned again. I felt I'd done the best I could to help."

Christy nodded absently, thinking about R. J. Wentworth. Maybe he had an alibi because he had hired someone else to commit the crime. Then she looked at Granny and sighed. She didn't want to think about the murder anymore. She wanted to enjoy her visit. "This is a fabulous meal. Let's talk about something pleasant. What's your latest project?"

"Scrapbooking." Granny launched into a description of the classes she was taking with a friend at a small craft shop nearby and how she hoped to take several shoeboxes full of keepsakes and display them in lovely scrapbooks.

The meal and the rest of the conversation left them both in good spirits. As Christy hugged Granny good-bye, she asked, "When are you coming to Summer Breeze for a visit? You owe us one."

"One of these days," Granny answered, looking a bit sad as Christy got into her car.

"That's what you always say," Christy teased. "I think you just don't want to get too far from Grits McCoy."

Granny huffed at that, complaining about Grits again as Lobo joined in with a round of barking.

As Christy drove home, she wished her grandmother would visit more. On the other hand, she was grateful that Granny, unlike many widows, had built a busy and contented life for herself. She knew Granny must feel lonely at times, but she never complained.

As she passed Seminole Road, Christy thought of Deerfield, and her memory flashed back to Ellen's bleak face. Christy decided that if she thought of a way to help, she would do it, despite her dad's warning not to get involved.

Her cell phone rang, and she saw the shop's number displayed on the screen.

"I'm just checking on you," Bobbie said in greeting.

"I'm fine. I just left Granny's and am heading back to Summer Breeze. Anything going on at the shop?"

"It's been a busy day, but no one has mentioned the jewelry box."

Christy sighed with relief. "I'm glad to hear that. I'm having dinner with Dan tonight, but call me if anything comes up."

"Will do. Have fun."

So word had not leaked out in Summer Breeze—not yet, at least. She knew it was only a matter of time.

∽

"How was your visit with your Granny?" Dan asked, studying his plate of grilled salmon.

"Good," Christy replied, trying to enjoy her grouper filet. Her stomach still felt stuffed from Granny's food, even though it had been several hours. "I went over to Deerfield to see if the jewelry box belonged there."

Dan looked up. "What happened?"

Christy recounted her conversation with the Browns. "Ellen and Vince feel the jewelry box and appraisal slip will prompt the authorities to reopen the investigation."

"That's good," Dan replied, looking at her. "You've been a great help to them. Tonight, let's not be sad. Let's talk about that trip to Alaska. Want to go?"

"I'd love to. That DVD we watched confirmed it for me," Christy said. "I should warn you, though: Mom and Dad may go along as chaperons. How funny is that?"

"You're kidding." Dan stared at her, the serious expression on his face indicating genuine concern. "A singles class ranging in age from twenty-five to fifty needs chaperons?"

Christy laughed. "Sorry," she said when he leaned back in his chair, looking slightly disturbed by her mirth. Even though he liked her parents, she could see he wasn't keen on having someone looking over his shoulder as though he were sixteen. "Well, it *is* a church-based event."

Dan took a huge swallow of iced tea.

Christy laughed again. "They were asked to go because someone was being polite. But no—Dad and Mom went to Alaska a couple of summers ago, and they aren't planning on a return trip."

Dan straightened in his chair and speared a piece of fish, his appetite restored. "Well, I didn't mean…" he began lamely.

"It's okay. I understand. The Phillipses are going. I suppose the elders in the church liked the idea of a married couple keeping an eye on all us wild singles." She winked and forced down another bite.

Dan shrugged and ate with obvious enjoyment while Christy pushed her food around her plate. Idly, she glanced around the restaurant that had become their favorite place to dine. It was small and quaint, with great food and service, and a spectacular view of the Gulf of Mexico. She enjoyed sitting by the wall of glass, peering out at the lights sparkling on the water.

The server appeared and refilled their glasses. Christy looked at Dan. "How did your meeting go today?"

"Mr. Filmore—that's the client I met for lunch—has some interesting ideas about an addition to his summer home."

Christy tried to follow the conversation, but her mind wandered until he suddenly stopped talking.

"You aren't paying attention to a word I've said."

She reached across the table and touched his hand. "I'm sorry. I just can't stop thinking about my visit with Ellen and Vince Brown."

He looked at her and sighed, shaking his head. She expected to hear him ask her to stay out of the investigation, but when Dan spoke, his words were a pleasant surprise.

"You've told me Kirby saved you from drowning years ago, and I see why you may feel compelled to help solve this case. So…let me help, too."

Christy stared at him, pleased with his suggestion. "What do you have in mind?"

"When you go out on one of your adventures, call me first so I can go with you. This time, I'd like the opportunity to protect you from dangerous people. Or protect you from yourself." He grinned.

She squeezed his hand. "It'll be good to have a partner."

6

Sunday

Christy and Seth nudged elbows just as they had done as children. They entered a side door of the church and turned into the pew where their mother sat waiting. Seth had begun to attend services again when he came home from FSU on the weekends. While he still didn't conform to dress shirt and pants for his father's sermons, his jeans and long-sleeved T-shirt were clean and well pressed.

Seth quit bumping Christy in an attempt to rile her and leaned around her to give his mother a pleasant smile. "What's for lunch?" he asked in a voice that could be heard from the back door.

Beth Castleman merely smiled and whispered back, "Your favorite—lasagna."

He gave her a thumbs-up and a silly quirk of the eyebrows as Grant came to the lectern. Glancing down at the family pew, the pastor's dark eyes glowed with pride before he turned back to read the morning scripture.

Seth opened a wrapper and popped a stick of gum in his mouth, while those around them followed the reading of scripture in their Bibles. Christy glanced again at her younger brother, who gave her a wide smile. He was such a charmer that people usually forgave his behavior or lack of manners.

As he chewed the gum with relish, he looked down at her simple black dress and made the familiar expression that indicated he thought she looked like a nerd. She couldn't resist jabbing him in the ribs.

Grant Castleman's voice rang out over the congregation. "Today I'd like to discuss a subject that has touched all of us at one time or another in our lives: grief."

That sentence brought Christy's attention back into focus. She ignored Seth and listened as her father relayed a message of hope in the dark hours of tragedy. Christy's thoughts moved to Deerfield. Vince had said Ellen pushed herself so hard in order to avoid feeling pain that she became ill. Although the tragedy had occurred eight years before, a veil of sadness shrouded the Brown family. Clearly they had not worked through their grief.

Christy recalled her reaction to the death of Chad, her fiancé, ten years ago. She had lashed out in anger, rather than facing the fact that Chad's carelessness and bad choices had led to his death. She had slowly worked through her pain until she found a measure of peace. When Dan came into her life, she felt she was ready for a relationship.

Her father closed his message and offered a prayer. The congregation sang "Amazing Grace."

"Can you join us for lunch?" Christy's mother whispered in her ear.

"Dan and I have plans. And to put your mind at ease, I turned the jewelry box and appraisal slip over to Ellen and Vince Brown."

Beth nodded with satisfaction, then faced the front of the church and continued singing.

As the service ended and people streamed out of the pews, Christy turned to Seth. "Want to go boating with Dan and me this afternoon?"

He looked as though an improper word might tumble out before he caught himself and heaved a sigh instead. "Wish I could, but I gotta get back to school and study for an exam tomorrow. I hate when professors give exams on Monday."

"I know. That's a bummer."

They reached the parking lot, and she gave him one last hearty jab to the ribs to make up for the ones he'd given her during the service. "Back to you," she said.

Seth dodged and chuckled. "Say hello to Dan," he said. "And try to keep him fooled until you've been married a day or two."

She made a face at him. "I don't need advice from a guy who never dates the same girl three times." The third date was always a deal breaker for him. "Good luck on your exam."

"Thanks," he called, heading toward his car.

Christy noticed Mrs. Ragland, the third-grade teacher at the local elementary school. "Good morning, Mrs. Ragland," she called as she walked over to speak to her.

"Christy! Nice to see you."

Mrs. Ragland was in her late fifties, but she had aged gracefully, possibly because she loved her work. She wore a white linen suit, simple earrings, and tortoise shell glasses beneath salt-and-pepper hair.

"I wanted to ask you about a little girl who came into our shop this week," Christy began, hoping to sound tactful. "Zeffie Adams."

"Oh, Zeffie." Mrs. Ragland nodded, her dark eyes shining behind her lens. "Such a bright child. She has the most amazing memory of any child I've ever taught." A look of sadness dimmed the bright eyes. "She misses school a lot because her grandmother is ill. I checked it out and was ashamed of myself for being so suspicious when I discovered Zeffie was telling the truth."

"Yes, I've spoken to Mrs. Adams. It's such a tragic situation."

Mrs. Ragland frowned. "I don't know a lot about Zeffie or her family. I just know that she could be at the top of the class if she were in regular attendance."

A moment of silence followed, and Christy realized Mrs. Ragland had told her all she knew. "Well." Christy smiled at her. "It's nice to see you again. Is your husband okay?"

"He's down with a cold, which is why he stayed home from church today. But I'm spoiling him with a lemon icebox pie."

"Sounds like the perfect cure," Christy called over her shoulder as she circled her car to reach the driver's side.

So Zeffie had an amazing memory. What, she wondered, was stored in the child's brain that might lead to Kirby's killer?

7

When Christy met Dan at the marina, the fried chicken she had purchased at the market deli and placed in a Tupperware container accomplished her purpose. As he peered down into the picnic basket of fried chicken, crusty rolls, and fresh fruit, he swallowed hard. "This looks great! I'm starving."

She didn't bother to detail her rush to the market. After all, she'd whipped up the brownies in her kitchen early this morning, and that qualified as home-cooked.

She'd met Dan in the parking lot of the marina to save time. He took the basket from her, and they headed toward the boat slips, but after a few steps, Dan stopped walking and looked at her.

"I should tell you something in case we see him."

"Him?" she repeated, glancing quickly at the long white building that housed the marina offices.

"R. J. Wentworth owns the marina. I'm sure by now you've heard his name if you had a conversation with the Browns."

Christy nodded. "He married Julie Clark after Kirby was killed. I'm afraid some people never forgave him for the way he chased her, particularly during the Strickland tragedy."

She looked at the Closed sign on the office door and wished this had been a Sunday R.J. chose to show up.

Dan's boat was a twenty-nine-foot fiberglass outboard sport, solid white. He'd had the seats reupholstered in a warm crimson, and Christy was almost as fond of it as he was. As soon as he started the boat and backed out of the slip, he took a deep breath and began to smile. Christy knew nothing relaxed him as much as being out on the Gulf with his boat. He fished occasionally, but his main enjoyment was riding for pleasure, exploring the Gulf and soaking up the sun.

"Ready for lunch?" she asked.

"More than ready." He smiled at her and eyed the picnic basket.

It was not as sunny as it had been the day before, and the temperature had dropped a few notches, but being out in the boat, gliding over the emerald waters, always seemed to work magic for both of them.

She served the food on thick paper plates and reached into the ice chest for drinks. They dug in, enjoying the food and the view.

"This is great," Dan commented.

Christy munched on a drumstick, staring out at the Gulf. Despite her effort to forget about the Kirby Strickland murder, her thoughts drifted back to the controversial man who owned this marina: R. J. Wentworth. Was it possible that he had been so crazy over Julie that he committed such a heinous crime? While he had one of those convenient air-tight alibis for the time of the murder, she wished she could ask him what he was doing on the road that day at Deerfield. How did he know Kirby would be returning to the house? Ellen had mentioned Julie's worry that R.J. was able to track her phone calls. Christy rolled that possibility around in her mind.

"What has you so deep in thought?" Dan asked, finishing off the last brownie.

She knew she should say something about the boat or the weather, but she decided to be honest. "I was thinking about what Vince Brown said yesterday..." Her voice trailed off at the disappointment clouding Dan's face.

"I know that troubles you, but could we just forget it today and have a good time?"

Christy nodded. Sunday was supposed to be a day of relaxation and rest. Why not take a break from the Strickland case?

A sputtering engine broke through her thoughts. Dan checked out the problem, and soon he had the engine running smoothly. After a couple of minutes, though, just as they were about to breathe a sigh of relief, the engine sputtered again, sounding even worse.

"We'd better not take any chances," Dan said. "Sounds like the engine is about to die on us. I'm heading back to the marina to find a mechanic."

They limped back to shore, Dan at the helm while Christy gathered up the remnants from their picnic and placed the empty soda cans in a trash bag. Just as Dan was guiding the boat into his slip at the marina, the engine gave a gasping sputter and then lapsed into an ugly silence. They floated into the slip.

"Close call," he said, glancing at her. "I had the boat checked out a couple of months ago, and it was fine. I don't like the kind of surprise we got today."

"You handled it well," she said, placing a hand on his shoulder.

He helped her onto the dock, then secured the boat. "I'm going to find the mechanic. One of the reasons I chose this marina was because there's always a mechanic on call."

"Go ahead. I'll stay here and watch the boat."

Dan grinned. "Give it a drink of water if it needs it." He turned, walking briskly toward a building on the north end of the marina.

Christy shoved her hands in her pockets and stared down the long line of boats docked side by side. They had agreed to relax and enjoy the day, and she couldn't go around solving mysteries just because she wrote them. Actually, she wrote historical mysteries, based on the legend and lore of nearby Shipwreck Island. Still, once she got curious about something, she was like… She looked out at a pelican skimming just above the surface of the water. *Like that pelican hungry for a fish.*

Deciding it couldn't hurt, she sauntered up to the office and peered in the window. Large, neat, and tidy. Otherwise, she couldn't tell much about the place R.J. frequented.

Turning, she gazed at the boats that filled the harbor, all sizes and shapes, interesting names painted on their sterns. There were other marinas in the area, but this one was by far the most popular. Extra perks were offered to the locals, which is why most people Christy knew kept their boats here.

The sound of music captured her attention, and she turned toward a sleek green and white yacht gliding into a nearby slip. A man stood on the third story of the bow, talking on a cell phone. Even from a distance, she could see he was deeply tanned, with black hair, dark eyes, and broad cheekbones. His T-shirt strained across his shoulders and chest, and as he ended his conversation and hooked the phone onto his belt, she noticed his tight jeans outlined every muscle in his long legs. In the background, Garth Brooks wailed out a tale of love.

The man looked down at her and waved. Christy tried to decide if she should just wave back and walk away, but he was already climbing down the ladder. As he jumped onto the boardwalk, quick as a cat, she noticed the Florida State insignia on his T-shirt. He looked like a former athlete, and as he turned to face her, the deep-set brown eyes and prominent cheekbones prompted a flashback. Where had she seen him?

"Hi." A smile flashed over his face, bringing into play the laugh lines forming on his forehead and bracketing his mouth as he tossed a rope to a dockhand standing at the bow of the yacht.

"Hi," she responded, looking back at the yacht. "Nice."

"Thanks. I've loved boats all my life, so I decided to get into a business that involved them. I broker boats from here to Key West, where I live."

She nodded, unable to resist testing him. "Do I know you?"

"Name's Wayne Crocker. What's yours?"

"Christy Castleman." Wayne Crocker. Kirby's friend? He could be Kirby's age, around thirty-seven or -eight, but the sun-wrinkled skin made him appear older.

She decided to take a chance. "I think we met at Deerfield years ago."

That announcement brought a quick change of mood. He lowered his eyes for a moment. "I haven't been there since…in years."

"My grandmother lives on the adjoining farm," Christy volunteered, wanting to keep the conversation going.

His eyes swung back to her. "Do you live up there?"

"No, I live in Summer Breeze, but I used to visit a lot when I was growing up. I always loved going to Deerfield." She swallowed and dove in again. "You were at the reunion, weren't you?"

He looked her over, obviously puzzled. "You must have been a kid then."

"I wasn't a kid, though I was younger than Kirby. Our families were always friends. You were on his football team, weren't you?" She recalled the headlines on the newspaper clipping Ellen had shown her. "I know about that game where you ran for the final touchdown when the Cougars made the state play-offs."

His expression changed completely. The dark eyes came to life, a grin played over his full lips, and he reached up to slick back his dark hair, slightly ruffled by the breeze kicking up out in the Gulf.

"Everybody on that team won the game. But yeah, I made the final touchdown."

"You and Kirby made the big plays. And you both looked good."

He grinned. "Yeah, I guess so. It was great being with those guys at the reunion. I came from the wrong side of the tracks, so to speak, but when I started high school and made the team, Kirby included me in his social circle. Everybody hung out at his house. On that last

Saturday, we must have gone over every game we ever played. I was living in Lynn Haven at the time, selling cars. I hadn't seen those guys in a while." He shook his head. "I couldn't believe it when I got a phone call the next day about Kirby. The next week I was a pall-bearer at his funeral." He shook his head. "Haven't been able to attend a funeral since."

Christy searched for the right words. "This has been a terrible tragedy for the Strickland family. They've had to deal with the knowledge that whoever killed Kirby went free."

His dark eyes had been staring into space, but he slowly focused on her.

Christy cleared her throat. "Did you have your own theory about who might have done it?"

He took a deep breath, obviously considering her question. He shoved his hands in his pockets, an action that surprised her, seeing that his jeans were so tight. "In crimes I read about and watch on TV, I'm always hearing the word *motive*. Who had the most to gain? When I ask myself that question, I get an obvious answer."

His next words rocked her back on her heels, a simple observa-tion that had been overshadowed by the confusion surrounding the case.

Before she could frame an appropriate comment, she glanced down the dock and saw Dan standing by his boat slip, staring at her.

"I'd better go," she said, turning on her heel.

Wayne called a "nice to meet you," but she didn't turn back. She felt guilty for leaving Dan to worry about his boat while she discussed the Strickland murder with Wayne Crocker. Particularly when she had vowed to give it a rest.

"What did the mechanic say?" she asked, as soon as she was in earshot.

"Needs a new part, which will have to be ordered. I'm just grateful we hadn't gone out very far when the problem started."

"So when can the boat be repaired?" Christy slipped her hand in his as he reached down for the picnic basket they had left on the dock.

"It'll take a few days." Dan looked up at the sky. "The clouds are rolling in, so we might have come in early anyway. At least we had a good lunch."

As they headed toward Dan's car, he cast a sidelong glance at her. "Who was that guy?"

Something in his voice made Christy ask, "Do you know him?"

"I saw him yesterday when I met Mr. Filmore here for lunch. Mr. Filmore wanted to see my boat and look around the marina. That guy was seated in the lounge, watching a football game on TV. Some guys were making a fuss over him, talking about the good old days. The lady tending the bar got in on the discussion. By the time we left, she and the guy you were talking to were getting really friendly."

"I bet he does a lot of that," Christy said.

"Yep, probably does."

"His name is Wayne Crocker," she said. "He played football with Kirby in high school, then got a scholarship to FSU. He was at the reunion that day."

Dan looked worried. "Be careful."

She linked her arm through his and stepped closer to his side. "I doubt I'll see him again. He made an interesting comment while we were talking, though. Everyone liked Kirby, and people want to believe this was a robbery that escalated into murder and that the crime was committed by people who didn't know the Stricklands. But when I asked Crocker what he thought, he said, 'Who had the motive? Vince got the family fortune. R.J. got the girl.'"

~

A shadow crept through the long stretch of woods on the hill above the Deerfield mansion. The woods had grown denser in eight years, but even then it had been easy to hide a car. Waiting had been the tough part that night so long ago, but there was no question about what had to be done. The motive warranted the risk.

Everyone thought Kirby was the greatest guy in the world, but he wasn't. Even Ellen had reminded him to lock up when he left, knowing what a scatterbrain he was. Aside from his short stint in the limelight during football seasons, Kirby was a real nerd. Even on the field, it was obvious to the crowd that he often forgot plays and threw wild passes. A computer brain, that's what he was. Not a businessman. Not someone who could run a big business like Strickland Timber. But then, all his life, Kirby'd had everything handed to him on a silver platter.

Still, Kirby shouldn't have died. If only he hadn't gone for the gun. What else could you do? You didn't just stand there and let someone shoot you.

The shadow turned away, walking back through the woods. Reliving that night had reinforced the theory of self-defense. There was no choice.

But who would believe that, knowing the motive?

8

Monday

I t was a clear sunny morning. Christy picked up the newspaper, then turned the key in the lock to open the shop. This was her day to work, and Bobbie had been grateful when she called last night.

"Jack and I didn't slow down all weekend. I'm worn slap out. What did you do with that jewelry box and appraisal slip?"

"Returned it to Ellen Strickland Brown. It's out of our hands now, so to speak."

"Hmm," Bobbie remarked, sounding doubtful.

Christy expected an uneventful day at the shop after such a hectic weekend. The tourists and weekend visitors had deserted the area, and even though the snowbirds had arrived, Mondays were usually slow. She had dressed casually in black pants and a tailored red blouse. Thinking of a long day on her feet, she had worn comfortable sandals.

She glanced at the front page of the paper, noting that the Gators were number four in the BCS rankings. She hoped Vince and Ellen had enjoyed watching the game, glad they found ways to enjoy their time together. She had wondered about that, with Ellen so highly charged and anxious.

The phone rang just as she tucked her purse under the counter, and she tried to sound cheerful as she answered.

"May I speak with Christy?"

"This is she." Christy recognized Ellen Brown's tense voice and wondered if just thinking of her had summoned Ellen to the phone. She smiled at such a silly thought.

"Christy, it's Ellen. I'm glad you're already open. Listen, two detectives will be coming in this morning to discuss the jewelry box with you." She rushed through her words, barely pausing to catch a breath. "As soon as Vince called, they came right out, and I think this time we're going to make some progress."

"I certainly hope so," Christy replied kindly. "I enjoyed my visit with you. I'll help any way I can."

"You already have. Oops, I'm due at the House of Ruth in five minutes. I do volunteer work there on Mondays."

"Well, you'd better hurry. I'll watch for the detectives." She barely got the words out before Ellen hung up.

Christy had just made a pot of coffee when it occurred to her that she should warn Molly's grandmother before the detectives came to her door. The woman was sick, and Christy believed little Zeffie and Molly were innocent victims in what had taken place.

Grabbing her keys and purse, she rushed to the shop door and flipped the sign to Back in Ten Minutes, then got in her car and turned down Fourth Street. Spotting Hilda Russell sweeping her front walk, Christy leaned out the window.

"Hi, Mrs. Russell. Do you know a Molly Adams and her grand-daughter Zeffie?"

"Sure do." Mrs. Russell leaned against her broom. "Molly cleaned houses for the neighbors for the first month they were here, but now she isn't well. You looking for her?"

When Christy nodded, the woman pointed toward the next block. "Third house down on the right. The older house. Don't think there's a number on the mailbox."

"Thanks." Christy rolled up the window and followed the directions. It was easy to spot the Adams house, the oldest one on the street of rentals. She hopped out of her SUV and hurried up the cracked sidewalk. She stepped onto the rickety wooden porch and knocked softly on the door.

She heard slow, labored steps move across thin floorboards, and the door opened a crack. A tall woman with thinning gray hair peered at her.

"Hi. Are you Mrs. Adams?" Christy inquired.

The woman nodded, taking in Christy's dark pants and red blouse.

"I'm Christy Castleman. We spoke on the phone."

The woman's expression changed immediately, and she opened the door. "Come in. Zeffie really likes you."

"And I like her." She followed the older woman into a tiny living room filled with cheap pine furnishings and took a seat on a couch left over from the sixties as her host settled into a rocking chair. Beside her, a table held several bottles of medication.

"I worry about Zeffie all the time," Molly said, folding her hands in the lap of her housedress. Her light brown eyes held Christy's in her gaze.

"You shouldn't. She seems to be doing fine."

The older woman looked at her lap. "She's doing okay now, but I worry about the future."

Christy couldn't follow that train of thought. "May I ask why?"

Molly hesitated, turning her hands over in her lap. "My health is no secret. If you haven't heard, you soon will." A deep sigh sank her chest. "I have lung cancer, and it's terminal. After my diagnosis, I decided if I was going to die, I would make the most of the time I had left. I've always wanted to live near the water, after being cooped up in an apartment in Montgomery most of my life. My cousin owns this house and made my dream come true. And Zeffie loves the beach. It helps me so much to see Zeffie happy here."

Christy tried to hide her dismay. "I'm sorry to hear about your condition. I'll be glad to help Zeffie in any way I can." The ache in her heart for Molly and Zeffie swelled to her throat, and she fought to keep her voice steady.

"We have no family—except for a cousin," Molly continued. "April was an only child. My husband died years ago—then April."

"What will happen to Zeffie?" Christy blurted, then clamped her lips together, regretting her outburst. "Sorry. I shouldn't be so personal."

Molly gave her a weak smile. "I don't mind, since you've been so nice to Zeffie. I've given my cousin Sally Carver power of attorney over my affairs. She has agreed to take Zeffie when…"

An awkward silence followed, and Christy shifted on the couch, gazing at some framed photographs on a bookcase.

"That's my daughter April," Molly explained.

Christy tried to conceal her surprise as she looked at the photographs of a young woman, drawing the same conclusion from all of them. While Zeffie was a beauty, April had been plain and sullen. Her hair was a bland shade of brown, her eyes dark beneath lids that seemed to droop in her large face. Other photos showed an overweight girl unhappy with herself.

"Zeffie was our angel. Didn't ever look like she belonged to us, so I knew God sent her." A pall of sadness slipped over Molly's face. "She's nothing like her mother. April was our only child, and I spoiled her rotten. Her dad left us when she was a teenager. Got himself killed in a barroom brawl shortly after."

Molly sighed. "I'm afraid her spoiled nature combined with her dad's genes made April as wild as a March wind. She ran with the wrong crowd in school, and after she graduated, she went to Panama City for a while, then came back pregnant. If she knew who the father was, she never said." She studied her long hands. "I fell in love with Zeffie the first time I saw her in the hospital nursery. We decided I would quit work and stay home with Zeffie and April would be the breadwinner. She could make more money than I could as a waitress, even with tips.

"So I took over raising Zeffie. After a couple years, April moved down to Fort Walton. Said she could get better jobs being a server in the touristy restaurants. I wouldn't let her take Zeffie, and she didn't argue about it. She knew the child was better off with me. She only came home a couple times a month. On her last visit, she brought that jewelry box home to Zeffie and gave me a beach picture. When I asked her about the picture, she said she got it at a garage sale. I assume she picked up the jewelry box at the same time."

"In Fort Walton?" Christy asked.

Molly nodded and began to cough, placing a rumpled handkerchief to her mouth. When the coughing subsided, she continued. "For your questions about the jewelry box, the girl who shared an apartment with April might know more."

Molly got out of the chair and went to a small desk, pulling open a drawer. She opened a worn little book and slowly fumbled through the pages.

"Her roommate was named Sheryl Wilcox. I have no idea where she is now. I haven't seen her since April's funeral. As I said, April was killed when her car hit a telephone pole."

She cleared her throat. "Well, Mrs. Adams, I know you have enough trouble, but I'm afraid I have some bad news. When I stripped the lining from the jewelry box, I found an appraisal slip that belonged in the home of a man who was killed in a robbery in 1998."

"Oh no!" Molly sank into her chair and grabbed a bottle of pills, shaking one into her palm. She reached for her water glass and took a sip, swallowing the pill, then looked at Christy and shook her head. "I swear I know nothing about it. Oh no."

"Then don't let this trouble you. I came here merely to warn you that legally I was obligated to give the appraisal slip and the jewelry box to the family of the deceased. I expect the authorities will reopen the case. You see, the killer was never caught." Christy tried to speak gently in consideration of the woman's delicate condition. "You'll probably be visited by a couple of detectives, but all you have to do is tell them just what you've told me. They aren't going to suspect you or Zeffie of anything."

Molly shook her gray head again. "April had her problems, and I never made excuses for her, but I knew her well enough to say she would never be involved in something like that. Of course, I can't speak for some of her friends, but maybe Sheryl Wilcox can."

Molly looked exhausted, and Christy regretted making her feel worse. Still, she was glad she had given her a tactful warning before the detectives arrived.

"I must get back to the shop," Christy said, clutching the armrest to pull herself up from the sagging sofa. "I'm sure the detectives will be more interested in talking with Sheryl Wilcox than you. And please let Zeffie come by to see me whenever she wants."

Hope glimmered in Molly's eyes. "That's so nice of you. She told me you work Monday and Friday, and she's already asked to go back and learn more about turning trash to treasure." Molly's pale lips attempted to smile.

"Good. And if there's anything I can do for you—run an errand, anything—please call. My father is Grant Castleman, pastor of Community Church, and his congregation is wonderful about reaching out to help wherever they can."

For the first time, a look of relief swept over Molly's worn face. "I knew you were a good woman. I'd like Zeffie to attend church if you could work that out."

"My mother teaches Sunday school, and nothing would make her happier than to pick up Zeffie and take her to her class." Christy glanced at her wristwatch. "I really must go."

"All right," Molly said. Her light brown eyes reflected her gratitude. "Please come again. You've been like a ray of sunlight to a weary old woman."

Christy smiled. "A very courageous woman," she corrected. "I'll see you again."

She hurried out of the house and back to the car, feeling a gloomy mood envelop her despite her attempt to be pleasant. She often forgot to count her blessings until she met someone like Molly Adams.

And Zeffie. Christy felt drawn even more to the bright young girl now that she'd heard more about her family. What would happen to her?

9

The two men who walked into the shop soon after Christy returned didn't need to introduce themselves. She could already guess who they were. The older man, short and white haired, cast curious glances around the shop, while the taller guy, long and lanky, spoke in a smooth, polite voice.

"Good morning," the younger one addressed her. "I'm Captain Taylor Davis, and this is Captain Kramer. We're with FDLE in Tallahassee. We've reopened the Strickland case and understand you're the lady who bought the jewelry box."

"That's right," she replied. "I assume you're the two gentlemen who worked the case in 1998?"

"Captain Kramer did. The other officer has retired. I've been assigned in his place," Captain Davis informed her.

"Always helps to bring a fresh pair of eyes to a case," Captain Kramer said, his voice deep and husky.

"Nice to meet you." Christy extended her hand to each of them.

She explained how she came to own the jewelry box and how she found the appraisal slip. She finished her story by supplying Molly Adams's name, clarifying that the box had been brought in by her granddaughter. "Since the jewelry box was given to Zeffie and her grandmother, I don't believe they know anything about the robbery."

"We can't assume anything," Captain Davis pointed out. "I understand the jewelry box belonged to Zeffie's mother."

"That's right. She died a few years ago."

"Sounds like we need to speak with the grandmother," Captain Davis said.

"I can give you the address, but you should know Mrs. Adams has terminal lung cancer. I hope you can be gentle with her."

Captain Davis softened at Christy's words. "We'll do that." He studied her for a moment. "Did you know the Strickland family?"

"Only as neighbors. My grandmother owns the adjoining farm."

Captain Davis handed her his card. "We'll be in touch. Give us a call if you think of anything that might help."

"Thanks for your help, Miss Castleman." Captain Kramer smiled and opened the door.

As they were leaving, Miz B, one of Christy's favorite people, entered the shop.

"How's my girl?" she asked with a wide smile. As usual, her brown eyes twinkled in her round dark face, and she wore a new hairstyle, this one with lots of brown curls and swirls around her face. Miz B had a passion for wigs, one that originated when she had cancer a few years back and chemotherapy took her hair. She was now in remission, and everyone in Summer Breeze kept her on their prayer list.

Christy smiled when she saw the Styrofoam container in Miz B's hands. Well known for the best restaurant in the area, Miz B was a fabulous cook who took pride in her variety of foods, but her main specialty was soul food.

"Brought you a little something for today. Bobbie has offered to host the Red Hats here on Thursday afternoon. She's going to teach us how to make fancy purses for Christmas. Then we'll get all dressed up and participate in the Christmas parade."

"You should! Glad to see you having fun. I know I'll be having fun when I bite into whatever you have in that dish."

"You looked a little pale at church." Miz B frowned. "I thought you needed something healthy, like turnip greens and baked apples with a side of meat loaf."

"Yum." Christy smiled. Miz B always had an excuse for her generosity. Christy knew she looked fine, but she decided to play the game. "I'm glad you realized I need to eat healthy."

While Miz B placed the container of food on the counter, Christy walked around to the cash register.

"Don't you go insulting a good deed," Miz B warned, an ominous threat flashing in her dark eyes.

"Okay," Christy quickly replied. You didn't argue with a six-foot-tall, two-hundred-pound woman when you were a mere five foot three.

"This is a gift," Miz B continued, "not somethin' to be paid for."

Christy turned to a colorful bouquet of scarves and selected one that resembled a Monet painting of water lilies with red accents. "Here you go. Make the other Red Hatters envious and drape this around your neck."

Miz B lit up, her big hand stroking the soft silk. "Won't I be something? You know our chapter's grown to thirty ladies? We're like a bunch of sisters who'd do anything for one another. And we have a mighty good time."

"Terrific. You deserve a good time."

"Well, your aunt's the life of the party. Don't know what we did to entertain ourselves before she hit town. I tell you, she's a bundle of fun." Miz B glanced over her shoulder. "I better get going. Junior will be goofing off in the kitchen instead of chopping onions for the hush puppies. Catfish and hush puppies are one of the specials today."

Christy gave her an affectionate hug and placed the scarf in a small gold shopping bag. "Before you go, I want to ask you something. Everybody comes into your place. Do you know R. J. Wentworth?"

"The one who owns the marina?"

"Yes, that's the one."

Miz B nodded. "I haven't seen him at my restaurant, but I know who he is."

"Do you recall hearing about the robbery and murder over in Washington County back in 1998? Kirby Strickland?"

Miz B hesitated, lifting her gaze to the ceiling for a moment. "I do recall that," she answered, looking back at Christy. "Why?"

"It took place near my grandmother's farm."

"Really?" Miz B's eyes widened even more.

"Really! She saw a strange sports car on the road the day of the murder. The car drove up and down twice. When the authorities checked my grandmother's statement, they learned that a car matching that description belonged to R. J. Wentworth."

Miz B put a hand to her chest. "No!"

"Yes, and while he had an alibi for that day and Granny's claim never got very far, there still seems to be some suspicion." Christy paused. "I should clarify that. The girl R.J. had been dating dropped him for Kirby. After she and Kirby became engaged, she claimed R.J. still followed her. I can't say if that's true, but later, after the tragedy, she married R.J."

Miz B's dark eyes had grown enormous. "I don't know that much about him. All I know is that my son Billy worked on the construction crew Mr. Wentworth hired to rework that marina. Billy wears his feelings on his sleeve, of course, but he and Mr. Wentworth didn't get along. One day Billy got mad and stormed off."

Christy leaned forward. "Why was that?"

Miz B shrugged. "Billy claimed Mr. Wentworth was hard to work for, that he was demanding and short tempered. Seemed real nervous all the time, Billy said."

Christy stared at Miz B, digesting this information. "Do you remember when it was that Billy worked for him?"

Miz B looked into space, silently counting with her fingers. "It was 1998, just before little Billy was born, which was May twenty-eighth. I think he had been working for the man a couple months that spring."

"I see." R.J. had moved fast, setting himself up in the area in order to be near Julie and her fiancé. It also placed him at a convenient location to speed up to Deerfield and back.

Miz B checked her gold wristwatch. "Hey, I gotta run. And your lunch is getting cold." Miz B looked her over, her hands crossed as she laced and unlaced her fingers. Christy recognized this familiar gesture as a signal her mind was working on something.

"You and that fine-looking man gettin' along all right?" she asked, a twinkle rising in her dark eyes.

"Dan and I are great," Christy reported.

"Mm, he sure is handsome. Makes me feel good just to look at him." A deep laugh rumbled through her as she gripped her gold shopping bag and ambled out the door and down the sidewalk to her baby blue Cadillac.

Christy watched her go, wishing she could talk to Billy. She'd really like to hear more about what R.J. was like that spring. It sounded like he was a bundle of nerves, though it made sense. He'd lost Julie to Kirby, then proceeded to try to keep tabs on her. Had his anxiety been prompted by a guilty conscience?

She turned to the container of food, deep in thought, and reached for her bottled water. She sat on a stool and opened the container, glancing at the clock. Already 12:15. The morning had flown by.

She was just finishing her last bite when Bobbie walked through the front door.

"I'm bored to death at home. Mind if I keep you company?"

Christy closed the Styrofoam box and studied her aunt, looking as cute as ever in a pink turtleneck and navy pants, her blond hair twisted up in the back.

"I'm glad you stopped by," Christy replied. "I need a break to run an errand."

"Sure," Bobbie said, flipping the pages of a new decorating magazine. "Does your errand have anything to do with Dan?"

Christy smiled. "In a way." After all, he kept his boat at R.J.'s marina.

"Listen, sweetie," Bobbie called, "can you be back by four? I have an appointment with Valerie for a shampoo and style."

"No problem." Christy grabbed her purse and car keys and hurried out the door.

She drove fast to the marina, constantly on the lookout for a patrol officer. *This is an impulsive thing to do,* she told herself. But when had that ever stopped her?

Checking the clock, she realized she had put herself on a tight schedule, driving to Destin and back in time for Bobbie to keep her appointment. There would be little time to question R.J. if she saw him, but what did she plan to ask?

This is also a foolish thing to do, she thought.

Nevertheless, she felt no inclination to turn around.

Christy pulled into the parking lot of the marina and looked around. A silver Jaguar parked near the office caught her eye. R.J.'s car, no doubt. She hopped out and strolled toward the board-walk, casually looking at the boats, pretending not to realize she stood directly in front of the office. Slowly, she turned and looked through the glass pane of the door. She saw a brightly lit office with FSU memorabilia decorating the walls, along with groupings of framed photographs. A man sat behind a desk, shuffling papers while talking on the phone.

Could this be R.J.? He hung up the telephone, then turned and glanced toward the window. Spotting her, he got up and hurried around the desk, and stepped out the door.

As she watched his approach, she realized he was not at all what she had expected. She would never label this short man with a big belly as handsome, although he might once have been. His hair was a dark blond worn in short layers, and his suntanned skin attested to hours out on the docks. He had a broad forehead, a slim nose, and thin lips, with a dimple in his chin that managed to add a touch of youth. Sunglasses obscured his eyes, and Christy felt a pang of disappointment. She read people by their eyes.

"Hi. Can I help you?" he asked pleasantly. Although he wore

casual clothes, she knew the crisp khakis, polo shirt, and cashmere sweater draped and tied under his collar had borne a hefty price tag. His leather moccasins were scuffed at the toe, but she'd bet they cost more than several pairs of her most expensive heels. "I'm R. J. Wentworth." He extended a thick hand with tapered nails.

"Christy Castleman," she responded, taking his hand.

"Nice to meet you," he replied, dropping her hand after a brief handshake. He was pleasant and friendly but all business.

"Christy Castleman," he repeated. "Aren't you one of the owners of that new shop in Summer Breeze? My wife mentioned it the other night. She also said you were a writer."

"Yes, that's me. Nice of you to remember. May I ask your wife's name?" She kept her demeanor innocent and calm.

"Julie. Julie Clark Wentworth. She owns a boutique at Seaside. Women love her clothes."

"Of course, I remember her now." She hesitated, wondering how to be tactful. She couldn't think of a way at the moment, so she decided to stretch the truth a bit. She called it elaborating.

"As a matter of fact, I believe I first met your wife years ago. Up…" She paused, looking regretful as she looked down at her hands.

"Where did you meet her?" R.J. asked, more interested now.

"It's been a long time. I believe I first met her up at Deerfield, the estate that adjoins my grandmother's farm in Washington County."

His pleasant expression disappeared like a Popsicle beneath a

July sun. "She used to spend time there, all right." He looked out at the water, shoving his hands deep in his pockets.

Christy waited to see if he'd say more.

"I'm not too popular up in those parts," he continued quietly. "People want to believe I cast myself in the role of jilted boyfriend, that I followed Julie around when she was seeing Kirby."

"Oh?"

He hesitated for a moment. "Sometimes. But I never meant any harm." He turned his face back to her. "And I certainly didn't have anything to do with what happened there. I've had to defend my actions so many times over the years that I've learned to just go ahead and explain before the suspicions start." He shrugged. "Guess that's why I'm running my mouth now. I have a bad habit of doing that."

His admission took Christy by surprise. She had never expected him to be so open about such a sensitive subject.

"When you say 'what happened there,' are you referring to the tragedy with Kirby?"

"Yeah. I feel rotten all of that happened to a nice family, but the worst thing I ever did was act like a fool where Julie was concerned."

Through the sunglasses, Christy felt his eyes upon her. He looked her directly in the eye, and she had a hunch that if he removed the sunglasses, she would see raw pain.

It was time to change the subject. "I came here to look for my boyfriend. He was having some trouble with his boat. I thought he might have stopped by over his lunch hour."

"Who's your boyfriend?"

"Dan Brockman. He keeps his boat in that slip down there." She pointed.

"Dan! A real gentleman. I wish everyone who kept their boats at the marina was as nice as that guy." The sadness that had dominated R.J.'s face moments before vanished surprisingly fast, Christy thought.

"I haven't seen Dan," he said, turning to look up and down the marina. "Want me to give him a message if I do?"

"No, that's okay. I'll run into him later."

To prolong the conversation, she considered mentioning the problem with the boat, but then discarded the idea. R.J. might call Dan to inquire. Naturally, R.J. would mention her stopping by, and Dan would guess her motive.

"Obviously he isn't here today, so I guess I misunderstood." She turned to leave, but wanted to end their conversation on a pleasant exchange. "I'll try to check out your wife's shop. I've heard great things about it."

"Do that," he said, watching her for a moment before he spun on his heel and headed down the boardwalk. He called a greeting to a man tying up his boat.

Christy was climbing the steps up from the boardwalk when she remembered Wayne Crocker. She looked down at the slip that normally held his big boat, but it was empty. She supposed he had gone back to Key West.

She hurried to her car, thinking about R.J. Maybe he'd had nothing to do with the crime, after all. Maybe his folly had been to love Julie so much that he made a spectacle of himself chasing her until he caught her.

As she slipped under the steering wheel, she had to ask herself what she'd accomplished by this quick trip. She had met R. J. Wentworth, talked with him, if only for a few minutes, and yet…he seemed candid. He didn't try to hide his role as the jilted boyfriend.

Christy cranked the engine and backed out of the parking spot, replaying the conversation in her mind. Her instincts told her he was not the killer, but she reminded herself that after all these years, he would have developed the right response at the mention of Kirby's name or any references to Deerfield.

When she arrived back at the shop, she opened the door to find Bobbie placing a small red tam on Zeffie Adams's head.

"Perfect timing," Bobbie called, a strange expression on her face. "Zeffie stopped by to see you and—"

"Why did you upset Grandma like that?" Zeffie whirled, glaring at Christy. "I thought you were my friend."

Stunned by her words, Christy walked back to the antique gold mirror where Zeffie and Bobbie stood, examining Zeffie's reflection. Bobbie reached over to the counter for a pair of red bead necklaces and draped them around Zeffie's neck. She looked like a doll with her blond hair and green eyes beneath the red felt tam.

"Honey, you'll be a celebrity." Bobbie knelt beside her. "You're the one who turned in the jewelry box."

Christy shot a thank-you glance in Bobbie's direction, then turned to Zeffie.

"If you and I hadn't discussed removing the lining from the jewelry box, I would never have found that appraisal slip. And it may help solve a murder. Don't you see? You've done everyone a favor."

"Really?" A look of dismay slipped over Zeffie's features.

"Didn't your grandmother tell you? I came to see her this morning to let her know the detectives would want to talk with her," Christy continued, placing her purse and car keys on the counter. "Their questioning her is just a routine procedure. They have to backtrack the trail of the jewelry box. I'm sorry if it upset her, and I'm sorry that you felt betrayed."

"Well…" Zeffie glanced at Bobbie. "Grandma wasn't feeling good when I left for school this morning, so maybe it wasn't just those strange men."

Christy touched the shoulder of Zeffie's white sweatshirt. She was wearing another pair of jeans, too short, and the same tennis shoes with the scuffed toe, but the shiny beads and red tam transformed her into a princess.

"Trust me." Christy patted her shoulder. "I *am* your friend. I wouldn't hurt you or your grandmother. But don't you see? This is going to catch a mean person who stole that jewelry box and…hurt someone over it."

"Killed him!" Zeffie blurted, looking horrified.

"But remember your grandmother said your mother probably got the jewelry box at a garage sale," Christy hastened to add. "The detectives are only checking out facts. That's what detectives are supposed to do."

"Yes!" Bobbie rearranged the beads on Zeffie's sweatshirt. "They were just doing their job. And you've been a big help. You know, the beads and the tam look so cute on you, I'd like you to have them."

Zeffie turned back to her reflection, stroking the shiny beads with her fingers. "They're so pretty."

"And you can be a little mascot for the Red Hatters," Bobbie added.

"What if Zeffie helps out when the ladies come to make their purses for Christmas?" Christy suggested. "She and I talked about starting a craft class for kids. She could help out and get some pointers."

"That would be so cool!" Zeffie said, clearly impressed. Then she frowned. "I don't know if Grandma would want me to accept the beads and hat."

"Of course she will," Christy replied. "I told her you were my friend. And now you have another friend in my aunt Bobbie."

"Yes, you do!" Bobbie affirmed. "Do you think you could help us with the purses? The ladies are coming here on Thursday afternoon with their supplies."

Zeffie nodded, the tam slipping a notch lower on her blond head. "I could come after school."

"Then it's settled!" Christy said, relieved Zeffie no longer saw her as a traitor.

"Oh, look at the time!" Bobbie gasped. "I'll be late to the beauty salon. Can I give you a ride home, Zeffie?"

"No, ma'am. It isn't far. I wouldn't want you to be late." Zeffie looked at Christy. "I'd better go so Grandma doesn't worry."

"Okay. But you don't have to wait until Thursday to come back," Christy called as Zeffie marched proudly toward the door, holding her head high.

"Thank you." She glanced once more at Christy as she followed Bobbie out the door.

∽

A shadow stood in the darkened doorway of a coffee shop that was closed for the off-season. Across the street, Christy Castleman moved around her shop, putting things away, preparing to close for the night.

Darkness had already descended over the quiet streets. Neither Christy nor the shop was of interest now; it was the little girl and her grandmother who presented a new threat. How much did they know?

And how much had Christy Castleman learned from them? Maybe it was time to find out.

11

Christy turned out the lights in the shop, locked the door, and hurried to her car. Most of the other shops were already closed, and the street was practically deserted.

Dan called earlier, asking if he could drop by this evening. She liked that idea and offered to make sandwiches for them. Then he mentioned he wanted to discuss something with her tonight, and her heart sank. He knew she'd been snooping at the marina.

But his next sentence offset that notion. "I'll see you soon, honey." His tone was lighthearted, tinged with an excitement she hadn't heard lately.

She arched an eyebrow as she turned her car down her street and swung into her driveway. The word *discuss* presented all sorts of interesting possibilities. Her mind had been swirling with them ever since she hung up the phone.

Dan arrived shortly after she got home, and they sat on barstools at her kitchen counter, enjoying the club sandwiches she had prepared. He didn't broach the topic in the first thirty minutes, so she filled up the time talking about Zeffie.

Dan reached for her hand. "I think it's great you're being so kind to her. When I get the boat repaired, maybe we can take her out with us."

Christy smiled. "I bet she'd love that."

She fiddled with the crust of her sandwich and thought about her visit to the marina earlier today. Dan seemed unaware of it, and while she was deciding how best to casually mention it, Dan broached the subject he wanted to discuss.

"A former client of mine, Wesley Parker from Montana, called today. You remember his was one of the first houses I designed, and he wanted it on a choice lot over at Rosemary Beach."

Christy nodded, trying to follow his words. "Oh," she suddenly remembered, "you mean that quaint yellow house with the gabled roof?"

"Right. So he called me today and offered to fly me up to Montana to look at some property he may develop on Flathead Lake."

She laid the sandwich on her plate and touched a napkin to her lips. "Flathead Lake?" she echoed. Confusion clouded her mind as she faced him, waiting to hear more. He looked very serious, and her appetite waned.

"His property is located an hour from Glacier National Park, overlooking the lake. He says the area is just being discovered by tourists. It sounds like an exciting opportunity. If you're okay with it, I'll call him back and accept."

"It sounds like a wonderful opportunity," she responded, wishing she could wrap some enthusiasm around her voice. "How long will you be gone?"

"I'm not sure. Would you like to come with me?"

She lowered her gaze to her plate. She couldn't just take off on short notice. She was a partner in a new business they were trying to build. Furthermore, she liked having time to plan for a trip.

She shook her head. "I'd love to, but I can't get away right now. Since this is a short business trip, you can probably accomplish more without me."

They turned back to their sandwiches, but she was no longer hungry.

"You don't seem very enthused about the idea," Dan said as he pushed his empty plate away.

She hesitated. "Oh, I think it's great that Mr. Parker wants your opinion. He knows a good architect when he sees one."

Dan reached over to rub his thumb against the corner of her mouth, and she grinned, imagining she probably had mayonnaise all over her lips.

"I'm going to try to get a flight out of Panama City tomorrow or the next day," he said, then glanced at his watch. "Where did the time go?" He folded his napkin and stood. "Sorry I have to be in a rush tonight. I should have planned better."

"When will I see you again?" she asked, looking into his eyes.

"Tomorrow night, if I don't leave until Wednesday. I'll call and let you know."

She nodded. "Great."

He stood and pulled her into his arms, giving her a warm, deep kiss. He studied her face for a moment, then glanced at the wall clock. "I really hate to leave, but I'm meeting with my foreman in half an hour to go over the week's schedule and be sure he understands exactly what has to be done while I'm away. Then I'll be up half the night packing and gathering up architectural plans to take with me."

She nodded absently, only half listening. She reminded herself of the lesson she had learned during their last breakup. *Don't be needy and possessive.*

She hugged him, then stepped back. "I think Mr. Parker will get good advice," she said. "After all, you're the best."

He cupped her chin in his broad hands. "You're making it difficult for me to leave." He kissed her again, but she gently pushed him away.

"You'll be late," she said, glancing at the clock.

"Okay, I'll call you." He turned toward the door.

Her eyes lingered on his dark hair, the broad shoulders and slim torso over long legs. He carried himself with dignity and pride, and yet he was the kindest man she'd ever known except for her father.

After he left, she turned the lock on the door and gathered up their plates, rinsed them and placed them in the dishwasher. She hesitated at the sink, looking through her kitchen window to the darkness beyond. She missed Dan already, and he hadn't even left. She closed the door of the dishwasher and absently twisted the dial to pots and pans, although none were loaded. The water swooshed loudly in the dishwasher as she marched into her office and flipped the light switch.

She needed to start another novel. Creating stories about historical characters had always been her therapy in the past. Best of all, she liked writing happy endings. One or two critics had termed them too idealistic, but she wrote them for all the readers in the world who needed happy endings. They didn't need another punch of reality.

She turned on the computer and stared blankly at the monitor as it flashed through its routine. She couldn't seem to focus on work. Like the paper that often jammed in her printer, her thoughts were stuck on her relationship with Dan.

It was useless trying to work when she couldn't generate any interest in her writing. She kept thinking about the glow in Dan's eyes when he'd told her about this new opportunity in Montana. If he gave Mr. Parker good advice and laid out a plan for him, then he would probably be offered a job overseeing the project to completion. How long would that take?

She pushed her chair back from her computer desk and stared up at the painting of a pirate ship.

She didn't want to leave Summer Breeze again, but if she regressed to being possessive and petty, Dan wouldn't ask her to go with him.

Glancing at the clock, she decided to go to bed and see what tomorrow would bring. When she reached her bedroom, her eyes fell on the Bible on her nightstand. She reached over and picked it up. The pages, worn tissue-soft, held notations and highlights throughout. She had never believed in the idea that one had to be so respectful of a Bible that it shouldn't be marked up. Her markings were references to passages that gave her strength and comfort.

She began to read some of the highlighted verses, finding the strength that work could not provide. Only the One who created her could understand her fears and doubts and provide her with fresh hope and promises on which she could rely.

12

Tuesday

She spent the night tossing and turning. When she woke in the morning, she blinked and looked around. Her covers looked as though they'd been whirled into a wad in the dryer. As she freshened up and went to the kitchen for her morning coffee and muffin, she decided to call Jack. She'd offer to take him to lunch if he promised to keep her laughing. Jack's humor had always appealed to her. He could make her laugh quicker and harder than anyone she knew. Even Dan.

As the coffee brewed, she picked up the phone and dialed his number.

"Ah, my sunshine girl." His deep voice rumbled over the line, the words filled with affection.

"So you broke down and got caller ID. Don't want to miss a call from Bobbie, right?"

"Or from you. Hey, I'm no tightwad. I just never cared who called until now. The other reason I never got caller ID was so you'd have to drive out to see me if you wanted to talk."

Christy smiled. "I should have known you'd have the perfect answer. I do want to see you, in fact. I wanted to invite you to lunch because I need a good laugh today, and I can always count on you for that."

"Hey, this is my lucky day. Getting taken to lunch by the prettiest woman in the panhandle, the second prettiest being your aunt. Anything wrong?"

She hesitated. "Dan's flying to Montana today or tomorrow. He's been asked to look over a project and give his opinion."

"Don't sound so gloomy. He'll only be gone a few days, and in the meantime, you get to have barbecue with me every day. And today I have a special place in mind."

"And where is that?" she asked, pouring coffee and smiling. Jack always seemed to know what to say to make her happy.

"Let's drive down to Mexico Beach and eat at the Hickory Pitt, Willie's place. You'll forget your city manners and start licking your fingers soon as you get a taste of his special barbecue sauce."

"Sounds wonderful. And since you live closer to Mexico Beach than I do, I'll get dressed and drive out to Rainbow Bay. We can leave from there."

"I love the way you think. And I'm glad you're taking time off to make an old man happy."

"Stop that. No one thinks of you as *old* and I doubt you think of yourself that way. See you in a couple of hours."

By the time Christy pulled into Jack's driveway, he was already out in the yard, dressed neatly in jeans and a denim shirt, with a wide smile that lit up his blue eyes. His eyes had once been darker, but a lifetime beneath the Florida sun had faded the deep blue to pale blue, and she thought of the morning sky. She liked this shade better. In fact, there was very little about Jack she didn't like. The man who had almost been her father-in-law had become a second dad instead, and she wrinkled her nose at him as he strode up to the driver's side.

"As fancy as your new car is, let's go in mine," Jack said in greeting.

"You don't trust my driving?"

"I'm of the old school, and you know it. I like to do the driving."

"Spare me the Back Bay philosophy." She wiggled over the arm rest and flopped into the passenger seat. "Get in and drive. It's full of gas, and knowing you, I bet you're running on your last fumes."

Jack was a stickler for keeping a full tank of gas, and they both knew it, but she loved teasing him almost as much as he loved handing it right back to her. She expected more debate, but he opened the door and slid in, mumbling something about 'you women with short legs' as he adjusted the seat.

"If you want a long-legged woman, you missed your chance two months ago with Roseann Cole," Christy said.

He threw back his head and roared with laughter. As his laughter subsided, he turned the key in the ignition, threw his arm up over the seat, and looked over his shoulder as he backed her SUV out of the drive.

Christy looked at Jack and smiled. She suddenly felt good, just being with him.

"So," he said, pulling onto the road. "Why are you so upset about Dan leaving town for a few days?" He shot her a worried glance. "I hope you're not gonna turn into one of those women who has to be in control of her man. You've never been that way before. Your aunt's not that way."

"Let's face it, Jack," she retorted. "I'll never have the charisma Bobbie has. She could talk you into anything, and before it was over, you'd think it was your idea."

"Nope! I don't play that game."

Christy turned to look out the window, hiding her smile. He was already playing that game; he just wouldn't admit it.

They turned onto the main highway, and Jack waved at Buster Greenwood as his white double-cab truck roared out from the convenience store. Buster grinned and waved back, his face as round as one of Miz B's dinner plates.

"Looks like Buster's put on a few more pounds," Christy commented, glancing back through the window.

"Buster likes to eat almost as much as he likes to fish."

"So now, when he stops for gas, Buster avails himself of Jed's doughnuts." She shook her head. Some people never worried about what they ate, just how often they ate.

"Let's get back to what we were talking about," Jack said, obviously prepared to offer his advice concerning Dan. Christy suspected he had been thinking about it since she called him earlier. "I think it's great someone respects Dan's talent enough to want his ideas all the way out in Montana."

"As long as all they want are ideas."

"What do you mean by that?"

Christy sighed. "Nothing."

Jack made a face. "I hate how you say *nothing* when that pretty little head of yours is just crammed with worries. You think this guy will want Dan to come to Montana to oversee the project?"

She lowered her gaze to her uneven nails. She needed a manicure. Maybe she'd go over to Valerie's shop and spoil herself. A manicure from Carol would make her feel great.

"If he went out to Montana, he wouldn't stay," Jack continued, refusing to let her drift away from the conversation. "He loves it here. He's got too much invested to leave."

She turned in the seat to face him. "You think so? I know he bought those ten acres, and he owns his own place and the property in his new development."

"And he has a more important investment: you."

The words warmed her heart, and she realized how much she'd needed to hear them.

"Christy, I approve of Dan more than any guy I've ever met. I'd like to see it work out for you."

She touched his arm. "Thanks, Jack."

He slowed down, and she looked up to see the sign for the Hickory Pitt. Her mind shot back to Vince Brown's suspicions about Willie Pitt concerning the robbery and murder. She hadn't planned it this way, but sizing up Willie and maybe getting his opinion on what happened at Deerfield would help her fixate on something other than Dan.

The square concrete building was nothing fancy, but hickory

smoke curled through the air like an aphrodisiac. Anyone with a taste for barbecue either turned into the driveway or did a U-turn after they passed and came back.

"We're early today. That's good." Jack steered the SUV into the parking lot and cut the engine. "My stomach's already growling. You hungry?"

"I hadn't thought about it, but now I'm starving," Christy replied, opening her door and hopping onto the graveled path that led up to the screen door. Within, the sounds of male laughter mingled with a ringing telephone and the hiss of smoke from the grill.

As soon as they entered the building, Christy spotted the man who had to be Willie. He towered behind the counter, a wide smile on his dark face, and was just lifting a Gators baseball cap to scratch his shiny bald head. *Big* best described him, as he stood well over six feet tall, with huge arms, a thick chest, and a quick, deep laugh that set the mood for all his customers. A white bib apron bore traces of his famous sauce, and he yelled through the open partition for the kitchen to dip up some extra sauce.

"My favorite customer just walked in," he called, as Christy and Jack settled into a booth with a planked table, scarred from use and punctuated with initials.

"Christy, this is Willie Pitt, the master of barbecue. And this"—Jack gestured dramatically at Christy—"is the prettiest, smartest young lady you'll ever meet."

Willie's big eyes lit with interest. "I have no doubt of that. What're you doing with this old codger?"

"He's my second dad," she responded, "and one of my dearest friends."

Willie put his wide hands on his hips and leaned back a notch. "Man, you've done yourself proud," he said, quirking a bushy eyebrow at Jack. Then he looked at Christy and spoke more seriously. "I know who you are, Miss Castleman. I've heard a lotta nice things about you, and not just from this dude."

"Okay, let's cut the bull and order," Jack said, looking across the table at Christy. "I'm having my usual barbecue ribs, but the chicken's great. Or if you just want a sandwich, his pulled pork is the best."

Christy nodded. "The sandwich is what I want." She glanced at the couple nearby who were each trying to gather a huge sandwich in their hands. "Looks like all I can manage."

"And I reckon you two want sweet tea," Willie said. "Jack always takes extra lemon."

"Jack just likes to be fussed over," Christy teased. "I'll take my tea the same as everyone else."

Willie chuckled. "Coming right up." He hurried across the small interior, moving with an easy grace that surprised her for a man of his size and build.

"He's funny," she said to Jack, as Willie shouted their orders into the kitchen. She noticed a middle-aged woman taking orders and a guy in his twenties delivering food. "You get special treatment here, I see. He's personally taking care of us."

"Yeah," Jack agreed, his eyes roaming across the half-dozen tables in the center of the room back to the booths along the wall. He folded his hands on the table and leaned forward, his voice lowered. "You see why I said he could never have been involved in that Strickland thing."

Actually, she couldn't see. Willie made a pleasant impression, but she had watched two other killers fool the community. Consequently, she reserved her judgments until she knew more about people and what motivated them. She had learned through bitter experience that some people lived double lives.

But she didn't want to sound cynical, so she merely nodded.

"I like this place," she said, enjoying the ambience. The board walls held all sorts of memorabilia. An old cast iron skillet hung on a rack, along with framed prints reminiscent of general stores and early farm days. She could see Willie was an avid football fan. Autographed pictures of several well-known players lined the walls, and since Elvis wailed out the second song in a row from the speakers in the ceiling, she suspected Willie was also an Elvis fan. Her guess was confirmed when she turned and looked at the wall behind her, where a poster featured Elvis in his famous white suit.

One of the servers delivered two king-size glasses of iced tea and a small bowl filled with lemon slices.

"I'd say you got extra lemon," Christy teased, selecting a ripe yellow slice and squeezing it into her tea.

"I always do."

Christy took a swallow of the sweet tea, relishing the taste. In the next minute, a fat round sandwich stuffed with pork sat on a white plate in front of her, with a dill pickle and potato chips.

"Ah, look at this." Jack cast a loving look at his platter. The stack of thick pork ribs, dripping with sauce, and mound of potato salad and slaw could feed three people Jack's size. Nevertheless, he dug in, obviously welcoming the challenge.

"You were right," Christy said, between mouthfuls. "This food is fantastic."

Jack wiped his mouth with a napkin. "Willie prides himself on his barbecue and insists on his staff doing the same."

Christy glanced back at big Willie, propped against the counter, teasing a guy seated on the barstool. He'd make an interesting match for Miz B. They had a lot in common with their restaurants, size, and affable nature.

Willie turned as though feeling her eyes upon him. Straightening his apron, he hurried to their table.

"Everything all right here?"

"Wonderful," Christy said. "This barbecue is everything Jack claimed it to be."

Willie chuckled, and Jack scooted over in the booth, moving his plate and glass. "Take a load off your feet and join us for a minute."

Willie glanced at Christy. "Well, if you want me to."

"We do," Christy said, smiling at him.

"We came here to eat and not to ask questions," Jack began, "but since we're here, something interesting happened at Christy's shop last week."

"My aunt and I have a shop in Summer Breeze," she explained. "We buy and sell everything from antiques to flea market finds. Anyway, a little girl brought in a jewelry box to sell."

Willie nodded. "News travels fast in these parts. I already heard about it." He looked at Jack. "I have a policeman friend who comes down here a couple times a week for barbecue. I reckon all the police on the coast are talking about what happened. You bought the box, right?"

Christy nodded. "When I cleaned it up and ripped out the old lining, I found an appraisal slip underneath. The slip gave Annabell Strickland's name and address. The jewelry box turned out to be the one taken from Deerfield the night Kirby was murdered."

Willie leaned back against the booth, heaving a sigh. "Awful, just awful what happened to that boy." He glanced at Jack. "Did you tell her I catered the barbecue the day he got killed?"

When Jack nodded, Willie shook his bald head, and all the humor of moments before drained from his face. His forehead rumpled into a network of frowns. "The Stricklands were good folks. I don't know who'd hurt Kirby."

He crossed his arms over his broad chest. "As Jack may have told you, I was on the suspect list in the beginning. The investigators found my fingerprints in the office and came after me like a bunch of bloodhounds starving for fresh meat. But I told them the truth. After the guests left and we cleaned up, Mr. Kirby asked if I wanted to be paid in cash or check. Naturally, I prefer cash." He glanced at Jack, who seemed to understand his reasoning. "I followed him into the front office and pulled back a chair to sit down while he opened a drawer and counted out cash. When I reached over to the desk, I left more fingerprints."

As Christy listened, she thought Willie seemed pretty straightforward about it all.

"I left there around four thirty when me and my guys had

cleaned up, and I never went back. Our pastor and his wife dropped by to visit that evening. Lou, my wife, had called them to come pray with us. She'd just got more bad news." He looked at Christy. "Her cancer had spread to her brain. She died two months later."

Christy leaned forward. "I'm sorry to hear that." She hesitated for a moment, trying to be tactful. "Willie, did you ever have suspicions about anyone? Did anyone show an unusual interest in the house the day of the barbecue?"

"Well, I did think of someone, but she wasn't there that day. I wondered about Della—that's the housekeeper who quit before Miss Annabell died. Not that she'd do it, but I felt like she was a link to someone who would."

"Really?" Christy stared at him. She hadn't heard anything about Della.

"Yes ma'am. She had a friend, Reuben Foster—well, he'd been a friend to her husband. When the detectives found out he had a connection to Della, they were quick to track him down and take fingerprints and DNA. But he didn't match up with anyone who'd been around that day or night, so that shot down my theory. I think he's in jail now, caught driving drunk again."

"So the authorities took a sample of his DNA? And Della too?" Christy repeated, wanting to be sure she had heard correctly.

"Yes ma'am. I know for a fact they took samples from everybody. I heard CSI from Tallahassee went over every empty pop can and paper plate in the trash. Everybody at the barbecue and me and my crew gave samples and got fingerprinted. Later, all the friends and neighbors had to do that."

Jack turned to Christy. "Willie had a booming restaurant in town, but all the gossip over the Strickland case hurt his business." He looked back at the big man beside him. "And I guess you wanted a change anyway after Lou passed."

"Yeah, I just wanted to get away from all the bad memories of that tragedy and the way Lou suffered..." He took a deep breath and glanced around his small café. "Anyway, I like it better down here. I don't have to cater anymore, and my regulars like Jack here don't mind driving a little further if my barbecue's worth it."

"Everybody knows you're the best." Jack pushed back his platter, still one third full. "Can't hold anymore."

Willie stood up. "Why don't I box it up for you? You can finish it off at home tonight."

"Great idea," Jack said, reaching for his billfold.

"Today it's on the house," Willie said. "Just seeing you and meeting this lovely young lady is a big pleasure for a fat old guy like me. If you'll come back," he added, glancing at Christy.

"Oh, I'll be back," she replied. "I can promise you that."

The food had been wonderful, and Willie had been a rich source of information.

13

Christy went jogging at the beach, then chose a side street back to her house, hoping to get rid of some pent-up emotions.

Dan had called from the airport on her drive home from lunch. He could get a flight out of Panama City at two and was hurrying to the gate. She had wished him a safe trip, they had said their love yous, and she had hung up, feeling a dip in her mood. As soon as she got home, she'd grabbed her running shoes and headed out, determined to lift her spirits.

She was only a few blocks from home when she spotted Deputy Arnold's big SUV. He stood on the sidewalk, waving a broad finger at a guy who had parked his motorcycle and stood listening to the lecture. "Organ donors, that's what you folks are. Don't you get on the bike again without a helmet."

"Yes sir." The red-faced young man hurried off.

Christy stood in the background, sipping the bottle of water she'd hooked on the belt of her running suit. "Hey, Deputy Arnold."

Big Bob, broad in body and head, had tried to pretend irritation when she solved two murders in the community, but in the final analysis, he appreciated her hard work.

As Bob turned, she smiled. "Glad to see you out saving lives."

Bob ignored her comment. "I want to ask you something. I understand the Strickland murder case has been reopened." He propped his big fists on his hips. "Everybody's talking about you being the one who bought the jewelry box and returned it to Ellen Brown. Now the sheriff in Washington County has called in FDLE. They stopped by my office yesterday."

Christy nodded. "They came to see me, too. I gave them the names of the people who sold me the box."

"Molly Adams. Or rather her granddaughter. The Strickland murder took place in another county, and I wasn't involved, but I've been asked to keep an eye on the Adams family for their protection."

At the end of the block near the school, Christy spotted Zeffie with her backpack, wearing the familiar sweatshirt and jeans. Today she also sported the shiny red beads.

"Speaking of angels, I hear the flutter of little wings. That's Zeffie Adams," Christy said, as the little girl waved at her. "The grand-daughter. Maybe this would be a good time for you to meet her."

Since Bob had five children of his own and possessed a soft spot in his heart for children, he turned his big frame and faced Zeffie as she approached.

"How was your day, Zeffie?" Christy asked.

"Okay," she responded pleasantly. Her green eyes widened, tak-ing in the looming presence of Bob Arnold.

"Zeffie, I'd like you to meet the man who protects us here in Summer Breeze. This is Deputy Arnold. And Deputy Arnold, say hello to Miss Zeffie Adams."

Zeffie giggled at the formal introduction. As Bob extended his big hand, she reached forward and took it, her small hand lost in his.

"Well, Zeffie," Bob said, sizing her up, "it's very nice to meet you."

"Do you catch criminals?" she asked, looking him over.

"I do my best, but we don't have many criminals here. This is a great place to live."

Her smile moved from Bob to Christy then back. "Maybe you can catch the person who once owned my jewelry box and arrest him for the awful thing he did."

Bob lifted his hand to stroke his broad cheek. "Everyone in this part of the country would like to solve that case."

"And Zeffie has already been a big help," Christy added. "If not for her, we'd never have found the appraisal slip. She's the one who gave us an important clue."

"Is that right?" Bob asked. "Then I have something for you, Zeffie."

He turned and strode back to his car, reaching into the backseat. He came back with a cigar box that he opened to reveal several round buttons like the smiley-face ones, only these read Good Citizen.

His normally serious face broke into a wide smile. "I give these to people who do good for the community. I think you've earned one."

Zeffie stared at the button he gave her. "Can I wear it all the time?"

"Sure you can," Bob replied, his demeanor indicating this wasn't something he normally did.

"Here, let me clip it on for you." Christy inserted the pin through Zeffie's sweatshirt and hooked it into the catch.

Zeffie touched it, pride lighting her eyes. "Oh, thank you! Grandma will be so proud."

Bob's big face, creased with the smile, turned serious again. "Gotta go. You girls keep on being good citizens."

"Yes sir," Zeffie called after him, "we will." Her green eyes lingered on his big SUV as he got in, rocking the front seat with his weight. Waving, he pulled out from the curb and drove off.

She turned to Christy. "Grandma had to go to the doctor today, and she said it'd be okay for me to stop by your shop for a while."

Christy hesitated. "Bobbie's there, but I have to drive over to Seaside." She caught herself before she explained why: to meet Julie Wentworth.

Zeffie fidgeted from one foot to the other. "I've never been to Seaside."

Christy's resolve crumpled. How could she refuse? She'd find a way to talk to Julie out of earshot from Zeffie.

"Then do you want to go home, put your books up, and leave your grandmother a note? We should be back by five or five thirty. I'll jog home, shower, and change clothes, and that'll give you a little time."

"Super!" Zeffie lit up. "I'm making so many nice friends." Her small hand touched the Good Citizen button, then moved to the shiny red beads Bobbie had given her.

"That's because everyone likes you, Zeffie. That should make you feel really good about yourself." Christy wanted to make this point, because Zeffie needed someone to instill her worth and give her confidence after being deserted by both parents. There was a limit to what a sick grandmother could do.

"Okay." Christy glanced at her watch. "It's 3:10. How about I pick you up around 3:45?"

"I'll be ready," Zeffie said, taking off at a run.

~

At exactly 3:45, Christy pulled into Molly Adams's driveway, and Zeffie shot out the front door. Apparently Molly had already returned, for she followed Zeffie onto the porch.

Christy got out of the car. "Hi, Mrs. Adams. I hope the detectives didn't upset you. Zeffie seemed to think they did."

Zeffie paused on the cracked sidewalk and looked back at her grandmother.

Molly returned her gaze. "Honey, remember I told you last night, the detectives weren't the reason I had to stay in bed. I…just didn't feel well."

Christy guessed the memory of April had brought on a depression. Even in the sunlight, Molly looked pale and she seemed to lean against the door for support.

"No, the men were real nice. I gave them Sheryl Wilcox's name in Fort Walton. Maybe she can help."

"Good." Christy looked at Zeffie. "See how you've helped in getting this case reopened?"

Zeffie looked pleased. She had removed the beads, washed her face, and brushed her straight hair until it gleamed like gold. She wore the red tam on her head.

Christy smiled. "I like that hat on you." The photographs of Zeffie's mother flashed through her memory. Mrs. Adams had been right. Zeffie bore no resemblance to April. Christy wondered about the mysterious father.

"You two have fun," Molly called hoarsely.

"Thanks," Christy replied. "We should be back by five or five thrity."

Molly nodded and smiled, then stepped back inside and closed the door.

As they drove to Seaside, Zeffie chatted merrily about the Thursday afternoon craft session when Bobbie would teach everyone how to make fancy purses.

"I love sequins and beads," she said.

Christy listened, nodding at the appropriate times. With meeting Julie on her mind, she had showered and shampooed her hair, still damp on the ends, and put on a pair of khakis and a V-neck cashmere sweater, recently purchased. It was that shade of sky blue she could never resist. The afternoon was wearing on, and the Gulf breezes would pick up soon, so the lightweight sweater seemed appropriate.

Zeffie turned to stare at the emerald waves breaking at the shoreline. "It's so different here from Montgomery. People are much friendlier."

"Yeah, Summer Breeze is a great place," Christy replied.

Zeffie was quiet for a moment, then surprised Christy with her next topic. "Momma always said she hated Montgomery. The last

time she came home, I thought she might take me back with her."
She sighed. "Anyway, Grandma wouldn't have let me go, and
Momma seemed like a stranger. Even though she brought me that
jewelry box, she didn't really seem to care about me." There was no
self-pity in Zeffie's voice. She merely related the facts.

"Momma kept lifting the lid on my jewelry box and listening to
that song. She said it made her think of someone a long time ago."
A heavy sigh followed, and she turned to look through the window
as they approached Seaside. "That was the last time I ever saw her."

14

C hristy turned into the ice cream shop. "Hey, I feel like something special. What about you?"

Zeffie grinned. "Me too."

They decided to share a banana split, with an extra dip of chocolate sauce. "I've never had a banana split," Zeffie admitted, dipping her spoon in the center of the sundae.

Looking at her, Christy realized Zeffie had missed many special treats in her life. She hoped the people of Summer Breeze would continue to spoil her, making her feel welcome, giving her little gifts.

After they left the ice cream shop, Christy spotted Julie's Boutique. "Let's go in here," she suggested. "We washed our hands after the ice cream, right?"

"I used extra soap," Zeffie boasted. The little red tam sat at a jaunty angle on her head, and beneath the tam, sunlight bounced off her long gold hair. When she looked up at Christy, an expression of tenderness filled her eyes. Christy smiled at her, thinking how rewarding it felt to see life in a fresh new way through the eyes of a child.

They opened the door of the boutique and crossed the threshold onto a lush white carpet. An ambience of wealth drifted through the air, from the crystal chandeliers to the exquisite clothes on padded hangers. Behind a glass counter, a woman placed a gleaming silver bracelet in a box.

"Hello," she called, a small yet friendly smile touching her glossed lips. She was a beautiful woman with small features, hazel eyes, and long dark hair with auburn highlights. Christy knew this had to be Julie.

She walked out from behind the counter, and Christy noticed how small and thin she was. She doubted she weighed more than ninety-eight pounds, though the thick, long hair and heavy jewelry would add a pound or two. She wore a brown pantsuit adorned with beads, chains, and gold cuff bracelets. Yet all of this paled in the sparkle of the huge diamond ring on her left hand.

"May I help you?" she asked in a soft voice.

"Maybe," Christy replied. "We're just browsing. My aunt has a birthday soon, and we're trying to find something for her."

"Oh? Does she like clothes, purses, jewelry?" Her eyes drifted down to Zeffie, and a quick smile touched her lips. "You have a Good Citizen badge," she observed. "Congratulations."

"Thank you. The sheriff gave it to me."

"Deputy Bob Arnold," Christy explained. "This is my friend, Zeffie Adams."

Julie's gaze moved to the little red tam.

"Aunt Bobbie gave me the hat," Zeffie said. She looked at Christy. "She told me to call her Aunt Bobbie." She turned back to Julie. "I don't have a real aunt."

"Oh." Confusion clouded Julie's hazel eyes.

"Zeffie, look at that display of purses on the back table," Christy said. "Why don't you check them out and get some ideas for the class on Thursday?"

As Zeffie hurried to the back of the shop, Christy turned to Julie. "I'm Christy Castleman."

"Of course." Julie extended her hand. "I've heard of you. Sorry to say I haven't read your mysteries, but I do know about your shop. I've been wanting to get down there ever since you opened."

"Thanks. I met your husband the other day."

She nodded and looked down at her hands, lacing her fingers together. "He mentioned you were a friend of the Stricklands." Julie looked at Christy, the hazel eyes bleak. "I'll never forgive myself for calling Kirby to go back to the house to pick up that list." Her voice had not modulated from the small, whispery tone, but a tremble vibrated through her words.

"You can't blame yourself," Christy replied softly. "How could anyone know such a thing would happen? I was away at that time, but as I understand it, a burglar came into the house and panicked. That could have happened anytime."

Julie nodded, yet Christy's words did not seem to comfort her. She sighed. "I just wish Ellen and I could be friends like before, but she's so bitter, and Vince makes it worse. They hated R.J., and now they hate me for marrying him. Vince wasn't Mrs. Strickland's first choice for a son-in-law, so I don't know why he's so quick to judge others."

Suddenly Julie seemed to think of something, and her long hair swirled about her face as she darted a glance at Zeffie. "Is that the little girl who sold you the jewelry box?" she whispered, turning back to Christy. "Everyone is talking about the box and the appraisal, and that the case is being reopened."

Wow, Christy thought. Willie had been right when he said news traveled fast.

She nodded. "Zeffie brought the box in. I believe her mother bought it at a garage sale. Unfortunately, we can't ask her; she was killed in a car wreck."

Julie's bracelets rattled as her hand shot to her mouth. "How horrible. What about the little girl?"

"She lives with her grandmother."

Zeffie walked up the aisle to them. "Those aren't the kind of purses we want to make. I think the ladies want something really fancy, with feathers and sequins. Did you find something for Aunt Bobbie?"

Christy noticed a lovely crystal brooch in a navy box in the showcase. "She'd love that brooch, I think."

"It is pretty, isn't it?" Julie removed the small box from its display beside other exquisite jewelry. She handed it to Christy.

Christy admired the brooch but almost gasped at the price. "Sorry. It's a bit over my budget." She started to hand it back, but Julie's hand stopped her.

"Since your family was friends with Kirby, why don't I knock it down to wholesale? And Zeffie"—she reached behind the counter and opened a drawer—"here's a little something for you." She handed Zeffie a thin gold bangle. "One of my customers ordered it for her granddaughter but then chose something else, so I'm stuck with it." She grinned. "You can have it if you like it."

Zeffie gasped, overwhelmed by the lovely little bracelet. "Thank you!" Impulsively, her arms flew around Julie's tiny waist.

"You're very welcome," Julie said, gently touching a strand of Zeffie's gold hair.

"Thanks for being so generous with us," Christy said, opening her shoulder bag to withdraw her billfold. She suspected the price Julie had offered on the brooch was below wholesale, but she also knew this was something Julie wanted to do, and as Miz B would say, she didn't want to offend a kindness. Christy laid some bills on the glass counter. "If you find something you like at our shop, I'll return the favor."

"Don't worry about it." Julie placed the purchase in a fancy gift bag, then glanced at Zeffie. "Do you want a bag for your bracelet?"

"Oh no!" Zeffie had already thrust the gold bangle on her wrist. "I'd like to wear it, if that's okay."

"Of course it's okay, if you promise to come back in." Julie extended a small hand to grasp Zeffie's. "And you can call me Aunt Julie if you want. I don't have an aunt either, just an uncle. I'm the only child in our small family."

"So am I!" Zeffie looked as though this made them blood kin.

"We'd better run," Christy said, glancing at an ornate French clock. "We'll have to push it to get you back when I promised."

Christy faced Julie again. "I'd like to talk with you again some time. About that night."

Julie nodded. "I'd love to see you again. Both of you." She looked at Zeffie with a hint of yearning. "I'm honored to be your aunt." She looked at Christy. "We can't have children, and I adore kids. I guess I relate to children more than adults."

Her words hung in the air, and Christy realized how fragile she seemed. She was the type who needed someone at her side, and apparently R.J. had done all the right things.

Another thought struck Christy: or had he done a wrong thing—something to ensure he kept the woman he deeply loved?

15

Too weary to cook or go out, Christy pulled a microwavable meal from her freezer and made a face. She disliked frozen meals, but at least this one contained veggies, which would be healthier than the peanut butter and jelly sandwich she would have eaten otherwise.

After picking over the meal and sipping her iced tea, she gave up. Pushing the dish aside, she sat on the barstool of the kitchen counter, her mind replaying each scene of the day. She'd gathered a wealth of information, beginning with Willie Pitt and ending with Julie. Now she tried to process it.

She had already put on her cotton pajamas and scuffs, so with her glass of tea in hand, she wandered into the living room and glanced idly around.

A blue chenille sofa and matching love seat dominated the small room. Glass end tables and a matching coffee table balanced the seating area. A Thomas Kinkade painting with a favorite psalm beneath the scene brightened the wall behind the love seat, and on the end wall, an entertainment center held a television and shelves of DVDs, magazines, and books.

She sank onto the sofa and reached past the home and fashion magazines scattered over her coffee table to pick up the pen and notepad that she always left there. She'd learned to keep a pen and pad in every room of the house in case an idea came to her about her novels or she saw or read something she wanted to jot down.

Suspects. She wrote the word across the top of the lined steno pad.

1. R. J. Wentworth

She paused, chewing on the end of the pen. He almost seemed too obvious. Unless, as Miz B suggested, he had hired a killer to make it look like a robbery. If so, the jewelry wouldn't have meant that much to him. Maybe that's how he paid the killer. As for the jewelry box, he'd probably tossed it out somewhere, and it had been retrieved and sold at a garage sale.

2. Willie Pitt

Vince had speculated about him, and yet Willie had a solid alibi, which Vince had hinted was odd.

3. Vince Brown

More than one person had noted that Vince had gained financially by marrying into the Strickland family and then taking over the farm and timber business after Kirby was murdered. A very strong motive for murder, but was he capable of it? He kept mentioning alibis—what was his? She shook that thought aside. He loved Ellen too much to kill her brother.

4. Della, the housekeeper

Willie had mentioned her as a link. One of her friends was bad news, he'd said. Willie obviously believed this man should be a suspect. What was his name? She leaned back against the cushion, trying to recall. Reuben?

She laid down her pen and walked back to the kitchen. Glancing at the notepad where she'd written Ellen's telephone number, she dialed.

She expected to get the answering machine, but to her surprise, Ellen answered.

"Hi, Ellen. It's Christy. Are you busy?"

"Just helping the boys with their homework. What's up?"

Christy tried to organize her thoughts. "Two detectives came by to see me. I told them everything I knew, then sent them to the Adams home. Mrs. Adams gave them the name of her daughter's roommate in Fort Walton. That's where she was living at the time."

"I still have my suspicions about the daughter. What's the name of this roommate?" Ellen asked tersely.

"Sheryl Wilcox. Ever heard of her?"

"No, but I've never heard of April Adams either."

"The detectives are going to Fort Walton to locate Sheryl and see if she can shed any light on where April got the jewelry box."

Ellen didn't respond to that.

"I wanted to ask you something, Ellen. I heard that the housekeeper, Della—"

"Della Young. What about her?"

"Do you know if she had a friend who was considered, well, a bit notorious?"

Ellen sighed. "They investigated him, I believe, but couldn't link him to the house. As for Della, I never knew her that well. Mother hired her while I was away at school. After Vince and I married and moved back, she was always busy vacuuming or cleaning when I stopped by. She didn't come in on weekends, and that's when I was most often here. When Mother and I went shopping, she'd drive into Lynn Haven."

She hesitated for a moment. "I do know Della quit right after Christmas. Mother never gave the reason. A week or two later, Mother died. Della came to the funeral and seemed all broken up, but I don't know anything about her personal life. Why?" The question was a demand. "Has someone heard something I should know?"

"No, the name just came up in conversation." Christy didn't want to say the name had come from Willie Pitt, whom Vince openly suspected. "Everyone down here is talking about the case." She paused, noting the silence on the other end. "Ellen, I have a personal interest in this because Kirby saved me from drowning when I was a girl."

"Really?" Ellen gasped. "I don't remember that."

"You weren't there. It was Fourth of July, 1987. My brother and I went up to Granny's for the annual community picnic at the lake."

"Tell me about it."

"I was eleven years old, learning to swim. I guess I needed a few more swimming lessons, because when I got out in deep water and began to flounder, I panicked. Kirby jumped in to save me. I've never forgotten how kind he was."

"I never heard about that," Ellen said, her voice filled with tenderness. "Ever since he died, people are always telling me wonderful stories about him, things I never knew. Kirby did so much for people, but he never bragged about it."

"I know. I always felt indebted to him. If there's any way I can help track down his killer now, I feel compelled to do that."

"I understand, and being a mystery writer, you probably have good instincts about people and situations like…this one."

"I don't know; I just feel a responsibility to explore anything I hear about. But I don't want to bother you."

"Oh no, you haven't." Ellen released a heavy sigh. "You've been a huge help from the day you brought the jewelry box, Christy."

The way Ellen drawled her name made Christy aware of how tired Ellen must feel, but it brought an even sharper memory of Kirby. Kirby talked slow and easy, drawled out her name as though it were spelled Christee. She closed her eyes as Ellen continued, but Christy wasn't listening. She could almost see and smell Kirby here in her kitchen, and when she looked down at her hands, they seemed to shrink. They were reaching, white-knuckled, for Kirby's strong arms as he pulled her to shore. Tears stung her eyes as she bit her lip. What could she do? She had to help.

"Don't you think?" Ellen asked.

Christy blinked, embarrassed by her blank silence. "I'm sorry, Ellen. What did you say?"

"I said I'm not giving any more statements to reporters. I refused to discuss it further. That's why I'd like you to keep me informed if you hear anything significant. Sometimes the family is the last to know. All we hear from the detectives is that they're working on it. No details."

"Ellen, I keep going back to the day of the barbecue. I know it's hard to believe anyone there would have killed Kirby, but maybe we should take a closer look at all the guys present that day. It seems to be a common theory that whoever came back merely wanted money, then panicked. I'm not sure what I'm babbling about, I just feel we're missing something."

"I know. So do I. I gave every name to the authorities during the first investigation. They seemed satisfied that no one here that day was involved."

Christy nodded. "By the way, I met Wayne Crocker at the marina. We just spoke for a minute, but he didn't really say anything helpful." Not that she could repeat. *Vince got the family fortune, R.J. got the girl.*

"Well, for someone who dropped out of college and worked as a salesman, I hear he's been quite successful. Hold on a minute." She could hear Ellen relaying a question, and then Vince's voice rumbled back a garbled reply.

"Vince says Wayne Crocker started out selling cars in Lynn Haven, worked his way up to selling boats in Panama City, and now owns his own boat brokering business and travels all over the coast. Vince wonders where he got the start-up money."

"Big commissions? Lots of sales?"

"Maybe. He's got the personality for it, but it does seem odd that out of all those guys, he appears to be the most successful financially. Vince says that may be something to think about."

Vince says. Vince seemed to have a list of suspects handy whenever asked.

"Ellen, I'll let you get back to the boys. Sorry to have bothered you."

"A call from you is never a bother. And thanks again, Christy, for bringing up the evidence that I think will lead us to whoever did it. At least, I'm placing all my hopes on that."

Christy tried to sound positive as she said good-bye, but she prayed this time the case wouldn't hit another dead end. That would be a double heartbreak for Ellen.

She carried the handset back to the living room and picked up the pen and notepad.

5. *Wayne Crocker*

She wrote his name slowly, rethinking her impression of him. Friendly, pleasant, yet in that short time, she only saw the surface of his personality. Still, he had appeared stricken when she mentioned Kirby, saying how Kirby had included a poor boy like him into the right social circle. She shook her head. He seemed like a long shot despite Vince's obvious suspicion. He'd had fifteen years to work his way to success, so his having money didn't seem so out of line to her.

Della…Reuben. She had to find out more about them. In the meantime, the detectives might make real progress once they located Sheryl Wilcox.

The phone rang again, and she read Dan's cell number on the caller ID. She grabbed it up and answered with a slow, breathy hello.

"Hey, if you're answering all your calls like that, I'd better grab the next flight out."

She burst into laughter. "Ever heard of caller ID?"

"Guess something that practical went out of my head. I'm looking at snow. Everywhere."

"Snow?" she asked, snuggling into a sofa pillow. "Are you freezing?"

"Actually, no. Wesley put me up in a condo right on the lake. I can stand here, sip hot coffee, and look at the most gorgeous view."

Her hopes plummeted, and she scolded herself. Did she actually *want* him to freeze and be miserable?

"Sounds great. Did you look at the property yet?"

"Yes, and it's fantastic. He has a gold-mine opportunity."

"Good. Now he can turn you loose, and you can come home to me."

"I do miss you," he said. "By the way, I called the marina to check on the progress of my boat. The mechanic had to order a part, but it should be up and running by the time I get back."

"Wonderful."

"R.J. said you stopped by there yesterday, looking for me. Did you really expect me to be there?"

She recognized the teasing in his tone and knew he wasn't mad, although he probably suspected she'd gone by to snoop.

"A lady who lives near the marina has a piece of furniture she wants to sell us." That much was true. "I just thought you might have stopped by to check on your boat."

"You couldn't call me?"

"No, I forgot to charge my phone, and my battery was dead." For once, she felt grateful for her forgetful nature. "And I didn't stay five minutes."

"So what did you think of R.J.?"

She winced. He knew her so well, knew exactly why she had gone. "He was nice. Like I told you, I was only there for five minutes."

"And you didn't mention it Monday night."

She flared. "Dan, this is beginning to make me feel like I'm being grilled."

The sound of his laughter made her sigh with relief. "I was intending to let it go, but I couldn't resist. Just stay out of trouble, okay?"

"Okay. Tell me what you've been doing since you got there. And how was the plane trip, other than long?"

General chitchat followed for the next half hour, and then they said their love yous and good-byes.

Later, as she wandered into the bedroom to prepare for bed, she began to hum the love song from the jewelry box. It did have a memorable refrain.

Christy's soprano voice hit notes that weren't there, and her parents had been relieved when she chose not to sing in the choir. Now she sang to herself or to the walls within her home, as loud and off-key as she wished.

"So when will I see you again?"

16

Wednesday

Christy faced a cloudy morning beyond her kitchen window, and the weatherman on her TV warned of storms and hurricane-like weather ahead. She turned the television off and walked down the hardwood hall, sipping her coffee. When she reached the master bath, she finished the coffee and placed the mug on the counter. She turned the shower on full force and began peeling off her pajamas. Her thoughts returned to Dan and the fact that he liked Montana.

You will not start worrying, she told herself, stepping into the shower.

An hour later, seated before her computer, she felt too mentally scattered to start a mystery novel, and from the crackle of thunder and warnings of bad weather, she knew she should unplug her computer, despite her surge protector. Still, her workaholic nature refused to let her wander through a day without a sense of accomplishment. She had to keep busy so she wouldn't miss Dan. Maybe she'd go into the shop, even though it wasn't her day to work. Or maybe she'd check out the thrift shop near Bay Point she'd heard about.

Or maybe she'd drive down to Mexico Beach and pay Willie Pitt a visit.

She knew Jack loved his barbecue, but she didn't want to involve him, since it would mean lingering for a meal. She'd go on the excuse of buying a bottle of the sauces she'd seen advertised for sale as they left the restaurant.

For the first time this morning, she felt energized. If she couldn't start another mystery on paper, she felt compelled to explore the real mystery of Kirby's death. Perhaps that explained why she couldn't concentrate on anything else.

She dressed in jeans and a long-sleeved shirt, then grabbed a rain jacket and headed out.

∽

Even at ten o'clock, the Hickory Pitt was humming. Christy pulled into the graveled driveway, parked, and hopped out. Dodging raindrops, she hurried up to the walkway. Enticing hickory smoke filled the air, and as she opened the screen door, she almost lunged headlong into Willie's broad chest.

"Well, you're a ray of sunshine on a dreary day. Wakes up a tired old dude like me," he said, looking down at her. "I was going out to buy more coffee, since I can't seem to drink enough to keep me going, but now I'm wide awake." He looked over her head. "Jack with you?"

"No." She glanced around the room, filled mostly with men at this hour, who were all turning to stare at her. "I just came down to pick up a bottle of your famous barbecue sauce."

He chuckled and spread a brawny arm. "Please come in."

She hurried to the shelf in the front of the café that held pints of dark red sauce, Willie's round face and wide smile centering the label.

"Neal, get the lady a drink while she waits. Iced tea?"

She turned back to him. "Iced tea in a cup to go, please. And just the usual amount of lemon. I'm not as demanding as Jack." She smiled at Willie and the young man behind the counter.

"Sounds like you're in a hurry," Willie said.

She nodded. "I'm taking the sauce to a meeting." She'd decide what kind of meeting later. She lowered her voice. "Willie, what was Reuben's last name?"

He arched an eyebrow and gave her a knowing look. "Did you have an ulterior motive for coming to buy my sauce?" he asked, teasing her with a grin.

"Yes. I'm bribing someone with it. The question is an afterthought."

"Reuben Foster. And I found out he finished his jail time. Went back to work painting."

"Where?"

A deep frown rumpled his forehead. "Don't know. Guess you could ask Della. They been on and off for years."

A red plastic cup brimming with sweet tea was placed in her hand. She took a sip and realized she should be buying his tea rather than his sauce.

"Mmm." She swallowed, relishing the taste. "Where would I find Della?"

He propped his hands on his hips and studied her more seriously. "You're really into this thing, aren't you? Haven't you ever heard that ole worn-out phrase, 'Curiosity killed the cat'?"

"I've heard it. It never bothered me, 'cause I'm not a cat."

He threw his head back and laughed his deep-chested laugh. "Last I heard, Della was in a nursing home over in Panama City."

He picked up the pint of sauce, walked around to the cash register, and rang up the sale.

Christy removed a ten-dollar bill from her billfold. "Maybe I can talk Jack into letting me tag along next time he gets a craving for barbecue."

"He better bring you." A playful threat underlined Willie's words. He leaned toward her and lowered his voice a notch. "Della had a bad stroke soon after Kirby was killed. I think she's in a wheelchair now."

"I'm sorry to hear that," Christy said, and for a moment they both stared at the bottle of sauce she held. She looked up at him, wanting to lighten the mood before she left. Her eyes roamed down the Alabama T-shirt that strained over his girth and the overalls that covered it.

"It's hard to tell if you're a Bama fan or a Gators fan," she said.

"My best answer is the one I always give: depends on who's playing."

"That's the right answer," Christy said, hugging her tea and sauce. She waved and left the café, dodging rain puddles. She hit the unlock button on her key remote and ran toward the car. Once inside, she plugged her cell phone into a hands-free mount to avoid the temptation of removing her hands from the steering wheel as the rain peppered down.

Back on the main highway leading to town, she tried to hold down her speed, since the highway was slick and people tended to get careless on rainy days. She adjusted the cell mount after dialing Bobbie at the shop. Bobbie's lilting voice filled the wire after the second ring.

"Hi, what's going on?" Christy asked in greeting.

"I'm doing some old-fashioned flirting," she replied saucily.

"Good. I need to speak to Jack."

"I didn't say it was Jack."

"But it is."

"No," Bobbie replied firmly, "it isn't. Why are you so interested?"

"I need to ask him something."

"Well, you'll have to wait until tonight. He's out fishing with J.T. today. Can you believe they'd go out on a day like this? At least they're fishing in another area, a freshwater creek where the fish are supposed to be grabbing bait. If you have nothing better to do, can you swing by here and pick up a bank deposit?"

Christy sighed. "Might as well." She wanted to see who was in their shop and had captured Bobbie's interest.

∽

When Christy turned down the block to the shop, she spotted a maroon Hummer 2 parked directly in front. She pulled in behind it, noting the Florida license tag from a different county. No one in Summer Breeze drove a Hummer. Or an H2.

Curiosity mounting, she tucked her shoulder bag strap over her arm and headed for the front door. When she stepped inside, her eyes widened at the sight of Wayne Crocker, who towered over Bobbie as she showed off a Big Ben clock she had restored.

"Hello," Christy called, cutting into her aunt's story about the clock.

Bobbie and Wayne turned toward her. He was neatly dressed in dark pants and a red polo. Both smiled.

"So this is your latest conquest?" Christy teased Bobbie.

"Don't I wish." Bobbie winked. "No, he's just a very good sport."

"Hello again." Wayne nodded at Christy.

Christy set her purse on the counter and joined them in the corner, where they studied the Big Ben. "I thought you'd gone to Key West," she said to Wayne.

"No. I took the boat down to Orlando for a day but came back. I put an option on a boat at Destin, and I've been hanging around until the Andersons made up their mind about it. They called last night to tell me they've decided to take it and that they're coming down this weekend to close the sale. They live in Knoxville, Tennessee, and want to use it for part of the year now that Mr. Anderson is retired."

"And lucky me"—Aunt Bobbie's blue eyes lit up—"the big estate sale that's been advertised all over Panama City was held this morning.

I met up with Wayne there, and he said he was looking for a clock for a houseboat. I told him I could design and build whatever he wanted. To prove my point, I invited him to the shop to show him what I had done to this cast-off Big Ben."

Christy turned toward Wayne. "What kind of clock do you want?"

He shrugged his wide shoulders. "That's the problem. I don't know."

Bobbie tilted her blond head and looked up at him. "I know where I can get a mariner's clock. A restaurant is going out of business, the Drifter. They want to sell everything, lock, stock and barrel, so to speak. They have a good-looking mariner's clock. Just needs a little polishing."

"Sounds good to me." Wayne turned to Christy. "Two detectives came by the marina last night, and someone referred them to my boat. They asked if I knew anything about a jewelry box that went missing the night of the murder."

He spread his big hands and shrugged. "I told them no one looked like they had sticky fingers or might want to sneak back later for a private tour of the house. But if anyone wanted to come back later, Kirby made it easy for them." He looked from Christy to Bobbie and back again. "He kept saying we had to wind things up by four because he had to leave at five to go to Tallahassee. Anyone in earshot, including the caterers, knew the house would be empty that night."

"Speaking of the jewelry box," Christy said, "it now seems it was bought at a garage sale over in Fort Walton, and that'll be tough to track down."

Wayne chewed his lip, obviously tying in the box with the detectives' questions to him. "So you think the jewelry box was taken the night the burglar broke in?"

Christy nodded. *If that's why he broke in.*

"Christy has taken little Zeffie Adams under her wing," Bobbie spoke up. "We worry about Zeffie, but it's Christy's nature to help whenever she can."

"Honey, you can't solve all the problems of the world," Wayne said. "That's what I used to tell Kirby."

Christy nodded sadly. "He was great, wasn't he?"

Wayne heaved a deep sigh. "Considering he was born and bred into money, he was great to us, most of the time. Sometimes he'd flaunt what he owned, then catch himself. His mother and sister were show-offs, though. With them, it was all about money and status."

Christy nodded. She could see how this would be true.

"Tell me honestly, what do you think of Vince?" Christy asked. Few people had said anything positive about him except her dad. Maybe Wayne would be different.

He shoved his hands in his pockets and rocked back on his heels. He rattled the change in his pocket, and Christy suspected he was trying to choose the right words. "I don't know him that well. What I know from Kirby is that Vince Brown elevated himself from a frat rat struggling to make his grades to marrying into a fortune. With

Kirby gone, Vince stepped into the family business and shared all Ellen inherited."

Christy nodded but felt the need to defend Vince. "From all reports, he's run the business well."

Wayne shrugged. "I really wouldn't know about that. Like I said, I never knew him that well."

"And R.J.?"

"I knew him better." He paused and chuckled. "He was a popular guy at Florida State. Always in love with Julie. I dated her on the sly, so I know she ran around on him some. Seemed to me she just used his influence to help her get through school."

"You dated her?" Christy jumped on this fact.

"I met her one summer at the beach. She was starting Florida State in the fall. Sweet, beautiful, but we didn't make it. She came from money, and I was a nobody. R.J. was always on her trail. He was one of those guys who knows everybody or wants to know them, always joining clubs and such. When Julie came to the campus, he introduced her around, helped her meet people who could get her on the cheerleading squad—but she tossed him aside like a dead fish when the right guy came along."

For a moment, his dark eyes were sad, reflective. "Even though she married R.J., I hear she isn't happy. I see him when I dock at the marina, but I try to steer clear of him when I can. He talks too much."

"How long were you at Florida State?" Christy asked innocently.

"I only lasted a semester, but I'll bet you already heard that." He grinned. "I'm not intellectual and didn't like the vigorous training required to make it in college ball. What I am is street smart and people smart, so I decided to do what I do best: be a salesman. Started out selling cars, working ten hours a day, seven days a week. Moved on to selling boats and worked even harder. Then one day the commissions started adding up, and I got into brokering boats."

"It takes a lot of hard work to be successful, doesn't it?" Bobbie asked. "I know from experience." She was fidgeting from one high heel to another, the way she often did when she could taste a sale.

"Okay, you two go on and take care of business," Christy said, walking around the counter to pick up the bank deposit. "This weather is getting worse."

"The restaurant that has the clock is only a couple blocks away," Bobbie said, hoisting a giant umbrella. Wayne took it from her, and with her arm tucked in his, they hurried to his car.

Christy pondered Wayne Crocker. Dan had warned her he was a ladies' man with conquests up and down the coast. Maybe Bobbie enjoyed flirting with him, but he held no real appeal for Christy. She missed Dan so much it hurt. The maroon Hummer pulled away from the curb, and Christy turned to the small portable television on the counter, tuning in the weather station.

The weatherman was announcing hurricane watches in their area. In some counties, the watches had been upgraded to warnings. She'd better do what she needed to do, then get home.

Remembering what Willie had told her about Della, she turned to the yellow pages and began to look up nursing homes. After several calls, she located Della Young in a small nursing home called Sunset Manor in a poor section of Panama City. She intended to pay Della a visit to see what information she could gather about the Stricklands. And Reuben Foster.

In less than ten minutes, the Hummer pulled up at the curb, and Bobbie hopped out, hoisting her umbrella as Wayne roared off.

Bobbie dashed under the door's awning, lowering her umbrella before she entered the shop. Judging from the smile on her face, she didn't care that her high heels were wet or that rain dripped from the cuffs of her pants.

"I think we have a sale," she said, blue eyes dancing. "He loves the mariner's clock, and I spoke with the owner. It's just a matter of getting the price right both ways."

"Terrific," Christy said. "Look, if you're back to stay, I need to run. And you should consider leaving early. We're under a hurricane watch."

"Right." Bobbie sighed. "I just realized how tired I am. Sure you don't want a cup of coffee before you go? I think the dampness makes me feel colder, or maybe I just want a pick-me-up."

Christy reached for her rain jacket. "I don't need coffee now. Thanks anyway. When will Jack return?"

"He didn't say. Cora Lee wanted them to come by for fried chicken when they were done fishing. I made an excuse not to join them. That woman uses too much grease for my taste."

Christy hadn't registered Bobbie's words beyond the fact that

Jack wouldn't be home early. "If you talk to him, would you ask him to call me if it isn't past ten tonight?"

"That's your bedtime?" Bobbie teased, spooning coffee into the coffee maker.

"Tonight it is. I didn't sleep well last night, and I'm wiped out."

"Aw, you just miss Dan."

"I talked with him last night. He'll be home Sunday, and I'll be so glad to see him."

Bobbie propped her elbows on the counter and gazed at her. "What a guy."

"You've done okay for yourself as well. Jack is one of the most lovable people I've ever known."

That brought a ripple of laughter from Bobbie. "Don't I know it! Oh Christy, I've never felt like this about any man. I'm fifty-one years old, been married three times, and here…" Her eyes filled with tears. "God has given us both a second chance. Every night I pray I don't mess it up."

Christy leaned over and kissed her aunt on the cheek. "You won't." She grabbed her purse and the sheet of paper where she'd written the address for Sunset Manor, then picked up an extra umbrella from the closet. "Gotta run. Talk to you later."

As Christy listened to the radio in her car, the announcer gave a high surf advisory, along with threats of more bad weather. How dumb was she, not turning around and heading home?

On the other hand, if she had to get in a basement or stairwell, she could do that in a nursing home as easily as anywhere else.

She'd been teased about having a built-in radar system when it came to people. Sometimes names set off strange alarms. The name *Della Young* rang in her head, louder than the distant warning of an approaching hurricane.

17

Traffic was light due to the rain and bad weather. In half an hour Christy pulled into the parking lot of Sunset Manor, an older white frame building with tables and chairs spaced about the yard, now collecting rain puddles. She parked in a visitor's space, hoisted her umbrella, and splashed her way up the wet sidewalk to the front door.

The door swung open, and she entered the foyer. As she lowered her umbrella and placed it beside the door, she noticed the receptionist, a small white-haired lady who sat with elbows propped on the desk, her eyelids fluttering as she nodded off to sleep. The sound of the wind tossing the fronds of the palm trees outside hadn't intruded on her nap.

"Hello," Christy called cheerfully.

The woman bolted upright in her chair and blinked.

"I'm here to visit Della Young," Christy explained.

The receptionist yawned and checked the clipboard on her desk. "Room 134. Fourth door on the right down that hall."

She indicated an arched hallway that led past a sideboard holding senior magazines, a floral display, and a cheerful Thought for the Day mounted on a tiny easel.

The fourth door on the right stood open, and two women

shared the small room. Della was easy to spot in her wheelchair in a far corner of the room, reading her Bible beneath the light of a floor lamp. The woman who shared the room with her lay in her bed, staring at the ceiling, oblivious to everything around her. A dark red curtain served as a partition to separate their beds.

Christy discreetly knocked on the doorframe, and Della turned around in her wheelchair. Silver-gray had overtaken her dark hair, and her light brown skin was smooth, despite the look of a woman in her late seventies. Her dark eyes appraised Christy curiously.

"Mrs. Young?" Christy asked.

"Yes," she answered in a low, pleasant voice.

"Mrs. Young, I'm Christy Castleman. I wanted to talk with you about the Strickland family."

The brown eyes widened above prominent cheekbones and gaunt cheeks, and her lips twitched. She stared at Christy for a moment, then closed her Bible and placed it on a table. "Have a seat." She indicated a chair nearby. "And just call me Della."

Christy found herself tiptoeing past the woman in the bed, although she continued to stare at the ceiling.

Della's tone was friendly, but she did not smile. "Why on earth do you want to talk to me about the Strickland family? That was so long ago." A heavy sigh followed her labored words.

Christy remembered Ellen saying Della went to Annabell Strickland's funeral and was all broken up, so she must have felt affection for the family. "Kirby Strickland's murder went unsolved for years, but something has happened to reopen the case."

Della was taking shorter breaths, her eyes piercing Christy's face. "What's happened?" she asked.

Christy explained who she was, about the shop she owned, and Zeffie Adams bringing in the jewelry box. She ended the story by detailing how she'd found the appraisal slip under the lining in the old box. "The box proved to belong to Annabell Strickland and was taken the night of the robbery when Kirby was killed."

Della reached into her pink floral housedress and withdrew a handkerchief, dabbing at the tears forming in her eyes. "I dusted that jewelry box a hundred times. Miss Annabell was always playing that little melody while she tried to figure out which pair of earrings to wear to some big party."

"You were very attached to her?" Christy asked gently.

"I was," Della answered slowly. "I worked for her for almost five years. Miss Annabell had her moods. She was a good-hearted woman, but things had to go her way, if you know what I mean. Her sudden death was a shock to me. I grieved for her, but now my tears are for Kirby. My husband—God rest his soul—and I never had children. Kirby was like a son to me, so wonderful. Gave me gifts every birthday, every Christmas."

"I knew Kirby too," Christy said. "My grandmother is Elsa Castleman, on the farm next door."

This clearly impressed Della. "Now there's a nice lady. How is she doing?"

"She's doing quite well, thank you. She still lives up at the farm alone, and she's in good health and keeps the community in food."

"Glad to hear her health is good." Della smiled. "If Miss Elsa ever brought over a cake, she always had time to talk to me. To her I was as special as the Strickland family."

Christy was touched by Della's words. She reached over and covered her hand. "Of course you're special."

Kindness warmed Della's dark eyes. "And I can see you're like your grandmother. If you had told me she was your grandmother when you first introduced yourself, I might have been more mannerly."

"You've been just fine," Christy replied, then hesitated. "I was wondering…you mentioned Kirby and Mrs. Strickland. How did you feel about Ellen?"

Della studied the prominent veins in her thin hands, folded in the lap of her pink housecoat. "Ellen was away most of the time, and I didn't know her that well. From what I observed when she visited, she was a little too spoiled to suit me," she said frankly. "She was so different from Kirby."

Christy nodded. "Everyone loved Kirby. What did you think of Vince Brown?"

Della hesitated for a moment, glancing out the window. "Don't really know him very well."

"Maybe I shouldn't ask, but did Miss Annabell approve of him?"

Della sighed. "I heard her say he came from good middle-class folks, but she thought Ellen needed someone to keep her in style. Reckon she wanted a doctor or a lawyer or someone in politics." She paused, and tears filled her dark eyes. "Kirby must have been like his father, although I never knew the man. He was dead when I went to work for them."

"Why do you think someone would kill a guy as pleasant and likable as Kirby?"

Della shook her head, looking miserable. "I don't know. I've always told those people who questioned me that I hadn't been there in three months, didn't know who'd been visiting. From everything I've heard about it, though, it just sounds like a robbery gone bad."

Christy nodded. "That's what it sounds like."

This theory had bothered Christy all along. In writing and researching her mystery novels, she tried not to be lazy and rely on convenient answers. Life was complicated; people were complicated. This robbery-gone-bad theory provided an excuse for not probing deeper, and perhaps this was what the killer had planned.

Silence stretched between them. "In case you're wondering why I'm so interested," Christy continued, "I feel a responsibility to help solve this case. Kirby saved me from drowning when I was a girl."

A look of tenderness crossed the older woman's face. "That's the way he was. Always did whatever he could to help people."

Christy nodded. "I also feel sorry for the little girl who brought me the jewelry box. Her name is Zeffie Adams. She has only her grandmother, who is dying of lung cancer. Zeffie sold me her jewelry box to help her grandma pay medical bills. She said it was a gift from her mother who was killed in a car wreck years ago."

Della listened carefully, watching Christy as she related the story. "Who was this little girl's mother?"

Christy watched for Della's response. "April Adams."

A tiny frown gathered on the bridge of the older woman's nose, bunching the thin brows together.

"Have you ever heard that name?" Christy asked, leaning forward in her chair, her hands folded over her knees.

"It has a familiar ring. But then, when you live as long as I have, all faces and names start to seem familiar." She paused. "April Adams," she repeated.

Christy was relieved to notice there was nothing wrong with Della's hearing. Unlike some people who didn't hear well or misunderstood what was said to them, this woman seemed to grasp every syllable.

"Della, I want to ask about someone else. Reuben Foster."

A sigh sank the woman's chest and her lips grew tight for a moment. Then she began to nod. "Yes, I knew Reuben Foster, but only as a friend of Sam's, my late husband. Reuben was African American, quiet and reserved, and worked with Sam for years. They were painters. One day Reuben saved his life. Sam fell from the top of a ladder. Reuben grabbed him, and they fell backwards. Reuben broke his fall, but as a result, Reuben always had back trouble."

Della pressed her head against her chair, closing her eyes, as though the memory had exhausted her. "I tried to help Reuben after Sam died, but I had to break ties with him, much as I hated to." Della hesitated, her eyes still closed. "I've tried to live my life by the Good Book, but I just couldn't keep loaning him money. Especially when I found out he was spending it on liquor."

"Did he respect your wishes to be left alone?"

She shook her head. "No. One day he came out to Deerfield, wanting to borrow money. He'd been drinking; otherwise he would have had better sense. When Miss Annabell saw him and overheard something about money, she ordered him off her property. Then she turned on me. She told me she wouldn't have riffraff like that at her door. I tried to explain that he'd saved my husband's life, but that didn't seem to matter. She started threatening to fire me, but before she could, I quit. She demanded the house key back, but I couldn't find it in my purse. I must have left it at home, but I never found it there either. I guess I just lost it, or else I left it on the kitchen counter. But she acted like she didn't believe me."

Della sighed. "Still, I felt awful when she died unexpectedly soon afterwards. I went to her funeral. I had another job by then. And it seemed like no time at all when I heard about Kirby. Guess I don't handle grief very well. I had a stroke that put me in the hospital, and I couldn't go to his funeral. About that time, Reuben got caught driving drunk and went to jail."

"Have you heard from him since?"

"He's tried over the years. I did hear from a friend that he's out of jail now."

The older woman looked exhausted, and Christy knew she should leave. She stood up and patted Della's shoulder. "I must go now. Thank you for talking to me."

Della smiled up at her. "I hope you'll visit again. I enjoyed talking to you."

Christy nodded. "Thanks, I'll try to do that."

She left the room, wishing she had brought flowers. Next time she would.

∾

A shadow moved beneath the swaying palms, steering clear of the streetlight on the corner. Wind howled across Summer Breeze, creating a noisy diversion. The threat of a hurricane had sent everyone for cover, which made the timing perfect for a close look at Christy Castleman's house and grounds. Within her house, lights burned, yet every window was covered with drapes or blinds. The car parked in the driveway verified her presence.

The shadow studied the adjoining yards, the proximity of neighbors. They huddled within the safety of their homes, cars in driveways and garages, curtains drawn.

The problem of a dog must be considered. The shadow crept along, listening carefully, ready to bolt if an animal alerted the neighborhood to the presence of a prowler. But there was no sound other than a television turned low.

Her yard was small, and the windows looked accessible to one who knew what to do. The shadow checked for a sign verifying an alarm system and, seeing none, crept across the backyard, stopping beside the meter box. The fluorescent light over the sink sent a white glow across the kitchen. The shadow could see a hall through the arched door, and surmised this was a typical ranch-style home.

The screen door quivered in the wind. Screens were easy to access with the right knife. A seven-foot fence separated the adjoining houses and yards. Perfect.

The shadow hesitated beside the window, hearing the distant

tones of a weatherman's report on late-night news. The living room or den. The light was on; she was in there now.

A grin curled the shadow's lips. Now was not the time to enter the house. First, a message would be left. If that didn't end her snooping, the shadow would be forced to get rough. And if that happened, little Miss Castleman wouldn't live to tell about it.

18

Thursday

Although a line of storms had crossed the Florida panhandle, causing damage in some areas, Summer Breeze remained safe, one of the pockets the heaviest winds and rains had missed. Farther south, the large system had veered away from the coast.

Christy spent the night tossing and turning. She checked the weather station at midnight and was assured the threat had passed. As she sat on her sofa watching the weather station, she turned on the lamp and picked up her pad of notes labeled Suspects.

She spent an hour processing the information she had collected on people who had motives, filling three pages with notes that included the latest information on Reuben Foster, Della, Julie and her indiscretions, and Wayne Crocker. As an afterthought, she added that Ellen Brown had expressed displeasure over the new detective's intense questioning, indicating she'd felt a threat of suspicion against her Vince.

Mulling over those facts, Christy put down the pen and pad, turned off the television and light, and padded down the hardwood hallway to her bedroom. She nestled in her bed, relieved that the moaning wind had subsided, and fell asleep.

～

When the radio alarm penetrated her thick sleep, Christy sat up in bed and blinked at the clock. She had set it for nine, knowing there was no special need to rise early. Her mind shot to the notes she had made at midnight. The storm had provided a good opportunity to put on paper some of the jumbled information she'd absorbed the past few days. Often, when she was writing novels, she crawled out of bed at odd hours to write down her ideas, and it had proven a blessing.

She stood up and stretched, then ambled into the bathroom, reaching for her robe on its hook behind the bathroom door. She snuggled into the lightweight robe, then leaned over the sink, turned on the warm water, and splashed her face. She put a warm terry cloth over her forehead, pressing lightly against eyes that felt gritty and blurred. Then she patted her skin dry with a hand towel, frowning as she did. Something bothered her, something she couldn't pinpoint.

Caffeine. She needed it. Thrusting her feet in her house shoes, she plodded from her blue bedroom to the kitchen, where the light over the sink greeted her. She hit the switch on the coffee machine and turned out the light. Staring idly into her backyard, she could see debris blown about by the wind—and something else. She pressed her face closer to the window. In the edge of the grass, near the kitchen window, the mud from the rain held a footprint. Or half a footprint.

A feeling of apprehension crawled over her, but she shook her head. The power meter was nearby; probably the meter man had checked it late yesterday.

She walked over to the wall phone, picked up the headset, and dialed the deputy's office. While the number rang, she glanced out the kitchen window, sighing with relief as a brave new sun followed the storm.

"Bob Arnold." The name filled the telephone wire, the tone his usual bold, no-nonsense manner. Just the sound of his voice was reassuring to her, and the anxiety she felt over the footprint vanished. Bob was always a phone call away.

"Good morning. It's Christy. How are you, friend?"

"Busy, as usual. You okay?"

She looked out the window again and realized the half-footprint was directly beside the meter box. It had to be the meter man. She decided not to overreact.

"What's happening with the Strickland case?" she asked, moving on to other thoughts. "Before you say FDLE is handling it, I'm sure you're staying informed."

"If I were, you know I couldn't pass anything on, Christy. I can't risk losing my job—even for you."

She nodded. "I know. That was a very nice thing you did for Zeffie, giving her a Good Citizen badge."

"Well, she earned it," he replied. "She's a sweetheart, isn't she?" His voice dropped a notch. "I understand her grandmother is terminal. What's gonna happen to Zeffie?"

As the coffee gurgled, Christy reached for her mug. "I don't know. It all depends on how fast this case gets solved."

"What do you mean by that?" She could almost see him bolting upright in his sagging office chair.

"Well," Christy said, glancing at the coffee dripping into the carafe, "until the killer is found, there's a cloud of suspicion around April Adams, her mother." She filled her Mystery Lady mug. "I want Zeffie protected from gossip."

"What about other family?" Bob inquired.

"Mrs. Adams did mention a cousin, but Zeffie isn't close to her."

"Still, if there's a blood relative..."

"There is. Somewhere. Neither Zeffie nor her grandmother knows who Zeffie's father is. I wish it would turn out that he's a decent guy who would take her."

Silence filled the other end of the wire. She knew why. The only time Bob was silent with her was when he was mad, which he didn't seem to be, or when his emotions started warring with his logic.

"The detectives located Sheryl Wilcox," he finally said, his voice lowered, "but she doesn't know where April got the jewelry box. She agrees with the grandmother, thinks it was at a garage sale. So now the detectives are searching the classifieds for garage and yard sales preceding the weeks April returned to Montgomery with a painting and jewelry box."

For someone who had just told her FDLE was working the case, Bob seemed to be quite informed. And yet she could tell all of them a thing or two. She took another sip of coffee and realized it was time to resort to her own methods of investigation. This case was moving too slowly for her impatient nature. And there was the safety of Zeffie and her grandmother to consider, which sharpened her determination to home in on what felt right.

"Well, I'll let you go, Bob. Thanks. Keep me informed, if you can. In the meantime, we're trying to keep Zeffie happy."

They said their good-byes and hung up. Christy grabbed a bran muffin, which she wrapped in a paper towel, then topped off her coffee. Armed with something to satisfy her stomach, she directed her thoughts toward satisfying her curiosity.

She headed toward her office, switched on the light, and sat in the desk chair.

She turned on her computer and sat eating her muffin and sipping coffee while the machine came to life. Reaching for the desk phone, she dialed her grandmother, who answered on the first ring. Granny sounded as though she'd been up since daylight, and probably had.

"Hi, Granny. Is Grits McCoy's dog still bothering you?"

"No," she answered pleasantly. "They're both behaving."

Christy smiled at that. "Well… I've been thinking about the Strickland murder. Can you think of anyone in the community back in 1998 who would have broken into the house for money? Someone on drugs, maybe?"

"Honey, after they tested all the people at the barbecue, the detectives made the rounds of the neighbors. If anybody around here had any kind of arrest record or had ever been in jail, that person got hauled in for questioning. Why, they even took a DNA sample and fingerprints from me! I don't know if they got everyone in the county, but I can tell you one thing for sure. Everybody loved the Stricklands. They gave so much to this community that everyone was ready to grab a weapon and go after the killer, only no one knew who it was."

"What about drifters, suspicious people hanging around town?"

"Nope. We don't get many drifters, and if we do, they don't stay long. There's nothing to keep them here. And Hal, the sheriff, knows everyone in the county. Don't think he didn't do his best to sniff out any likely suspect. The Avertons had a nephew visiting from New York, and they grilled that poor boy so hard, he packed up and left the next day."

Christy sighed. "I see."

Reuben Foster jumped into her mind. She thought about what Della had told her and wondered why she hadn't mentioned his name to Bob. For some reason, she felt Reuben Foster held an important piece to this puzzle.

"Granny, I have another phone call I need to make, so I'll let you go. Maybe I can get back for a visit soon."

"I'm counting on it."

Christy hung up the phone and then dialed Bob's number again.

When he answered, she simply said, "Reuben Foster. What about him?"

"He's already been questioned," Bob reported. "Neither his DNA or fingerprints were found anywhere in the house."

Christy wasn't ready to let it go. "Where is he? How'd you find him?"

"Christy, you know I can't divulge that information."

"Well, I guess Zeffie and I are just going to have to come down to your office and sit there until we get some information on Reuben."

He heaved a sigh that she chose to ignore. "He's on welfare. Picks up odd jobs here and there. I understand he's been hanging out at Ned's convenience store near Rainbow Bay the past few days. But stay away from him. I'm telling you, he doesn't know anything."

"Okay." Christy tried to sound convincing. "Doesn't hurt to ask. I won't bother you again."

"I certainly hope not." Bob tried to sound gruff, but Christy knew him too well. When it came to their friendship, he was all bark and no bite.

Back at her computer, she inserted a disk and opened her special criminal database program, the one she had come by secretly. Having a friend in the FBI had its rewards.

She began her search with Reuben Foster, who showed only a few DUIs, the last one resulting in jail time. No other incriminating reports.

She tried every name on her suspect list: R. J. Wentworth, Vince Brown, Wayne Crocker, Della Young, and even Ellen Brown. Unlike the other times she had used this program to investigate suspects, she found nothing more than two speeding tickets—one for Ellen Brown, one for Wayne Crocker.

She tried Sheryl Wilcox. To her surprise, she read about an arrest for prostitution.

Curious, she typed in the name April Adams. A DUI during her stint at Panama City Beach, then the car wreck in Fort Walton, a bottle of prescription pain pills found on the floorboard. No charges of prostitution.

Christy felt relieved. Zeffie did not deserve a mother who sold her body. April had messed up her life, but not as badly as some people.

She removed the disk, disappointed that her sneaky little search hadn't uncovered something important. This was how she had sniffed out the right direction to take when tracking down criminals in the past.

Zipping over to her e-mail account, she found a message from Dan. He was returning late Sunday afternoon. She shot back a happy reply: "I'll treat you to dinner."

A smile crossed her lips and remained on her face the rest of the morning.

❦

After a run at Shipwreck Island, her lungs filled with fresh air and her mind humming with adrenaline, one fact rose to the forefront of Christy's mind as she unlocked her back door and hurried to her bedroom. She had to find Reuben Foster.

In record time, she showered and shampooed her hair. After

whisking it into a damp ponytail, she changed into jeans and a long-sleeved T-shirt. She planned to attend the Red Hatters purse class later in the day and see Zeffie, but first she had a plan—a plan that would begin with a returned phone call.

The caller ID on her nightstand showed Jack's home phone. She grabbed the receiver, already smiling.

"Hey, good-looking," she called merrily.

"What do you want?" Jack growled.

"You *are* good-looking. My aunt certainly thinks so."

"How do you always know just what to say? 'Specially to a wrin-kled old cuss like me." The voice softened, and Christy thought she heard a chuckle.

"How was the fishing trip?" she asked.

"Lousy. The fish weren't biting, and J.T. spent the day yakking about Cora Lee."

"Sounds like it didn't improve your mood," she said, thinking he sounded crankier than usual.

"That's not why you called. You still pining after Dan?"

"No, I am not," she snapped, then caught herself. "He calls every night and will be flying home Sunday." She attempted to sweeten her tone. "How about a favor for a favor?"

"That's a new way of putting it. What do you need from me?"

"Actually, I have something you're going to love."

"Your aunt's gonna move in with me."

"Nope. With her, it'll have to be marriage."

"Just teasing. I wouldn't ask her to do that. Move in, I mean."

"You didn't say you wouldn't ask her to marry you. I seem to recall you referring to her as the gal you intended to marry."

"And that's not what you called to talk about, either."

She sighed. He knew her too well. "I have a pint of Willie's special barbecue sauce so you and J.T. can host a barbecue or you and Bobbie can devour it at your own cookout."

"Hey, I've been craving barbecue." He began to sound like the mellow guy she loved. "And his sauce is the best. But wait a minute."

She winced, knowing he'd figured out her real motive.

"You made a trip down there to buy the sauce," he said. "Tell me you didn't."

"I did, and Willie was very nice. Do you ever hang out at Ned's convenience store?"

He paused. "It always takes me a minute to catch up with you. I stop by for gas occasionally, but I don't hang out, as you call it. Why? What's Ned done?"

"Nothing. I was just hoping you'd meet me there in half an hour. A character I need to ask about hangs out there, and I'd prefer to have you along."

"I would prefer to be along! See you there in half an hour."

~

When she turned into Ned's convenience store thirty minutes later, Christy spotted Jack seated on the popular bench locals used to swap stories.

She got out of her car, barbecue sauce in hand, and Jack jumped up. From his jeans and wrinkled shirt, she could see he'd neglected his morning routine. She wondered how late he'd stayed out with J.T. and Cora Lee. The slight stubble of whiskers on his face proved his haste in meeting her here. He'd probably been kicked back in his recliner, reading a fishing magazine, with plans to do as little as possible today. Sometimes he preferred that.

"Only Ned and the peanut farmer are here," he reported, his voice lowered. "Who're you looking for?"

"Here." She thrust the bottle of sauce into his hand, and he grinned with satisfaction. "Did I ask you if you ever heard of a Reuben Foster?"

"Didn't Willie mention him?"

"Yeah. He's been in and out of jail, and I was told he sometimes hangs out here."

Jack glanced around the deserted parking lot of the gas station. "I could ask Ned about him. But first, you gotta tell me why."

She studied Jack's craggy face. "Promise you won't give me a lecture on snooping or being overly curious? It involves the Strickland investigation."

He sighed. "Christy, you're a successful mystery writer because you have a knack for solving puzzles, and you don't need to apologize for your curiosity. It's part of who you are."

She stared at him for a moment, then gave him a hug. "Why don't other people see it that way?"

He sighed and grinned, the faded blue eyes deep and reflective.

"Maybe they haven't had the kind of life lessons I've had. Years ago, I learned to face facts and accept them."

"You're so wise," she said, meaning it.

"Skip the flattery. What makes you think this Foster might have been involved?"

"He was friends with the husband of the Stricklands' house-keeper, Della." She gave him a rundown of what she had learned from Della. When she'd finished the story, she looked intently at him. "Remember, your friend Willie said Reuben was bad news. I think he may have stolen Della's missing key to the Strickland house."

Jack glanced at his truck. "Let me put this sauce away, and we'll have a talk with Ned."

Christy squared her shoulders and looked around the parking lot. A truck pulled in beside the gas pumps, and a young man dressed in work clothes climbed out.

"Okay," Jack said when he returned. "Just let me do the talking."

She nodded and followed him into the convenience store. Hard candy in glass jars sat on the counter, along with assorted candy bars, chewing gum, and boxes of doughnuts. The big attraction was obviously the opportunity to buy a lottery ticket, because a middle-aged man in overalls was studying the rack of choices while laying out some dollar bills at the cash register.

Christy could smell strong coffee and spotted a huge stainless-steel coffee machine on a back counter. Behind the front counter, an older man with white hair and a mustache held court. This, Christy concluded, must be Ned.

"Good luck," he called to the man who was thrusting lottery tickets in his pants pocket. He turned to Christy and Jack. "Jack Watson! Anytime you want to bring in someone who looks like her, you get free coffee and doughnuts!"

"Behave, Ned," Jack said good-naturedly, glancing around the store. "Slow morning?"

"Yeah, this is Thursday, remember? Folks get paid tomorrow. That's when I make most of my sales." He stared at Christy.

"Ned, this is Christy Castleman," Jack said, "a friend of mine from Summer Breeze."

Ned nodded. "Pleased to meet you." He looked at Jack with a question in his eyes.

Christy sighed. She might as well satisfy his curiosity. "I was Chad's fiancée. Jack and I stay in touch."

An apology slid over the man's face, and he looked at Jack as though searching for words.

"Ned, I'm looking for someone who comes in here," Jack said, easing the awkward moment. "Guy named Reuben Foster. African American."

Ned frowned. "I think that's the guy painting the big red barn at the Wilson farm. A good painter, I hear, if you can keep him off the booze. He may have finished the job by now, though. I don't know. Reckon you could drive down to the Wilson farm—go through the four-way stop, and the farm's a coupla miles down on the left."

Jack nodded. "I know where it is. And that's a good idea—I'd like to see what kind of job he does. In case I miss him, let me give you my phone number. Have him call me. I need an outbuilding painted."

Ned scrambled for a stubby pencil, tore off a page from his receipt book, and wrote Jack's number on the back. "Sure, Jack. I'll tell him if he comes in."

Christy reached into a jar for a couple of peppermint sticks and noting the price, dumped some change on the counter.

"Thanks." Ned smiled. "Stop by again."

Christy nodded. "I will."

As they walked out, Christy thrust a peppermint in Jack's shirt pocket.

He looked at her. "Now I guess you want to ride over to the Wilson farm."

"Yep." She grinned up at him. "Do you mind?"

"Does it matter?" He chuckled as he pulled the peppermint stick from his pocket, tore off the end of the wrapper, and began to chew on it. "You're like a shark when it smells blood," he said, grinning at her.

"Keeps life interesting, doesn't it?"

Without asking which vehicle they should take, Christy hoisted herself up into Jack's truck.

As they drove the short distance to the Wilson farm, Christy said, "I guess I'm just following my instincts."

Jack quirked an eyebrow. "Well, I've learned to trust your instincts. You're usually on target." He reached the four-way stop, hit his signal to turn into the farm's driveway, but then hesitated as a truck with a cattle trailer pulled out.

The driver rolled down the window. "Can I help you folks?"

"Yeah," Jack called, giving the driver a friendly grin. "We're looking for the guy who's painting the Wilsons' barn. I need some work done."

"He finished up three days ago. Did a good job, but haven't seen him since. You could ask Mr. Wilson how to get in touch with him, but he and his wife left for the airport this morning to fly up to Kentucky to see their new grandbaby. Said they'd be back in a week."

Christy's hopes sank. "Would anyone else know how to reach this guy?" she asked, leaning over Jack.

"Nope. Don't even know how Mr. Wilson got his name, but he'd be the one to ask."

"Okay, thanks a lot." Jack waved as he did a U-turn in the road. "There's no point in grilling anyone else," he said to Christy. "We've hit a dead end for now. We'll have to wait on the Wilsons or hope Foster gets my message and calls me."

"Would it be rude to try to reach the Wilsons up in Kentucky?"

"It'd be more than rude; it'd be ridiculous. And you'd come off so obvious you'll run Foster off before we can track him down. Just try to be patient." He took a deep breath and grinned. "Tell your aunt I'm looking forward to tonight."

"Okay, I will," she replied as Jack roared into the parking lot of the convenience store and pulled up to Christy's SUV.

She turned to him. "Thanks, Jack. You're a true friend."

He grinned. "I know. Anytime you need me, just call."

She nodded, blew him a kiss, then climbed into her SUV. She backed out of the parking lot and pressed the accelerator to the floor as she headed back to Summer Breeze.

19

Christy's mind zipped through the information she had gathered and landed on the next person she wanted to speak to—Sheryl Wilcox. She knew April in those last days better than anyone. But Christy wasn't about to call the detectives working the case and ask for her number.

As she turned down the street to the shop, Christy could see cars lined up all the way to the end of the block. The Christmas purse project must be a huge success. She grabbed the last available spot across the street, half a block down.

Reaching under the front seat, she pulled out a phone directory. She flipped over to the Fort Walton section, and searched the Wilcox names. No Sheryl listed. How had the detectives found her? She frowned and shoved the book back under the seat. Maybe her number was unlisted. She grabbed her cell phone and dialed 411, but was told there was no one by that name, not even with an unlisted number.

Strike two.

She got out of the car and crossed the street, glancing through the window of the ice cream shop. She saw several Red Hatters waiting in line for ice cream and smiled. Their little project was perking up the local economy as well.

Christy paused outside their shop to look at its name—I Saw It First—swirled in red cursive across the plate glass window. Aunt Bobbie had chosen the perfect name, she thought, and as she opened the door to loud chatter and laughter, she realized just how much she enjoyed being co-owner of this unique shop. Turning trash to treasure, discovering unused "stuff" in people's attics and making it useful again, had proved to be a rewarding project.

She studied her aunt as Bobbie explained the basics of knitting and crocheting. "You can choose whichever one appeals to you when making your purses," she finished, her blue eyes twinkling.

Bobbie had taught her family and everyone in Summer Breeze that one must look beyond the flaws and find the promise. Bobbie had done that with her life and set an example for others to do so.

"I'm running late," a voice called behind Christy.

She turned to see Valerie hurrying through the door, dressed in her trademark denim vest, plaid shirt, and jeans.

"Thought I couldn't make it, but I had a cancellation for a perm," Valerie said, slightly breathless. She was a pretty woman, not only because she took pride in styling her blond hair and wearing the latest fashions, but also because she always wore a smile that put a sparkle in her hazel eyes.

"Valerie, will you close the door, please? You're causing a draft," Miz B yelled, angling around to see what had disturbed Bobbie's demonstration.

At least a dozen women crowded around the six-foot-long table that had been set up in the center aisle. Zeffie, perched on a tall stool, wore a rhinestone tiara on her blond head. Upon seeing Christy, she hopped down from the stool and ran to meet her. She motioned for her to bend down so she could whisper.

"I've been made an honorary princess. They had a crowning ceremony for me." She spoke as though the mayor had just given her the key to Summer Breeze.

"That's great," Christy whispered. "You look fabulous with the tiara."

"So let's get busy," Bobbie said. "I've got sequins and beads and chains to add to the purses, but we have to do the basics first."

"I haven't knitted in ten years," Joy said.

"No problem." Bobbie smiled at her, pushing up the sleeves of her silk shirt. "It'll come back to you the minute you start." She glanced at Christy. "Want to join us?"

Zeffie tugged at her hand, and Christy followed her over. "I'd love to, but I have to be someplace in a minute. I just wanted to pop in and say hi."

She was greeted with a chorus of "Hello, how are you?"

"I was wondering…" While she had their attention, it couldn't hurt to ask. "How many of you know people in Fort Walton?"

Tess Nixon turned in her chair and looked at Christy. "I was born and raised there. Just moved to Summer Breeze a couple years ago when we opened the motel."

Christy's hopes soared. "Did you ever know an April Adams?"

Tess shook her head. "No, did she live in Fort Walton?"

"Not for long. What about Sheryl Wilcox?"

Tess looked thoughtful. "I think so. I believe that's Nadine

Wilcox's daughter." She reached in her purse and withdrew her cell. "I can tell you in just a minute."

As Tess dialed, Christy walked over to Zeffie and whispered in her ear. "I hope you don't mind if I mention your mother's name. We're still trying to find the lady she lived with who might know about the garage sale."

Zeffie nodded, reaching up to adjust her tiara. "It's okay. I understand."

"How's your grandmother?" Christy asked, idly stroking a strand of blond hair.

"A little better," she said. "She's glad everyone has been so nice to me."

"Got it!" Tess shouted, closing her cell phone and writing something on her palm. "Sheryl is Nadine's middle daughter. She's married now but still lives in Fort Walton." She thrust her palm toward Christy. "I don't have her address, but here's her phone number."

Christy stared at the numbers printed on the woman's hand. She couldn't believe it had been so easy.

"Here." Bobbie handed her a pen and pad.

Christy copied down the number, then tore the sheet off and handed the pad back to Bobbie.

"Thanks very much," she said. "I'll let you ladies get back to work."

No one asked why she wanted to find Sheryl Wilcox. They were already describing the kinds of purses they wanted to make for themselves or for someone else for Christmas. Even Zeffie had gone over to look at Bobbie's assortment of feathers and sequins.

Grateful she didn't have to explain, Christy hurried out of the front door and practically ran to her car. The clock on the dash read four thirty. With the phone number before her, she dialed. After several rings, an answering machine picked up with a brief message. She left her cell and home phone numbers and asked Sheryl to call her as soon as possible. "It concerns April Adams's mother, so I'd really appreciate it if you'd call."

She hung up and stared into space. Now what? There was no point driving to Fort Walton if she didn't know where to look for Sheryl. And she didn't want to seem overeager and scare her off.

She sighed, suddenly aware of how tired she felt. She hadn't slowed down all day after a sleepless night. Deciding to be sensible at last, she drove to Miz B's rambling restaurant that more closely resembled a huge country home. After ordering a healthy meal to go, Christy peered into the dining room, hoping to see her old friend Jamie, who waitressed there, but she was nowhere in sight. When her boxed meal arrived, she paid, then hurried back to her car and headed home.

As she drove, questions about Sheryl Wilcox filled her mind. Could she be the key to unlocking the mystery of April? If not, she could at least tell Christy more than she knew about April now.

∽

When she arrived home, Christy saw a manila envelope stamped with the return address of Community Church propped against her back door. Balancing her food and purse, she unlocked the door and picked up the envelope. After kicking the door closed with her heel, she opened the clasp on the envelope and shook out an eight-by-ten black-and-white photo of her smiling parents. A Post-it note was stuck to the back.

Think we'll use this one for the church directory. What do you think? Keep the proof. Love, Mom

Christy smiled, placing her container of food on the eating bar along with her purse and keys. Then she went to the living room and laid the photo on the coffee table. Her eyes lingered on her petite blond mother seated beside Christy's dad and wearing the usual warm smile. Warmth flooded her heart as she studied her father's dark hair—sprouting threads of gray at the temples—kind brown eyes, and smile that invited people to open their hearts to him.

She returned to the kitchen, sank onto a stool, and opened the container of food. Kicking off her sandals, she rested her feet on the rung of the eating bar as she devoured her food.

"Thank God for Miz B," she said, relishing every bite.

She finished up and placed her silverware in the dishwasher. As she wiped off the eating bar, her gaze paused on a small bottle of fingernail polish Valerie had given her on her last visit to the shop for a haircut. "Try this great autumn color," she'd said, tucking the bottle in Christy's purse.

Christy picked up the bottle and read the label. Burnt Crimson.

She laughed, glancing at her short nails, neatly buffed. Then she looked down at her toenails and winced. Uncapping the polish, she sat on one barstool and propped her foot up on the other, meticulously painting her plain nails. As she did, she replayed the day's events in her mind.

She had to find Sheryl Wilcox. Glancing at her answering machine again, she read the "0" on the display one more time. She'd left her cell phone on all afternoon, but there had been no calls from Sheryl. Patience was not one of her virtues, but there was nothing she could do but wait. And hope.

She finished the last toe and sighed as she studied her Burnt Crimson nails. At least her feet would look better, even if they didn't feel better. She recapped the bottle and grabbed a paper towel. Wiping her hands, she wandered into the living room and sank onto the sofa. She snuggled her weary body beneath the afghan Granny had made, while keeping her toes out to dry, and picked up the television remote.

Idly, she surfed the channels until she found an old black-and-white movie she'd seen before, starring actors she adored. She placed the remote on the coffee table and settled back to watch, but fell asleep before it was over.

⚮

"Seems like that painter's getting awful popular," Ned said to the stranger at the convenience store. "First Jack Watson and that pretty

young lady, then those detectives, and now you. Like I've told everybody else, Reuben Foster hasn't been here for several days. The guys
from the Wilson farm said he finished their barn and left. Reckon
Foster's moved on somewhere else. I've got about three different
numbers written over there on my pad for him to call, if he shows
up again."

"You don't need to add mine," the stranger replied. "Sounds like
he's got all the work he needs. I'll find another painter."

Ned nodded, looking at the stranger. "That's a good-looking
pair of sunglasses. I don't wear 'em, cause I lose every pair I ever get."

The stranger thanked Ned and said good night.

Ned locked up the cash register and glanced at the clock. Closing time was ten minutes ago, and he was ready for Beverly's pork
chops and fried okra. He thrust a handful of apples in a brown sack
and started turning out lights. Maybe tonight he'd talk her into an
apple pie.

20

Friday

Blinking, Christy sat up and looked at the daylight seeping through her blinds. For the first time in the three years she'd owned this house, she'd spent the night on the sofa. Sighing with contentment, she snuggled back into the sofa pillows. The phone rang, but she decided to let the answering machine take the call.

The machine picked up, and Bobbie's voice floated to her from the kitchen. "Hey, hon. I was just wondering if you're running late for work, but obviously you're on the way. See you soon."

Christy bolted up, glancing at the clock. Nine. What was she thinking? This was her day to work at the shop. She ran to the bedroom, hugging her arms to warm up. The temperature had dropped after the rain, and she opened her closet and pulled out a red ribbed turtleneck and navy Dockers.

Twenty minutes later, as she pulled up in front of the shop, she spotted Wayne Crocker's maroon Hummer. Bobbie must have made the sale.

When she entered, Wayne held the mariner's clock under one arm, handing Bobbie a check with his free hand.

"You found a clock," Christy said.

"Your aunt bargained with the guy and got a better price than I could have done."

"It just needed dusting off and a screw tightened here and there," Bobbie said, looking at the check. "You don't need to pay me this much."

"You found it for me. And your time's worth something."

"Well thanks, Wayne." Bobbie smiled.

Christy thought of something and decided to ask. "Wayne, when you visited Kirby's house, did you ever meet the housekeeper, Della Young?"

"Mrs. Strickland had a housekeeper, but I don't remember her name. Sorry."

Christy shrugged. "It's not really important."

"Her name does sound familiar, though." Wayne studied her. "Maybe I heard Kirby mention her. Or maybe someone mentioned her during the first investigation."

"Did you ever hear of a Reuben Foster?" Christy asked.

He frowned. "I think the detectives asked about him. But no, I don't know him either."

She decided to try a different approach. "You mentioned going out with Julie years ago. Do you know of anyone else who did?"

"Nope. Like I told you, I met her at the beach with some girl-friends, and believe me, she was there to have a good time. So we did."

A hint of their good time drifted in the air, leaving Christy and Bobbie to draw their own conclusions.

He looked down at his clock. "Gotta go. The Andersons are coming, and I have some paperwork left to finish on the houseboat."

"Don't you want me to wrap the clock for you?" Bobbie asked eagerly.

"No need. I'm gonna hang it on the wall in the houseboat soon as I get back."

"Well, thanks again."

Wayne glanced at Christy. "Take care," he said, then turned and walked out the front door.

Christy stared after him. His admission about a relationship with Julie gave her something to think about. No one else had mentioned Julie with other guys, but maybe she'd been discreet where R.J. was concerned. Christy felt sure Julie had been faithful to Kirby, but the fact remained that Julie hadn't always been true to R.J. That gave her a moment's pause.

Her thoughts returned to Sheryl Wilcox. Although Christy had been in a hurry to get to work this morning, she'd glanced at the answering machine in passing. Sheryl hadn't returned her call, either on her home phone or on her cell.

Automatically, her eyes dropped to the office phone. She hadn't left this number. Maybe she should try again.

When she called, she got the answering machine. She repeated her first message, adding the number of the office phone.

Wondering how the investigation was going, she decided to call Ellen. The phone rang long enough that she expected the answering machine to pick up, but suddenly Ellen answered, her voice terse and strident above the steady tapping of Bobbie's hammer in the work-room behind Christy.

"Hi, Ellen. It's Christy. Just wanted to check on you."

"Well, I'm not too happy, Christy."

That much was obvious from her tone. "What's wrong?"

"Apparently, the detectives aren't getting anywhere in their second attempt to find Kirby's murderer, so they've decided to turn the spotlight on us."

"What do you mean?"

"They said they're tracking down leads on a garage sale in Fort Walton, but they've been back here twice, with that new guy going over the same questions, like we might not tell the same story as before. Or to be more frank, like we have something to hide. To be honest, I'm quite upset about it."

"I can see why. I don't understand what they're doing."

There was a pause, then a deep sigh. "Well, there's always been criticism of Vince from people who were jealous. We married for love, pure and simple. He didn't know my status when he met me. We were at the University of Florida, for heaven's sake. I didn't even bring him home that year. During the summer, we worked at a dude ranch in Colorado because we both love horses and farm life. We had a lot in common and knew we were right together."

Her voice softened. "Vince would have been successful in whatever career he chose. He came from a humble background, but he's made the family business even more successful than before. If anyone has gained from this marriage, it's me."

As Christy listened, it made perfect sense to her. "And I'm sure your mother appreciated what he accomplished as well."

There was a moment's hesitation from Ellen, and Christy sensed either she'd said the wrong thing or had opened a topic the other woman didn't want to discuss.

"Actually," Ellen replied, "Vince didn't take over the business until after…Kirby was gone."

"But I thought Kirby did Web designs," Christy blurted. She'd been under the impression the timber business had a manager in those days.

"He did that on the side. He loved it. In his last couple of years, he wanted to devote himself full time to Web designing, but he knew Mother expected him to keep the family business going. Frankly, the business had begun to flounder, but Mother died before she had an opportunity to see that Vince could be a lot more than just an assistant bank manager." After a momentary pause, she explained. "He was working at a bank in Panama City."

Christy recalled what Della had said about Annabell's ambitions for Ellen. She also recalled that Vince had said Julie called *their apartment* when Kirby had gone missing. An apartment rather than a house was probably not in Annabell's aspirations for her only daughter.

She realized an awkward silence had descended on the conversation and tried to fill in the gap. "Ellen, try not to worry. Maybe as those detectives check out the people who hosted garage sales, they'll find the person who owned the jewelry box. In the meantime, try not to read anything into the detectives' questions. I believe they're just double-checking all the facts."

"Maybe you're right, Christy. It just…feels different this time. I keep wondering if someone has said something to make them suspicious of Vince."

"But who would? Or why?"

"That's what I've been asking myself," Ellen said. "Hey, Christy, someone's at the door, so I'd better run. Thanks for calling."

They said their good-byes and hung up. Christy stared at the phone. She hadn't mentioned Sheryl Wilcox, but then, why would she? She had nothing to tell. If Captain Davis was asking Vince and Ellen lots of questions, maybe he was onto something. And maybe this time the investigation wouldn't end up a cold case.

∾

Christy polished off a late lunch of an apple and a pimento cheese sandwich, a leftover she'd found in plastic wrap in the fridge. Still, it had been good enough with a bottle of cold water.

As she tossed the remnants into the wastebasket, wiping her mouth with a napkin, she heard a roar out front. A tour bus angled its way into the curb, taking up all available space. The shop was quickly becoming a destination for those in search of craft ideas, antiques, or browsing. It was a favorite for senior citizens, because many of their items dated back to the last century, bringing a sense of nostalgia. "My mother had one of these," or "When we first married we bought one of those," were words Christy heard often.

The door swung open, and an eager group of older men and women entered, their eyes widening at the contents within the shop.

Christy took a deep breath, fixed a bright smile on her face, and went forward to accommodate them.

They spent half an hour in the shop, asking a million questions, until finally Christy grabbed the phone and located Bobbie at a home a few blocks away, where she was bargaining with a woman for a Duncan Phyfe sofa. When Christy whispered that the shop was full and she needed help, Bobbie assured her she'd be there in a flash.

And she was. The minute Bobbie walked through the door, she stepped right into the group and began explaining each item with pride and joy. Christy backed up to the French chair, removed the 1940s evening gown, and sank down. She felt as old as the dress and completely exhausted. Bobbie, on the contrary, sparkled with life as she explained how she had converted an old window frame into a lovely mirrored hall accessory.

The phone rang again, and Christy dragged herself over to the counter, grateful for an opportunity to make herself useful.

As she answered by saying, "I Saw It First," there was a slight hesitation on the other end.

Then a woman's voice abruptly said, "I must have the wrong number."

"Wait!" Christy said, stopping her before she hung up. "Are you returning a call to Christy Castleman?"

"Yes, but I don't know a Christy Castleman." The voice spoke in a raspy, indifferent tone.

"I'm Christy. If you're Sheryl, I really need to talk to you."

"Why do you want to talk to me?"

"It concerns Molly Adams. Did you know she's dying?"

There was a momentary pause, during which the loud laughter in the shop prompted Christy to stick her finger in the ear not pressed against the phone.

"No, I didn't know that," Sheryl replied, a change in her tone. "Two detectives came to ask some weird questions about a jewelry box. I don't know where April got that jewelry box—at a garage sale, I think. But they didn't say nothing about her mother."

"Well, Molly and little Zeffie are friends of mine. What I want to talk to you about concerns both of them. When could you meet me for coffee?"

"Can't we talk about this over the phone?"

"No, I'm at work. When can you meet me?" She was determined not to let this woman get away.

"I could meet you at Joe's Diner here in Fort Walton tomorrow around one o'clock. But I won't have long."

"That's fine. It won't take long. I'm just trying to help April's little girl. I'll explain it to you. By the way, I don't live in Fort Walton. Can you give me the address of that diner?"

Christy grabbed a pen and jotted the address down on the pad, writing as fast as she could since Sheryl sounded hurried.

"Okay. I'm five-three with long brown hair," Christy said, waiting for Sheryl to give a description.

"I'll find you." Sheryl made it sound as though Christy would be the obvious stranger in the diner.

Christy breathed a sigh of relief and hung up. Bobbie nudged her, motioning toward the woman extending a handful of cash.

"Oh, sorry," Christy said, taking the price tag and ringing up the amount on the cash register.

∾

After work, Christy felt tense and anxious. She drove to the park and grabbed her running shoes from the trunk. She needed some physical exercise to loosen the tension. For the next forty-five minutes, she jogged along the trails, relishing the fresh air as her pent-up energy flowed into her muscles and her feet pounded the trail.

As she ran, her mind replayed the facts on Kirby's barbecue and murder, along with each suspect on her list. Another scenario played through her mind.

R. J. Wentworth hadn't been the only man in Julie's life before Kirby came along. If she was willing to have a fling at the beach with Wayne Crocker, who else had she seen over the years? Had R.J. been double-crossed without knowing it? Or had the truth exploded in his face suddenly, making him crazy enough to do something drastic? Something he would regret for the rest of his life?

She ran faster, nodding absently to other runners on the trail as her mind picked up speed with her body.

What about Julie? She had seemed so convincing that day in her shop when she told Christy about forgetting the invitation list and calling Kirby to go back for it. And yet, a simple return home had cost Kirby his life. Had someone broken in to steal, or had someone been waiting for him? Someone who wanted the murder to look like a burglary and thus grabbed the easiest, most valuable item in haste—Mrs. Strickland's jewelry box?

Christy stopped running and leaned against a tree to stretch out her legs, her breath jerking through her chest. Further up the trail, a black crow swooped into a grassy area and began feeding on a dead bird. She hated crows. And she hated the way her thoughts, like a vulture, began to feed on dark possibilities. Still, a question persisted, pecking at her peace of mind.

Had Julie sent R.J. back to kill Kirby? And if so, why?

Mrs. Strickland's estate had been scheduled for final settlement the week after Kirby was murdered. Had Kirby left a will? Had he already designated his fiancée as the recipient of his life insurance? Had the depression and suicidal behavior that frightened Julie's father been just an act?

Why? Why would Julie kill Kirby if she loved him?

Despite her actions, had R.J. been her real love all along?

Was R.J.'s father wealthy enough to set him up for life with a large marina? When Christy had spoken to Bobbie about R.J. and Julie, Bobbie was quick to mention that their Rosemary Beach home looked like it belonged to a movie star. She had toured it during the Home and Garden show. And what about the huge diamond on Julie's left hand? Ten thousand dollars would be a low estimate of its cost, Christy figured. Not to mention the exclusive shop, which must hold over a hundred thousand dollars' worth of inventory.

Was the small, sweet woman with the soft whispery voice a little girl who never grew up? Who wanted to play dress-up with clothes and jewelry and be worshiped and waited on by a man who would die for her?

Or kill for her?

"Hey, Christy," a female voice called to her.

She turned to see a college girl from church, out getting some exercise with her boyfriend.

"Hey," Christy called back, waving to them.

She blinked herself back to reality. Her feet felt like concrete blocks as she plodded back to the car, and exhaustion settled over her like dust settling over the park. It had been a long day, and the tour group at the shop had taken a huge dose of her energy. Perhaps being tired had made her prey to darker thoughts, and yet she'd learned to listen to the voices that spoke to her when an investigation was under way, just as the characters in her books spoke to her, telling her what to write. She knew her mental wiring differed from others, but she viewed it as a strength that should not be taken for granted.

She hit the remote on her keys to open the car door and then sank gratefully into the front seat. The towel and bottle of water on the passenger seat were welcome sights, and she wiped her face and gulped water into her parched throat.

Heaving a sigh, she recapped the bottle and started the car. As she drove home, she lowered the window, deeply inhaling the fresh autumn air. She wished the breeze could drift through her brain, cleansing it of the ominous thoughts that lingered.

Her memory drifted back over the years. She could feel the cold lake on her skin, the panic that filled her chest as she gulped for air and got mouthfuls of water instead. Then she saw in her mind's eye the kind eyes of Kirby Strickland, felt his strong arms around her.

"Kirby," she said, gripping the wheel tighter, "we're going to catch your killer. I promise you that."

Energized by that thought, she turned into her neighborhood. The cozy glow of streetlamps illuminated the grassy yards of homes along the way, and she felt a sense of peace as she pulled into her driveway. She hopped out of the car, keys and purse in hand, and hurried to the back door.

Which stood open.

Had she been that scatterbrained? She paused and reached inside the door, flipping on the kitchen light. The kitchen looked normal, but something wasn't right. Reaching into her purse, she grabbed her cell phone and flipped it open. She had taken only a few steps into the kitchen when she looked through the opening from the eating bar to the living room and felt a chill.

The blinds on the back window flapped gently in the breeze coming through the shattered windowpane.

She knew she hadn't left the lamp on the end table on, but it burned brightly, highlighting the white accent pillow on the sofa.

Her gaze froze on the pillow, propped conspicuously so that big red letters, shaped from Burnt Crimson fingernail polish, greeted her.

Back off.

Her breath caught as she ran out of the house and dived back into her car and quickly hit the automatic lock. She dialed Bob's private number as she raced through the streets to the deputy sheriff's office.

It wasn't until Bob sat her down with a hot cup of coffee that the trembling subsided.

"Ronnie," he hollered into the back office, "get a crew. We're going to Christy's house." He spun around in his office chair. "You want to call your dad, or shall I?"

Christy sighed. "I'll call him." He stood, and she mirrored his movement. "I need to get some of my things. I'll follow you guys back."

He paused at the door. "Only if you let us go in first, and you don't get in our way. I don't want anything to happen to you," he said, his voice gentle. His big arm circled her shoulders.

She nodded. "Thanks, Bob."

When they arrived back at her home, she let Bob and Ronnie check out the house while she waited in the car. After he returned to the brightly lit back porch and waved to her, she hopped out and went inside.

She had heard other people talk about how violated they felt when someone broke into their home, touched and stole their belongings, and now she understood. It was soon apparent, however, that nothing was missing. The intruder had a mission for breaking into her home. The ugly red stain on her accent pillow—*Back off*—was a mild warning compared to the other thing he had done.

She stood beside Bob, staring at the photograph of her parents in the center of the coffee table. Two round globs of fingernail polish centered each forehead like a gunshot wound.

"Let's get out of here," Bob said gently. "Pack an overnight bag. We'll go to your parents' home."

Christy had frozen in time and space, trying to absorb the message some monster had left her. A very sick monster. "I hate to worry my parents," she said in a voice so weak she wondered if Bob could hear her.

"It's time we all got worried. You're not coming back to this house until it's been dusted for fingerprints and vacuumed for any evidence of who did this." Bob glanced around the room again, his features tight. "Let's hope a stray hair fell from this lowlife's head."

All she could do at this point was obey, and with Bob leading the way, she went to the center of refuge, her parents' home.

～

Grant and Beth Castleman did not take the news well. While Grant managed to speak calmly, he looked as though his face had been painted with chalk for a Halloween carnival. Beth forced some chicken soup into Christy, along with a glass of milk, and then Christy called Dan.

"I'll take the first flight out tomorrow," he said. "You stay put." His voice softened. "Christy, I love you more than anyone in the world. Please take care of yourself until I get home."

"Don't worry. I have lots of people watching over me," she said.

It wasn't until she was snuggled into her old bedroom that her conversation with Sheryl Wilcox drifted into her muddled thoughts. Was that conversation the cause of the red letters on her pillow, the targets on her parents' foreheads?

She clenched her eyes tightly shut. No, that hideous deed came directly from the person who took Kirby's life and now feared being exposed in this new investigation, where everyone was being examined more closely.

Christy sat up in bed, staring through the darkness to the crystal angel figurine on the dresser, its hands clasped in prayer, its head lowered. Following the angel's example, she clasped her hands together and closed her eyes.

"God, please help us bring this murderer to justice," she whispered into the darkness.

∽

There was an APB out on Reuben Foster, but the fool was still hanging around.

The shadow waited in the alley where Foster's green truck was parked. The only reason people hadn't recognized Foster was because he wore a baseball cap pulled low on his forehead and probably sat in the back of the bar, away from the crowd. No doubt he was tanking up for courage, and then he planned to sneak off in his truck and hide out somewhere.

The shadow waited patiently, leaning against a Dumpster in the dark alley near the back door of the bar. The door opened and the shadow flattened against the building, but Foster was too drunk to notice as he stumbled toward his old truck.

Just as he reached for the door handle, the stranger lifted the gun and fired. Foster crumpled. Another shot rang out, as though confirming the mark; then the shadow shoved the gun deep in a pocket and hurried up the alley, turning down a side street.

Shouts erupted in the darkness, echoing into the night. In the next five minutes, a siren screamed in the background, but the shadow was already in the car, driving slowly through town.

Saturday

The first flight Dan could book would arrive in Panama City around four o'clock in the afternoon. Christy offered to pick him up, but he refused, saying he'd left his car at the airport.

"I'll come to your parents' home," he said.

Too antsy to stay home, she convinced her parents she would be perfectly safe at the shop with Bobbie, who had been apprised of the situation late last night.

When Christy entered the shop, dressed casually, her hair whisked into a ponytail, she knew from a glance in the mirror that her face betrayed her feelings. The person who had tried to warn her off had only angered her. Her emotions were still churning over having her home violated with such an ugly threat, but the initial fear was gone, replaced by a firm determination.

She would find the person who had killed Kirby. She was onto the killer, and the killer knew it. She knew it too. No matter what anyone said, she wasn't about to back off.

But she kept this to herself and stayed away from her home as she had promised. Bob had called earlier that day, saying nothing obvious had been found, but it would take the crime unit a few days to finish their work. By now every neighbor on the block must know what had happened, and that alone discouraged her from returning.

"Oh, honey!" Bobbie rushed up as Christy put her purse on the counter. Despite Bobbie's soft pink blush, her face looked pale, and the usual sparkle in her blue eyes was gone. Her small arms flew around Christy, hugging her with surprising strength for such a petite lady. "I've been so worried about you."

"No need to worry," Christy assured her. "I've probably never been safer." She glanced around the shop. "Will you be afraid if I hang out here?"

"Of course not. Jack's on his way over now. You know how he is. There will be, you know, protection in the trunk of his car. But," she quickly added, "he has a permit."

Christy nodded, heading for the coffeepot. She was still trying to figure out what to do about Sheryl. As she poured coffee, she decided to find the detective's card and give him a call.

Jack walked through the door. His face wore the familiar look of worry—tensed features and tight lips. His eyes looked a bit red as well. Lack of sleep, she imagined.

"I'm fine," she called out, her courage flowing back at the sight of Jack. "So don't start making noises about being careful."

"Me?" he said gruffly, reaching for the coffeepot. "I'd bet my new fishing boat that's all you've heard for the last twelve hours."

"That's a bet you wouldn't lose," she said, clinking her mug to his in a toast.

Bobbie reached out to Jack, and Christy turned her head as they folded into a quick embrace. She strolled away from them, walking over to the forties evening gown. Maybe she'd buy it and throw a costume party. It'd be fun to escape back to another century when life seemed simpler.

Of course it wasn't. A war, loss of lives, and complications she couldn't even imagine existed then. She looked at the cell phone in her hand. And all the modern technology had not been invented.

She opened her phone and checked her messages, finding only the usual hourly check from her mom. Christy called her back, quickly reassuring her.

As she hung up, Jack stood before her, looking concerned. "How can I help?" he asked.

She sneaked a look at the clock. Did she dare?

"We could take a little ride," she said. "It would calm my nerves to look at the ocean, escape the phones, that kind of thing."

"Sure." He drained his coffee mug and placed it on the counter, just as she had done. He turned to Bobbie. "Are you afraid to stay by yourself?"

"Are you kidding? Not after what you hid in the back room of the shop. And I know how to use it too."

"Use what?" Christy asked, concerned Bobbie might do something foolish.

"He calls it a hog leg," Bobbie said, laughing. "But don't worry, I'd never use it. I've got a scream that will bring every shop owner on the block pouring in here. And a deputy's car has already cruised past three times this morning."

"Good." Jack brightened. "We won't be gone long."

"Stay as long as you like. I'm having another crafts class in an hour."

Jack grimaced. "Come on, squirt. We're outta here."

Christy grabbed her purse and strolled out the door with Jack as though she hadn't a care in the world.

"Wanna drive down the beach?" he asked as they rolled away from the shop.

"Actually, I thought it would be fun to drive to Fort Walton," Christy replied. "I haven't been there in a while."

He stared at her. "That's more than the 'little drive' you suggested."

She sighed. "Jack, I promised to meet Sheryl Wilcox at one o'clock. She has nothing to do with what happened last night," she hastened to add, seeing his blue eyes take on a edge of anger. "And besides, if you're with me, I'll be safe."

"But will I be?" he mumbled, turning onto the highway leading to Fort Walton.

"Come on, Jack. You've never been afraid of anything in your life."

He heaved a sigh and glanced at her. "Just out of curiosity, what'll it take to make you follow Bob's orders and stay out of this crazy investigation? Especially after the threat you got last night?"

"It'll take finding Kirby's killer, and someone made a big mistake last night. My stubborn streak pops out when someone tries to bully me."

"I noticed that," he said. "You gotta promise you won't tell any-one we talked to this woman. Well, I guess you can't do that if it turns out to be important. Your aunt will take that hog leg to me, and Dan…" He sighed. "Dan'll nail my hide to J.T.'s barn door."

She swatted his shoulder. "Stop it. When Dan gets back, I'll practically be under house arrest. This is my only chance, and see—I've chosen the man I trust the most to help me."

He threw back his head and roared with laughter. "Even when I know you're twisting me around that little finger of yours, I just go right ahead and do whatever you ask."

"Jack, that's part of your charm. You have a sense of adventure."

"Maybe neither of us has any sense at all."

But he pressed the accelerator harder, and they shot down the highway toward Fort Walton.

22

Jack and Christy sat in a booth at Joe's Diner, watching the front door. The décor of the diner duplicated many of the popular fifties diners specializing in cherry Cokes, malts, and hamburgers. A row of barstools ran the length of the counter. When Christy and Jack had entered at 12:45, the diner overflowed with customers, and they had to wait for one of the few booths along the wall, grabbing the one nearest the front door the minute the couple got up to pay their bill. They ordered hamburgers and malts and ate quickly, their eyes on the entrance.

While they ate, Christy expressed to Jack everything that had troubled her the night before concerning Julie and R.J.

Jack shook his head doubtfully. "I think that theory may be a long shot, Christy. So Julie had a fling at the beach. Maybe she just wanted a change."

"Maybe," Christy agreed, staring out the window at the road.

The memory of that conversation faded as a woman walked through the front door of the diner and looked around. She was a sturdy woman in her forties, with spiked red hair and freckles she didn't bother to hide with makeup. She wore jean shorts and a loose T-shirt advertising a local bar. When her eyes turned to Christy, she marched to their table.

"Christy?"

"Sheryl?"

She nodded, glancing suspiciously at Jack.

"Sheryl, this is my friend, Jack Watson."

"Hi, Sheryl. Want to have lunch with us?" Jack asked politely.

Sheryl looked from Jack to Christy, then shook her head. "Don't have time, but thanks." She slid in beside Christy and looked her over. "What's wrong with Molly?"

"Lung cancer. She hasn't long to live. Zeffie is an adorable little girl."

Sheryl heaved a sigh, folded her plump hands on the table, and fell silent for a moment. "April had a picture of Zeffie on her dresser in the bedroom. She was just a little thing, but she looked so sweet."

"Did April ever say who Zeffie's father was?"

"No. She went with a lotta men and, like I said, Zeffie was born before I ever met April. We were both single in those days, hanging out at bars. Still, if I'd had a little girl like Zeffie somewhere, I don't know that I'd have taken the path April did. But then, April operated on self-destruct. She tried to come off tough, but she was one of the neediest people I ever met. She was always on a crash diet, and she'd change her hair color every week. She wanted to find someone who would take care of her."

Sheryl looked from Christy to Jack, then back to Christy. "Two detectives came to see me, wanting to know about a jewelry box she had. All I remembered about it was the song it played. She played it over and over. One day I stomped in her room and told her I was sick of hearing it. She said she was taking it to her daughter that weekend, and she did. She was always going to garage sales. I know she bought a picture she hung in the living room about that time at a garage sale and that she was giving it to her mom. I think she probably bought the jewelry box at the same time."

She accepted the glass of water a server put before her but waved aside a menu. "I told them detectives that April always checked the classified ads in the newspaper for garage and yard sales. That if they wanted to find the owner of the jewelry box, the best way was to check the classifieds for a couple of weeks before April's last trip to Montgomery. Haven't heard from them since." She sighed. "And I hope I don't."

"A couple weeks after April got that jewelry box," Sheryl continued, "I moved in with Bo, my boyfriend. He didn't want me hanging around April anymore. I felt awful when I heard she'd had a car wreck and died."

"Did she move here from Panama City?" Christy asked.

Sheryl nodded. "She worked as a waitress there for a while, but I think she went home to Montgomery. That's where Zeffie was born. Then later, she moved down here. Said she could make more money. Other than that, she didn't talk about her past to me."

Sheryl took a big gulp of water, then slid out of the booth. "That's all I know to tell you except that I'm sorry about the grandmother. What'll happen to the kid? Bo and I got married, and we have five kids. The thought of that little girl without a mom breaks my heart."

Christy shook her head. "Molly has a cousin in Montgomery who's willing to take Zeffie, but I'm not sure that's what Zeffie wants."

Sheryl heaved a sigh. "Such is life." She hesitated for a moment, and Christy sensed she wanted to say something.

"Is there anything else, anything at all that you can think of? If we could clear this up, Zeffie wouldn't have to spend the rest of her life wondering if her mother was involved in a murder."

"I know." Sheryl's big face registered sadness. "I've been racking my brain to remember something. This morning I did. Might sound silly..."

"Sheryl, I promise you, nothing you say to me will sound silly. Tell me anything you remember. After all, you seem to have known April better than anyone else during the last year of her life."

"That's why I've been racking my brain. Once when I went in her room to borrow some earrings, she opened up that jewelry box and handed them to me. Then she said, 'Tex isn't going to fill up this jewelry box like he promised. I know he'll break up with me.' Sheryl had no confidence in herself, but then, Tex was no bargain either."

Christy's heart beat faster. "Who is Tex?"

"A bartender April was seeing for a while. The way she mentioned him in the same breath with the jewelry box made me think he knew something about it. Or maybe she just showed it to him after she bought it. It was just a hunch. Probably doesn't mean anything."

Christy glanced at Jack, who was staring at Sheryl, as though he, too, thought she might be on to something. "Sheryl, I put a lot of stock in a woman's intuition. I think it's worth checking out," she said. "Tell me about this guy."

"Everybody calls him Tex. Used to talk about how great Texas was. One night some drunk yelled, 'If it's so great, why don't you go home?'" Sheryl laughed at the remark, then turned serious again. "Tex Dunn. He runs the Salty Dog Saloon over on Booker Street. It's the toughest bar in town. He's built like a bull; in fact, he's also the bouncer there. You two might wanna steer clear of him."

Sheryl sighed. "I think Tex was the only man who really cared for April, but they didn't last long. She kept pushing him to get married." Sheryl snorted. "Tex ain't the marrying kind. April had issues about men always taking off, so she usually set herself up for a breakup before someone dumped her. Guess she never got over her dad running out on them. She and her mother had a rough time of it. Said she always wore thrift-store clothes and had learned when she was young, the best deals she could get were not at department store sales but at garage sales."

She stared out the window, as though reliving the past, and then looked at Christy. "I can tell you really care about little Zeffie."

"Did you tell the detectives about Tex?" Christy asked.

Sheryl shook her head. "Nah, they broke up before she got killed. Tex has a heart of gold. He'd never be involved in anything like that Strickland murder."

Christy wondered if she'd just heard the real reason Sheryl hadn't mentioned Tex to the detectives.

"Well, thanks a lot, Sheryl," she replied, aware the other woman was waiting for a response. "I'll let you know how things turn out. As for what you've told me, you've given me some real insight into April's life, and I thank you very much."

Every freckle on Sheryl's face seemed to dance as her lips broke into a wide smile, crinkling her dry skin. "Hey, thanks." She looked at Jack. "Nice to have met you. Looks like you've got yourself a good woman here."

It wasn't until Sheryl left that the two of them covered their mouths and snickered at her assumption they were a couple.

"I thought she was going to say I had a good daughter," Jack said, looking pleased.

Christy smiled. "You see, I'm always telling you that you're an attractive man. I knew you and Bobbie would be perfect for each other."

He grinned, picking up the bill. "Let's go see Tex."

∽

When they pulled into the parking lot of the seedy bar on Booker Street, Christy took a deep breath and bolstered her nerve. "We'll just kind of wade into the subject."

"*We* won't do anything," Jack said. "You aren't going in that joint." He looked east to west, north to south. "Lock the doors."

"What will you say to him?" Christy asked, oblivious to any danger.

"From what Sheryl says, he's a man's kind of man. He's not

gonna spill his guts to a pretty little thing like you. Just trust me. I may be in there awhile, but I'll find out about April Adams."

She rolled down the window as he crossed in front of the truck. "Jack, be careful. And don't stay if it looks like you might have a problem. Here." She thrust her cell phone out the window. "Take my phone."

He waved the suggestion aside. "In case you hadn't noticed, I know how to take care of myself. I've been doing it for fifty-some-odd years."

He disappeared inside the bar, leaving Christy in the truck to wait.

Drumming her fingers on the armrest, she watched the clock on the dash. After twenty agonizing minutes, she decided she'd give Jack another five, and then she was going in, cell phone in hand.

Four minutes later, Jack walked out of the bar, followed by a huge, brawny guy who lumbered across the street toward the car. She heard a loud chuckle from the big man as Jack rattled off a joke, or what she thought was a joke. She could only hear a few words. Her eyes sneaked back to Tex. She had a general impression of a bald guy dressed in black with heavily tattooed arms displayed by a sleeveless T-shirt.

She held her breath. Had the jewelry box belonged to this guy? If so, why was Jack acting friendly? Well, that might be the smart thing to do so as not to appear suspicious. She fidgeted, her hand gripping the cell phone tighter. This was one of the toughest-looking men she'd ever seen. Her gaze slid to Jack, who looked cool and calm.

As they approached the car, Jack smiled at her. "Relax, Christy.

Tex, this is Christy Castleman, the lady I was telling you about. Christy, this is Tex Dunn. And Tex, if you don't mind, tone down the language a bit. Christy's pretty straight-laced." Jack nudged Tex and winked at her.

Tex nodded. "Pleased to meet you, ma'am."

Christy nodded back. "You too."

"Hey, I wanted to tell ya I'm sorry to hear about April's momma. I know April loved the kid, even if she didn't go visit much. She said she could never believe the little girl really belonged to her, that she was too pretty."

"Oh, she said that?"

Tex nodded, towering above her outside the window. "When I asked who the dad was, she wouldn't say. 'Didn't matter,' she said, 'it was a one-time fling.' Then she added somethin' kinda funny. She said, 'At least he was different from the others.' Thanks to him, she had a beautiful child who looked more like him than her."

Christy stared at Tex, trying to digest that information. April did know who Zeffie's father was, but she'd never told anyone, not even Sheryl.

"Tell her where April got the jewelry box, Tex," Jack prompted.

"I gave that jewelry box to her," Tex admitted.

Christy felt as though he had just tossed a bomb in her lap.

"Tex got the jewelry box from a guy who worked for him, then passed it on to April," Jack explained.

She turned to Tex, her heart pounding. "Who was he?"

Tex shook his head. "Already told Jack, I don't know. A tall black dude. He worked for me about a week, and when he finished, I paid him in cash and he left."

"Do you remember exactly when he worked for you?"

"It was right before the bar's one-year anniversary celebration, July Fourth in 1998. So I'd say, the last of June."

"Did anyone else know him?"

He shook his head. "He was only here that week, but he's a good painter, I'll say that for him."

"And you don't recognize the name Reuben Foster?" Jack asked.

"Nope."

Christy hesitated, glancing at Jack. Still, she had to ask. "What about the name Willie Pitt?"

He frowned. "Now that name's more familiar. I'm sure I've heard it."

"Well," Jack drawled, "you probably have. He's the best barbecue guy in Bay County."

Tex shook his head. "I'm the oddball down here who doesn't like barbecue. Coulda heard of him from someone at the bar. Hey, I wish I could remember, but you're talking about 1998, and my old brain don't hold onto much anymore. I hear people's names all day and night."

Christy nodded, her hopes plummeting. "I understand."

"April used to come in the bar a lot, and we became friends." He paused, looking down for a moment as though thinking about something. "I cared for April. I know people used her, but I cared about her. To me, she seemed like a frightened, insecure woman who just needed someone to love and understand her. I guess you could say we bonded for a while. It tore me up when she got killed."

He shoved his hands in the pockets of his jeans, and the tattoos seemed to wiggle on his bare arms. "But back to the jewelry box. This guy, whatever his name was, who painted the outside of the bar, moonlighted doing odd jobs. Couple of days before payday, he asked for an advance. I don't give advances!"

He turned and looked back at the bar, pointing toward the side street that paralleled the building. "We stood out there on the sidewalk; I was looking over the paint job. His beat-up old truck was parked at the curb, and I noticed it held some old tools, a worn out old gym bag, and that little brown box." His sentences ran together and Christy wondered how he did that without taking a breath.

He looked back at Christy. "When he saw me looking in the bed of his truck, he went over and picked up the box. He said he got it when he cleaned out a garage for a guy who wanted stuff hauled off to the Dumpster, so he dumped the garbage bags but kept the gym bag for himself. Opened up the gym bag and found the jewelry box, decided to keep it too."

"But it was supposed to be hauled to the Dumpster," Christy interjected, wanting to get the facts straight.

Tex nodded. "The painter showed it to me. I lifted the lid, and it played a pretty tune. I thought April might like it, so I said, 'Okay, I'll give you ten bucks for it.' He took my money, finished the job on Friday. I paid him in cash and never saw him again."

Christy found herself taking extra breaths for him. He pulled a pack of cigarettes from the single pocket on his T-shirt, looked at her, then stuffed them back in the pocket.

For the first time, Jack looked deadly serious. "Tex, do you remember what kind of truck he was driving?"

Tex looked down again. Beads of perspiration gathered like raindrops on his bald head. She wondered if he were reading his answers off the pavement. Automatically, she thrust her head out the window to see nothing but dirty pavement.

"I just remember a beat-up old truck, maybe a Ford." He looked up again. "I was glad when he finished up, because it was a sore spot to my bar."

Christy glanced around, thinking the surrounding neighborhood was only a few notches above a sore spot.

"Tex, did Jack tell you everyone feels sorry for Zeffie because her mom is gone and she never knew her dad? And now her grandmother, who has cared for her all this time, is dying."

Tex nodded. A hint of a tear glistened in one eye. "That's terrible, just terrible. April loved that little gal. Maybe folks thought she didn't since she didn't live with her, but she did. First thing she said when I gave her the music box was, 'Now I'll have something pretty to take Zeffie.'"

Suddenly, Christy had an idea. In a way, it was a risky thing to do, but she always listened to her instincts. "Would you like to meet her sometime?"

Tex actually blushed. She would have bet her life that nothing would make this man blush. Now she realized he had a tender heart, and she could see why he understood April better than other people had.

"I'd like to see her, I really would, but she's better off not knowing somebody who looked like me was in her momma's past."

Jack was staring at her, and she knew he agreed with Tex.

"You could say some nice things about April, as you have to us," Christy persisted. "I think that would make Zeffie feel better about her mother and about herself. I'm afraid she hasn't heard many good things about her mother."

Tex shifted from one booted foot to the other and reached for his cigarettes again.

Christy braced herself. "Go ahead and smoke. You don't need to feel uncomfortable with me."

"Well, all this has got my nerves balled up," he said, pausing long enough to light his cigarette, take a deep puff, then turn his head and blow the smoke away from Christy. "If you think something I could say might make that little gal feel better about her momma, I'd be glad to do it. I'd like to do that much for April." He hesitated. "On second thought, she wouldn't have to know I ever had a thing with her mother. I could just be a…"

"You own a business, and that makes you a businessman," Jack supplied.

Christy nodded. "That's right. Why don't I give you a call when I find a good time for you to meet her? Can you drive over to Summer Breeze, or do you want me to bring her…"

"Oh no, ma'am, don't bring her here. It'd be a pleasure to drive over there whenever you find the right time."

Jack clamped a hand on his shoulder. "Thanks, Tex. If you hear anything, give me a call." He looked at Christy. "I left my number with him when we were inside, so we'll be in touch. For now, we gotta track down this guy who sold you the music box."

"You think he killed that Strickland guy?" Fire danced in Tex's blue eyes. "I'll ask everybody who works at the bar, everybody who comes in the bar. Maybe I can come up with a name."

"Thanks, Tex," Christy said.

Jack moved around the car and climbed in behind the wheel.

Christy extended her hand to Tex. "It was nice meeting you."

For a split second, he looked suspicious, as though she were playing with him, but as she smiled into his eyes, his face softened and his big hand reached out to shake hers.

"We'll be talking with you, Tex," Jack called.

He nodded and stepped back from the car, puffing deeply on his cigarette as he watched them drive away.

Neither Christy nor Jack spoke for several seconds.

"You'd better call Bob Arnold," Jack said at last.

Christy nodded. "I know. The guy who wanted everything thrown in the Dumpster didn't want that jewelry box found."

She dialed Bob's office number on her cell phone, but his secretary informed her he was out on an investigation. She hesitated, recalling what Sheryl had said about being questioned.

"Thank you." She hung up.

"Why didn't you leave word for him to call?" Jack asked.

"I'd rather talk to him in person."

Her thoughts returned to Willie, and she took a deep breath.

She hated to bring it up, but there was no avoiding the topic now. "Jack, I know you don't think Willie is capable of doing anything like this, but…" She didn't know what else to say.

"I don't know what I think," Jack said, staring at the road, his forehead rumpled with a deep frown. "Might as well go ahead and tell you: I heard Willie talking to a customer one day. The guy was asking him if he still did any painting on the side. Willie said no, that he gave that up years ago, when his barbecue business got going."

"So he *was* a painter at one time," Christy repeated, relieved that Jack was beginning to see both sides of the situation.

"And he wouldn't have reason to go back to Fort Walton because he lived in Panama City before he moved to Mexico Beach."

Jack turned and looked at her. "We never thought to ask Tex how he found this mysterious painter."

Christy slapped her forehead. "No. I never thought of that."

"I'll call him when I get home."

Her cell phone rang.

"Aunt Christy." Zeffie's voice was trembling. "Grandma is bad. She told me to call 911, and they've taken her to the hospital." She could hear the tears in Zeffie's voice. "I don't know what to do."

"I'll be right there. Where are you?"

"In the waiting area of the emergency room. I saw Aunt Julie in the parking lot. Her house cleaner had surgery. She's with me now."

"Let me speak with her, please." Christy grabbed Jack's arm tight. He let go of the wheel with one arm and squeezed her hand.

"Christy." Julie sounded nervous. "Can you come to the hospital? It's...crucial."

"I'm on my way. Can you stay with her till I get there?"

"Of course."

"Thanks. Be there in ten minutes." She hung up, sick with worry.

"Listen to me," Jack said. "I'll get you to the hospital, and you just stay there and take care of that little girl. I'll let everyone know what's going on."

Christy nodded. She could tell from the sound of Julie's voice that Molly Adams might be dying soon. Her heart beat faster; she'd have to notify the cousin in Montgomery.

"Be strong," he said, gripping her arm.

She saw that Jack's face had drained of color, and suddenly she remembered he had been through two terrible crises himself—first his wife, then his son. "Go see Bobbie," she said, reaching forward to peck him on the cheek.

They pulled into the hospital, and she hopped out of the car and ran through the doors of the emergency department.

The lady at the reception desk was named Ruth, and Christy knew her from church. When Christy explained why she had come, Ruth nodded. "Mrs. Wentworth asked me to send you back when you arrived."

She directed her through the double doors to the waiting room. Julie was talking on her cell phone with one hand and holding Zeffie with the other. When Zeffie spotted Christy, she broke free and ran to her, wrapping her arms around Christy's waist.

"It's okay, honey. We're here for you. I won't leave you, I promise."

A doctor walked quickly toward them, looking from Julie to Christy. "I need to speak with a family member," he said.

"Zeffie is the only family here," Christy said, looking pointedly at the doctor. She had to make him understand this was a delicate situation. "I'm their closest friend. She has a cousin in Montgomery that I can call."

He nodded. "Then you'd better do that. I'm admitting her to ICU." He hesitated, looking down at Zeffie and back at Christy. When Zeffie buried her face in Christy's arms, the doctor shook his head at Christy. "She isn't going to make it." He mouthed the words so that Christy understood.

"Thank you. Is she conscious?"

"She's in and out. I don't want anyone talking to her right now. We need to work with her."

"I understand," she said. "We'll wait until she's settled in ICU." Zeffie looked up at her.

Julie walked over to them after the doctor left, looking helpless. "How can I help?"

"You've helped by being here. Thank you so much, Julie." Christy looked at the somber faces populating the waiting area. It seemed to her that the oxygen had been sucked out of the room. "Let's walk out in the sunshine for a minute." She had to talk to Zeffie, and she didn't want to do it here.

The three of them strolled outside and found a deserted spot in the late afternoon sun. For a split second, the horrible suspicions Christy had entertained about Julie shot through her mind, and she felt like a jerk.

At that moment, a silver Jaguar pulled up to the curb and a man got out. Without the sunglasses, R.J.'s eyes glittered green in the sunlight as he rushed to his wife's side. "Honey, you sounded so upset," he said to Julie, placing an arm around her.

Zeffie turned back to stare at the brick exterior of the hospital. "Granny said I shouldn't be afraid if I ever had to come here with her. She said I was born in this hospital."

"Oh?" Christy asked, following Zeffie's gaze. "Well, it hasn't changed a lot in eight years—they added a wing onto the back, I think."

She glanced at Julie and R.J., who were both staring wide-eyed at Zeffie. Julie had withdrawn a billfold from her purse and opened it to a set of pictures. Christy tried to see what they were looking at, but all she could make out was a photograph of a little boy. Then, as they both looked from the picture to Zeffie, an idea popped into Christy's head. She studied R.J., then Zeffie.

At the same time, Zeffie turned to look at R.J. Two pairs of green eyes surveyed one another, and the same frown pulled at their mouths. R.J.'s chin held a big dimple, Zeffie's a small one.

"Could you excuse us for a moment?" Julie asked, thrusting her billfold back in her purse.

"Certainly," Christy replied, confused by the unspoken thoughts that seemed to hover in the air.

Julie and R.J. walked a comfortable distance and began to talk quietly.

The roar of a car engine diverted Christy's thoughts as a baby blue Cadillac screeched into the parking lot and double-parked. Miz B rolled out. "I just saw Jack at the red light," she called, hurrying toward them. She leaned down and gathered Zeffie in her broad arms. "You have a lot of friends here, baby. We're gonna help."

"Excuse me for a minute," Christy said, concerned by the distressed look on Julie's face as she kept glancing over her shoulder at Zeffie. Christy had a vague idea about what they might be discussing, but she didn't want to intrude. Just then, however, Julie motioned to her.

"Be right back," she said to Zeffie, then walked to Julie's side.

"Christy...we were just talking. This might seem like an odd question, but what did Zeffie's mother look like? Did she live here in Panama City?"

Christy faced two people whose tense emotions sat squarely on their face. She kept her voice calm, as though she hadn't an inkling what had set them off.

"I never met her, but I saw a couple pictures of her at Mrs. Adams's home. April had brown hair and eyes. And I believe she may have been working as a waitress at a restaurant in the Panama City beach area when Zeffie was born."

"Thank you," Julie replied, her voice tense, her cheeks flushed. R.J., on the other hand, had blanched and was shoving his hand through his dark blond hair.

Sensing the tension, Christy cleared her throat. "I'd better take Zeffie back inside."

She was only a few steps away when Julie's voice carried to her.

"R.J., you and some buddies came down here fishing a lot that spring. Remember? I got mad at you Memorial Day weekend because you were gone on my birthday."

"We celebrated when I got back," he reminded her.

"Yeah, well, from what your buddies said, you did more drinking and carousing than fishing."

When Christy reached them, Miz B was draping a familiar scarf around Zeffie's shoulders. It was the one Christy had given her.

Miz B looked at Christy. "It was the prettiest thing I had to give."

Christy hugged her. "Thanks, Miz B."

Julie and R.J. rejoined them, and Julie reached for Zeffie's hand. "Zeffie, when's your birthday?"

Zeffie looked puzzled. "February 13. Grandma always told me I was her Valentine."

Miz B filled up the silence that followed by reporting she had called her prayer chain, then spoken with Christy's dad at the church. Only Zeffie seemed to hear. Christy, Julie, and R.J. were working the math in their heads, and the numbers came out right.

Zeffie turned back to Julie. "Why'd you ask about my birthday?"

"Because R.J.'s birthday is in a week," Julie replied calmly, but her face told a different story. "I thought if your birthday was close, we'd make it a double party." She broke off for an awkward second. "When the time is right, I mean."

Zeffie smiled, but her gaze shot back to the hospital. "I want to see about Grandma."

"Of course," Christy said, gripping her hand. When she glanced back, R.J. stared at Zeffie as though he'd never seen her before.

"We'll come back later," Julie called after them.

"Me too," Miz B added.

As the others left, Christy turned to Zeffie, who held her hand tightly.

"Zeffie, we have to call your grandmother's cousin. Do you know her name and number?"

Zeffie frowned. "Uncle Bailey and Aunt Sally Carver. I don't know their telephone number, but they live in Montgomery. They don't call very often."

"That's okay. I can call Information. But you do understand, don't you, honey, that your grandmother's condition is very serious?"

"She may die," Zeffie blurted and burst into tears.

Christy gathered her into her arms, holding her close, saying nothing as the little girl cried her heart out. When the crying had subsided to sniffles and Zeffie had blown her nose and wiped her face with the Kleenex Christy gave her, they returned to the waiting room.

They sat down, and Christy punched in the number for Information on her cell phone. In a few minutes, she had Sally Carver on the line.

"Mrs. Carver, we need a family member here at the hospital. Mrs. Adams is critical. The doctor feels it's necessary for you to come."

"Is Molly going to die?" Sally asked. There was more panic than sadness in her voice.

"The doctor thinks so."

"We'll leave as soon as we can get packed," Sally said. "How is Zeffie?"

"She's very concerned about her grandma. I'll tell her you said hello," she added, although neither Sally nor Zeffie expressed a desire to speak to one another.

Christy replaced her cell phone in her purse and turned to Zeffie, who had flopped back against the chair. "We have to be strong for Grandma," Christy said, picking up Zeffie's hand again. "You aren't going through this alone. You have lots of friends here who love you."

Zeffie nodded, running Miz B's silk scarf through her fingers.

The next time the waiting room door opened, Christy spotted her parents hurrying toward them.

"Zeffie, you haven't met my parents," Christy said, "but they feel as though they know you."

"Christy talks about you all the time," Beth said, smiling at Zeffie. "I planned to come pick you up to attend my Sunday school class."

Christy gestured toward her father. "Zeffie, this is my father, Grant Castleman. Remember, I told you he's the pastor at Community Church."

Zeffie fixed her sad green eyes on his face. "Will you pray for Grandma?"

"Of course I will. In the meantime, could we pray for you?" he asked gently, taking a seat beside her.

After the prayer, Grant talked gently with Zeffie as he held her small hand in his. Beth called Christy aside.

"We're worried sick about you. Has Bob found out anything?"

"Not yet. But Dan's plane comes in at four o'clock, and I can promise you he won't let me out of his sight."

"I hope you're planning to stay with us again tonight."

"We'll see. Right now, let's worry about Zeffie."

Beth nodded, glancing at her. "We'd like to do something nice for her, maybe buy her a pretty new outfit. She wears about a size ten, right? It's hard to tell. She's so thin."

"That would be great. The clothes she wears don't fit her," Christy added, glancing at the little girl.

"I'm pretty sure she's a ten. If not, I can always exchange the clothes."

"Thanks, Mom." Christy hugged her mother.

Christy's parents offered to relieve her so she could get a snack, but she wasn't hungry and Zeffie wasn't interested in food.

A doctor came in to announce that Mrs. Adams had been moved to the intensive care unit but it would be at least an hour before anyone could see her.

"In the meantime, you can move up to the third-floor waiting room," he said.

Zeffie tucked her hand in Christy's as they headed toward the elevator. Christy tried to give Zeffie an encouraging smile, but the doctor's grim face lingered in her memory.

∾

The parking lot of the hospital had filled up quickly. Not a vacant space anywhere. Still, it might not be smart to park where the family was coming and going. A block away, the vehicle wouldn't be noticed under the shade of a live oak.

The stranger fastened the tag on his shirt pocket, then checked it in the visor mirror: "Associate Pastor, Fellowship Church, Panama City."

Satisfied this would get him past the usual guardians, he put on a pair of wide sunglasses, got out of the car, and hurried up the sidewalk, head down.

No familiar faces around the reception desk. He took the first exit to the stairwell, walking up the three flights. He'd called ahead to see where Molly Adams had been taken. At the top of the third set of stairs, he opened the door and stepped slowly into the hallway. He was familiar with the hospital; the family waiting area was to his left, the nurses' station to the right, beside the double doors leading into ICU.

The stranger approached a serious-faced nurse behind the glass cubicle and smiled. "I'm a friend of the family." He indicated his badge. "The congregation wanted me to check on Mrs. Adams."

The nurse softened a bit, reading the tag on his shirt. "The family is down in the waiting area," she pointed.

"Good," he said, glancing toward the waiting room then back to her. "Will it be possible for me to pray with Mrs. Adams when you admit family?"

The woman hesitated. "You could pray for her," she said, nodding, "but I'm not sure she would hear you. She's in a coma. You must know that."

He dropped his head. "This is so sad. Well, thanks a lot."

He turned as though heading toward the waiting room, but as soon as the nurse returned to the chart she was studying, he shifted his direction and made for the stairs.

23

Although Dan's plane didn't arrive until four o'clock, he'd been working his phone all day. By seven o'clock that evening, Christy's new security system had been installed. By eight, the two of them were seated in the waiting room of the hospital, comforting little Zeffie. Christy gripped Dan's hand, thrilled to have him back at her side.

Dan was whispering to her about the security system when Zeffie pressed her arm. "It's time for us to go in," she said.

Christy stood, aware that others were forming a line headed into ICU. Apparently, the unit was full of critical patients.

A nurse led them to a small glass room, where tubes and monitors dominated Molly's space.

"Grandma?" Zeffie asked, her voice trembling.

Molly's pale lids remained closed; the only movement of the woman's body was her chest moving slowly up and down in shallow breaths. An oxygen mask covered her nose and mouth, and just looking at her was enough to assure Christy that Zeffie didn't need to see her like this.

Still, Zeffie squared her shoulders and tried again. She stepped closer to the bed, wrapping her small hand around her grandmother's arm. "Grandma, it's me, Zeffie. I'm here."

For a moment, it seemed the eyes would open. The lashes fluttered, but then she grew still again.

Zeffie's face looked as white as the sterile walls and sheets. Christy reached for her hand. "Let's let her sleep."

Zeffie didn't object as they slipped quietly out of the huge area of cubicles. Nurses sat before monitors, and the swoosh of machines saving lives dominated the silence. The awful pall of death and dying overhung the room, and Christy feared she would start hyperventilating if they didn't get out soon.

As they walked back through the double doors and returned to the waiting room, a couple seated in the far corner jumped to their feet. They looked in their early fifties, both conservatively dressed, both wearing expressions of alarm.

"Hello, Zeffie." The woman rushed over and knelt beside Zeffie, then hesitated, as though unsure whether to shake hands or hug her.

"Hi," Zeffie said, reluctantly taking her hand.

The woman looked up at Christy. "You must be Miss Castleman."

"I'm Christy," she said, shaking her hand. "And you're Mrs. Carver?"

"Yes, and this is my husband, Bailey."

"How do you do?" His tone was more formal. He looked down at Zeffie and smiled. "Hello, young lady."

"Hello." Christy could feel Zeffie inching closer to her.

"How is Molly?" Sally asked, standing again. She was thin and straight, her short brown hair peppered with gray, while her husband was completely gray. They looked like they hadn't updated their wardrobes in a few years.

"Why don't we sit down?" Mr. Carver had the presence of mind to suggest.

Christy explained the situation, and tears formed in Sally's eyes. "I should have come down to visit her more often."

"I'm glad you're here now," Christy said, placing a hand on her arm. Zeffie looked as though she was about to start crying again, and Christy leaned toward the couple. "Zeffie and I are exhausted. We've been here for hours. Would you mind relieving us?"

"Oh," Sally said, looking from Christy to Zeffie, "of course you're exhausted. We'll be staying at the house."

"Since you're going to be here for a while tonight, is it okay if Zeffie comes home with me? I have a spare bedroom." And Dan had already told her he'd be sleeping on the couch until the killer was caught. Between him and the alarm system, Christy had no qualms about returning home.

Sally hesitated as she studied Zeffie. "Do you want to stay with Christy?"

"Yes ma'am."

The Carvers stared at Zeffie. Her response had been quick and firm, and Christy suspected they were wondering how well they would all get along.

"Then we'll go." Christy pulled out a business card and handed it to Mrs. Carver. "That has my home, cell, and business numbers on it. Please call if you need Zeffie...or me."

"I doubt we'll stay here at the hospital all night," Mr. Carver said. "After the drive down…"

"And since we can only go in every two hours," Mrs. Carver hastened to add.

Christy thought they could do whatever they pleased. They had no need to explain themselves to her.

They said a quick good-night to Zeffie since she was already hurrying ahead with Dan at her side. As the three of them stepped onto the elevator, Christy glanced at her. She had squared her shoulders again and set her chin firmly. Christy felt like crying even if Zeffie wouldn't. The poor child had been through so much in her short life. She had learned to accept reality in a way most children her age could not begin to imagine.

After a quick stop by Zeffie's house for some clothes, they arrived at Christy's, where Dan settled down before the television and Christy and Zeffie prepared for bed. Zeffie crawled in Christy's bed, and Christy smiled, not objecting.

Thoughts swirled through Christy's brain as she tiptoed down the hall to her office. She dialed Bobbie's number at home, looking for Jack, and of course he was there.

"What can we do?" he asked quickly. "I called Big Bob. He'll be at the hospital tomorrow morning to talk to Zeffie. Oh, and I called Tex back to see where he hired the painter. He said he just happened by. Well actually, he was sitting at the bar having a drink and mentioned he was a painter. Tex checked him out, asked for a reference. The guy didn't have one but offered to paint the back wall for Tex to see, and if he liked his work he would finish the job. If he didn't like it, he'd quit."

"Sounds pretty sure of himself," she said. Willie's extrovert personality rose to the front of her mind. "I have an idea."

"I expected that."

"I'm going to invite Tex to come over and see Zeffie as soon as he can."

"Here's his number." Jack recited the digits.

Christy jotted it down, said good-bye, and then dialed Tex. She could hear music and loud voices in the background as she asked for him.

"Who wants to know?" a bold voice asked.

"Christy Castleman," she replied.

"Hey, Christy. It's me, Tex."

"Listen, I don't think Molly Adams is going to last long. It'd be great if you'd come to the hospital around ten o' clock tomorrow morning. I'll have Zeffie there, and this would be your opportunity to say nice things about her mother. She's very upset, and I think this would help her a lot."

"I'd be honored to help. The hospital in Panama City?"

"Waiting room on the third floor of ICU."

"See you then."

As she hung up, another thought leaped into the melee of jumbled logic: the resemblance between Zeffie and R.J. But what if R.J. had been involved in Kirby's murder? They had to find the killer before Zeffie found out who her father was. All this could be a crazy coincidence.

You don't believe in coincidences, Christy told herself, yawning.

24

Sunday

Christy did not sleep well. Zeffie had slept with her, tossing and fidgeting. Since Christy was a light sleeper, she decided one of them should sleep in the guest bedroom the next night.

The smell of coffee drifted to her, and she smiled with contentment. Dan must be up. He'd spent an hour last night going over the security system with her, explaining the keypad, and had even taped a reminder on her door to turn it off or on.

"I'd advise leaving it on for a while."

"You're better than a security system," she had said, as they locked doors.

"Yeah, but if my car is parked in your driveway for too long, the neighbors will be calling the pastor of Community Church."

Christy slipped out of bed and hurried to the bathroom to dress. She found Dan at the eating bar, sipping the coffee he'd made. She noticed from the sack on the bar that he'd already been out for sausage and biscuits for all of them.

"You're wonderful," she said, planting a kiss on his cheek on her way to the coffeepot.

"Glad you feel that way. Can I trust you to stay safe, with the new alarm system and the cell phone in your hand?"

"Of course you can. You know," she said, pouring her coffee, "I've read that once a person breaks in a home, he doesn't return."

"I hate to remind you of this, but he didn't break in to steal anything," Dan said, standing.

It was unusual to see Dan looking rumpled and unshaven, but she knew he'd come straight from the airport to the hospital last night, then remained with her and Zeffie.

"Why don't you go home and get some rest?"

He stretched and yawned. "I have to confess, that sofa doesn't quite fit me."

She laughed, then thought of something. "You said last night you really feel good about the Montana project. I want to hear more."

He nodded, grabbing a napkin and dabbing at the coffee she had dribbled down her chin. "There'll be time for that."

"Christy?" Zeffie's voice rang out.

"I'll call you later," Dan said, heading for the back door. "And the alarm is on."

"Right. Thanks a bunch."

Later, fed and feeling better, Christy and Zeffie drove to the hospital. The sun beamed through their windshield, even though the temperature had dropped into the forties the night before. Christy insisted on Zeffie bringing a sweater, and Christy had dressed in heavier clothing as well.

"I'm glad this Sunday is a pretty day," Christy said, trying to fill the silence that absorbed them as they pulled into the hospital parking lot. From the corner of her eye, she saw Zeffie tense.

"I hope Grandma gets better," Zeffie said hopefully. "I believe in miracles."

Christy smiled at her. She didn't know what to say. The fact that her grandmother had lived so long with lung cancer was already a miracle.

She avoided the subject by asking Zeffie to help look for a parking space, and when she pointed one out, Christy wiggled the SUV in with just enough room for them to get their doors open.

They hurried into the hospital and crossed the lobby, and Christy pressed the up button on the elevator.

Zeffie began to fold and unfold her hands. "Christy, I don't want to go live with the Carvers," she blurted.

Christy paused. "You haven't had a chance to get to know them or for them to get to know you. They care about you. I can see that." She lifted a strand of Zeffie's blond hair, then laid it back on the shoulder of the new pink T-shirt she had bought for her. What she had told Zeffie was true, but she knew Zeffie was trying to imagine herself living with strangers who seemed so much older than they actually were.

When they reached the waiting room of the ICU, Christy was surprised to see Julie seated beside Sally Carver. Mr. Carver was nowhere around. Even from a distance, Christy could see the dark shadows under Sally's eyes, as though she had barely slept. Julie, in contrast, looked wide awake and spoke in an animated tone. Across the room, Christy could hear snippets of her conversation.

"R.J. owns a large marina, and I have a prosperous boutique."

Christy paused, her hand on Zeffie's shoulder. Neither Julie nor Sally seemed aware of their presence.

"And," Julie continued, "I can't have children." Her voice broke.

Suddenly it occurred to Christy what Julie might be trying to convey to Sally Carver. Would Sally, Zeffie's guardian, be willing to let Zeffie go if by some miracle R.J. proved to be her biological father? The cool light of morning always seemed to bring things into perspective. Today the idea of R.J. being Zeffie's father seemed a long shot, but Christy could see Julie hoped it was true.

"Let's say hello," Christy said, nudging Zeffie as they crossed the room to Sally and Julie.

"Hello," Julie beamed, her attention focused on Zeffie as she reached out to squeeze her hand.

"Good morning." Sally offered a weak smile. "Family members were allowed to go in fifteen minutes ago. Molly didn't respond to me," she said, then turned to Zeffie. "I know she wants to see you."

"I want to see her," Zeffie said, taking a seat next to Julie, rather than Sally.

For a moment, no one spoke. Then Christy thought of something.

"I'll be back in a few minutes. I need to make a couple of phone calls."

Sally nodded. "We'll be fine, won't we, Zeffie?"

Zeffie glanced at Sally with a somber expression and nodded.

Christy hurried down the hall to a small waiting room, unoccupied at this hour. She needed to think, and she did that best on her own. The click of high heels approaching the room turned her toward the door, and Julie rushed in, wringing her hands.

"Christy, could I talk to you?"

Julie's face was pale except for the twin spots of color on her cheekbones. Not blush, Christy noted, but rather a case of nerves.

"Of course. What's on your mind?" Christy asked, although she already knew the answer.

Julie laced her fingers before her as her gaze dropped to her sage green skirt and matching blouse. The fabric was soft, draping around her thin body, a perfect background for the ropes of beads and silver bracelets she wore. She continued to stare at her skirt in silence, as though the words she wanted to say were embroidered on her clothes.

Christy decided to make it easy for her.

"Julie, I can guess what's on your mind. From our conversation yesterday and the words I couldn't help overhearing a few minutes ago, you and R.J. have some hope that he's Zeffie's biological father."

Julie's head shot up, her long hair bouncing on her shoulders, her dark eyes huge.

"Yes! Oh yes, Christy. We've been up all night, hoping, praying…," her voice trailed.

Christy knew they were in a precarious situation, one for which she had no answers. She just knew Zeffie seemed to adore Julie, and the feeling appeared to be mutual.

"What do you plan to do?" Christy asked.

Julie bit her lip. "I know Mrs. Carver is Zeffie's guardian and has power of attorney over everything. She has Zeffie's birth certificate in a file, and with the proper paperwork, we could do a DNA test. With their consent, of course," she added in a rush.

Just then, Grant and Beth Castleman paused at the door. "Good morning," Grant called.

"Good morning," Christy and Julie replied in unison.

"Julie, have you met my parents?"

After she had made the introductions, Julie hurried off, allowing Christy to have privacy with her parents.

Beth was carrying a large shopping bag with the logo of a children's shop from the mall. Her parents had obviously gone there yesterday after leaving the hospital. Her father had his Bible tucked under his arm. Both were dressed for church, where they would be going when they left here.

"What's going on, honey?" her dad asked, studying her face. "And how are you?"

"I'm just fine." She began to tell him about her security system, but he nodded as though he understood.

"I had a long talk with Dan late yesterday," he said.

Suddenly it made sense to Christy why her mother had ceased to call her every hour.

"I also spoke with Bob, who'll be here shortly." Grant frowned. "Nothing yet on who broke into your place."

"Dad, let's talk about Zeffie."

She explained about the Carvers and Zeffie's wish not to live with them. "Mrs. Adams's condition is the same," she concluded. She decided not to comment on her conversation with Julie.

Her dad nodded, studying his shoes. Beth began pulling outfits out of the shopping bag for Christy's approval.

"Mom, they look just right, and I know she'll love them."

"How should I give these to her? I mean, I don't want it to seem like charity."

Christy stared at the cute jeans, pretty tops, and two nice dresses. "Just tell her you heard she liked pretty clothes and you wanted to do something to make her feel better."

"Right. Are you coming?"

"In a minute. The woman with her is Sally Carver. Zeffie will be going to live with her." Christy hesitated, thinking that maybe a DNA test would be a good idea.

Grant and Beth exchanged a glance. "Come down when you feel like it," Grant said.

They left, and Christy tried to focus her thoughts.

Could R.J. be Zeffie's father? Kirby's murderer had not been identified yet. It would be more damaging to Zeffie to learn R.J. was her father, only to learn that he also was a murderer.

Christy got up and started out the door, then spotted Big Bob huffing down the hall. For once, she was overjoyed to see him. She motioned him into the side room.

He was clean shaven, dressed in casual clothes rather than his uniform, and his big face wore an expression of genuine concern. "I just spoke with a doctor. He told me Mrs. Adams's blood pressure is dropping."

"Oh," Christy replied, glancing toward the waiting room where Zeffie sat.

"Dan tells me you've put in a security system," Bob said. "We're working hard on the break-in, but we haven't found anything yet, so you stick tight to your family."

Christy nodded. "Right now, I'm worried about Mrs. Adams and Zeffie."

Bob blew out a frustrated sigh and shoved his big hands in his pockets. "That poor little girl. We'd try to adopt her if we didn't already have five to feed and educate."

Christy touched his arm. "You have to be tough, I know, but I really like your tender side."

His big lips slid into a grin. "She's a cutie." Then he turned serious again. "Who is this Tex Jack told me about?"

"He's our link to the man who may have originally possessed the jewelry box."

"And just what are you doing—"

Christy cut him off. "What's going on with the investigation?"

Bob looked like a thundercloud about to erupt, but he took a slow, deep breath and glanced up and down the hall. "Seems to me that narrows it down to Willie Pitt—despite his so-called alibi—or Reuben Foster. And we can't find Reuben Foster anywhere."

"Really?" she asked, her hopes sinking.

"But we will," he assured her.

"Tex is coming here this morning. Maybe he'll remember something. Come on." She looped her hand through his big arm. "Come down and say hello to Zeffie. She's wearing her Good Citizen badge today."

In the waiting room, Zeffie was beaming over the clothes Beth was showing her. Big Bob walked over to meet Sally Carver, who glanced at the round, black clock on the wall.

"My husband, Bailey, should be here any minute."

Zeffie spotted Big Bob and ran over to hug him. Bob wrapped her in his large arms, and for a moment he looked as though he might actually shed a tear.

"I'll be back in a minute," Christy said, walking out of the room.

She was so close to tears herself that anything would set her off now. She knew she still had an hour and a half before taking Zeffie in to see her grandmother, so she walked to the elevator, punched the button, and rode down to the first floor. Her shoulder bag swinging from her arm, she strolled out onto the sidewalk, looking up at the sky. She was grateful for the sunlight, hoping it would boost everyone's mood. And then, as she turned her head to look across the parking lot, she spotted Dan walking briskly toward her, a smile on his face.

"How's it going?" he asked, giving her a quick hug and kiss.

She caught him up on what had happened so far. They were just turning to enter the hospital when Christy spotted Tex. She blinked and stared. He wore a fresh, long-sleeved shirt, hiding his tattoos, and a pair of clean jeans. His face was neatly shaven, and he looked respectable. As he came closer, she saw he had even removed the earrings.

"Tex, thanks so much for coming." She made the introductions between Dan and Tex, and they shook hands. Dan was trying to treat him like an old friend, but Tex kept looking around, seeming slightly uncomfortable.

"Tex, have you thought of anything else?"

His lips made an O as he blew out a sigh. "I asked around. My assistant, who's been with me since I opened, thinks Foster was his name."

"Reuben Foster?" Christy asked, hopefully.

"He just remembers Foster."

They talked as they entered the hospital, then crossed the lobby and rode up the elevator. Stepping into the waiting room, Christy glanced at the clock. They still had some time before family could enter the ICU. Bailey Carver had joined his wife, and Big Bob sat talking to Zeffie. As they approached, Christy heard Bob talking about the Christmas parade, asking Zeffie if she'd like to ride on a float as the mascot for Summer Breeze.

A smile lit the girl's face, bringing the dimple into play. Christy hated to interrupt the moment, but she could feel Tex lagging behind. "Be right back," she said to him.

She stopped in front of Big Bob. "Deputy Arnold, I'm so sorry to interrupt, but a friend of Zeffie's mother has made a special trip over from Fort Walton to visit Zeffie."

Big Bob's eyebrow hiked as his eyes shot toward Tex.

"Zeffie, could you come over and say hello to Tex?" Christy asked. "In fact, we might walk down to the drink machines."

Zeffie got out of her chair, and Dan gave her a hug, then sat down next to Big Bob. Zeffie followed Christy to where Tex stood, looking nervous. The three of them left the waiting room and walked toward the vending area.

"Zeffie, this is Tex. Tex, this is Zeffie," Christy said.

"How do you do, Zeffie?" Tex bowed. "I knew your momma when she lived in Fort Walton. She used to tell me you were the best gift of her life."

Zeffie stopped walking, and her mouth fell open as she stared up at Tex in disbelief. She glanced doubtfully at Christy.

Christy threw her hands in the air. "I know nothing about your momma, so don't think I told this man what to say."

"Zeffie, I realize you don't know me," Tex said, as they reached the refreshment center, "but I wouldn't lie to you about your mother."

Zeffie looked him up and down. "How'd you know my momma?"

"She used to come into my place of business," Tex replied. "We became friends, and sometimes we went out to eat together."

"Well, she never had much time to eat with me," Zeffie said, looking defensive.

"What would you like to drink?" Tex asked, pulling quarters from his pocket.

Zeffie studied the drink machine and pointed to her selection.

"Nothing for me, thanks," Christy said.

With two cold cans of Sprite in Tex's big hands, they found seats nearby.

"I'm sorry about your grandmother," he said. "I never knew her, but I wanted to come over and pay my respects. And I wanted you to know that your mother had a good heart and that she really loved you."

Zeffie stared deep into his eyes, watching with fascination as he popped the can open and handed it to her. "Thank you," she mumbled.

"You might be wondering why she lived down here, rather than up in Montgomery with you, but the truth is, you can make more money down here. She wanted to save up some money for you."

Zeffie's expression changed, and a look of relief crossed her face, followed by a new light in her eyes.

"Thanks for telling us this, Tex," Christy said.

"Can I call you Uncle Tex?" Zeffie asked.

Tex's eyes widened, and then a smile creased his big face. " 'Course you can."

Dan peered around the corner. "It's almost time for family to go in and visit."

Zeffie jumped up, spilling her drink. "That's okay," Tex said, pulling a clean handkerchief from his pocket to mop up the floor. "You go see your grandmother."

Zeffie hesitated. "Thanks for coming to see me. And thanks for what you said."

Tears gathered in her eyes as she spoke. Christy put a hand on her shoulder and guided her down the hall. "Thanks, again, Tex," Christy called over her shoulder.

Deputy Arnold stood in the door of the waiting room, looking as though he were waiting to speak with Tex.

"Tex told Zeffie some wonderful things about her mother," Christy said as they walked past Big Bob. She met his eyes and hoped he could read her warning. *Go easy.*

Holding hands, Christy and Zeffie entered the sterile world of monitors and tubes and approached Molly's bedside. Her eyes were open and the oxygen mask had been removed, freeing her to talk.

"Grandma," Zeffie said, reaching out to grasp her hand. "Please get well."

"Zeffie." Molly paused and tried to get a deeper breath. "I'm so grateful we've had these years together. You've been the best little girl a grandmother could ask for. I wish you could know how much I love you."

"I do know, Grandma." Zeffie's voice cracked, and tears streamed down her cheeks. "And I love you that much too."

The woman's eyes rose to Christy. "Thank you for being a good friend."

Her words were spoken with difficulty, and Christy wanted to say as much as she could without intruding on a private moment between Zeffie and her grandmother.

"Mrs. Adams, I want you to know that Zeffie will be fine. I promise to see to that."

"God bless you," she said to Christy. Then, as she looked back at Zeffie, tears filled her eyes. "Always be a good girl," she said, her tone so low that Zeffie had to lean forward to hear her. She closed her eyes.

Christy grasped Zeffie's hand. "Your grandmother wants to go back to sleep, so let's not tire her out."

Reluctantly, Zeffie followed Christy out of the room as a grim-faced nurse stood in the doorway.

The waiting room that had seemed so airless before now felt fresh compared to the smell and feel of death that seemed to cover the ICU. Looking around, Christy saw that Deputy Arnold was gone, along with Tex. Dan sat alone, flipping through a magazine. Julie and R.J. were talking quietly with the Carvers, whose faces were grim.

At that moment, however, Sally reached into the deep tote she had been carrying and removed a file folder. She glanced at her husband, who gave a quick nod. Then Sally handed the file to Julie.

Julie opened the file, and Christy could see a birth certificate in front, backed up by more paperwork that looked official. R.J. was motioning to a hospital employee wearing a lab technician tag.

As Zeffie and Christy approached, R.J. and Julie stood and smiled down at her.

"Hello, Aunt Julie," Zeffie said as Julie held out her arms.

R.J. still had that odd look about him as he studied Zeffie, his eyes lingering on her blond hair.

"Zeffie, R.J. and I would like to ask a favor of you," Julie said, glancing back at the Carvers, who were talking seriously. "Do you know anything about DNA?"

"Yes ma'am," Zeffie replied, her eyes moving toward R.J.

Christy bit her lip, wishing they had not chosen this time to approach the subject. After all, she still had suspicions about R.J.

"Zeffie," R.J. said, "I met your mother April in Panama City, and we were friends. I…" He stumbled, looking at Julie for support.

"You want to take my DNA?" Zeffie said, surprising all of them with her quick mind.

"Would you be willing to do that?" Julie asked. "They just swab your cheek."

Zeffie shot a glance toward the Carvers, who nodded back to her. "Yes ma'am."

The three of them disappeared from the waiting room only a few seconds before a doctor emerged from ICU. He looked around the waiting room, then walked toward Sally and Bailey Carver.

"I'm sorry to tell you this, but Mrs. Adams just passed away."

Sally burst into tears, covering her mouth with her hands, while Bailey looked genuinely upset, his arm encircling his wife's shoulders.

"We'll be taking the body back to Montgomery for burial," Bailey said.

Sally wiped the tears from her cheeks and composed herself. "Zeffie seems uncomfortable around us," Sally said slowly.

"We aren't used to having children around," Bailey added, "but we'll try to adjust to her."

But will she adjust to you? Christy wanted to ask.

"Sally," Bailey continued, "we'd best gather up our things and those of the girl. Don't forget the sack of new clothes. There's nothing else to be done here. I've left the business card of the funeral home in Montgomery at the nurses' station."

"Excuse me," Dan said. He, too, stared at Bailey, who seemed so mechanical about everything. "Would you prefer for us to drive Zeffie up later? I mean"—he glanced at Christy—"I'm sure she has lots of clothes and things to pack."

Bailey shook his head. "No, thank you. It's best to get this over with."

At that moment, Julie and R.J. appeared with Zeffie, who was smiling at Julie. When she turned to face the Carvers, Christy, and Dan, their tears and somber expressions reflected the bad news.

"No!" Zeffie cried.

Sally walked over to put an arm around Zeffie's heaving shoulders. "She's gone to heaven, honey. Now we have to go pack your things so we can drive back to Montgomery. That's where they're taking her."

Zeffie looked horrified. She turned helplessly to Christy.

"Dan and I will drive up later." Christy tried to sound reassuring, but in her own ears, her voice lacked the encouragement she wanted for Zeffie.

Zeffie turned and looked at R.J. and Julie, tears streaming down her face.

"And we'll drive up when we know the arrangements," Julie said.

"Yes, I'll let everyone know," Sally Carver informed them. "I have Christy's number."

"Come along now," Bailey said. "We must hurry."

Christy, Dan, Julie, and R.J. stared after the older couple walking down the hall with Zeffie. Sally clutched the shopping bag of clothes, but no one held Zeffie's hand.

Julie began to cry softly as R.J. gathered her in his arms, still staring after Zeffie.

"When will you know?" Christy managed to ask.

"Soon, I hope," R.J. replied, watching Zeffie until she was out of sight.

Dan took Christy's arm. "We'll talk to you later," he said.

He and Christy walked out of the hospital. Once they were alone, Dan turned to her and said, "After hearing the name Foster, Deputy Arnold asked Tex to come down to the office to take a look at mug shots. Maybe we're finally getting somewhere."

Christy merely stared at him, trying to comprehend all that had happened. Molly Adams had died. Zeffie gave a sample of her DNA to see if R.J. might be her father. And Kirby Strickland's murder was still unsolved.

25

Dan volunteered to deliver the few possessions Zeffie had left at Christy's to the Carver house where Zeffie and Molly had lived. Christy had been crying for the past half hour and couldn't bear to face Zeffie again. She had no idea what would happen, but one thing had become clear to Christy since she left the hospital.

Kirby's murder had to be solved. If R.J. had anything to do with it, Zeffie must not be hurt again.

As she stretched out on the sofa with a cup of tea, waiting for Dan to return, the phone rang. She picked up the headset and heard Ellen's voice on the other end.

"Hi, Christy. I called to invite you to join us for dinner tonight. Vince saw Wayne Crocker at the golf course today, and they decided we should get together at one of our favorite restaurants near Lynn Haven."

"That's very nice of you, Ellen, but I don't know. Dan and I just left the hospital. Molly Adams died—that's the mother of April Adams."

There was a moment of silence. Then Ellen's voice softened. "What will happen to the child now?"

Christy sighed, depressed by the answer. "Her closest relatives are an older couple from Montgomery. She's gone home with them."

"I'm sorry to hear the woman died." Ellen's usual rapid speech had slowed and sounded sincere.

"There's one thing you should know," Christy said. "It seems Reuben Foster is the one who had the jewelry box."

Ellen gasped. "The guy who came out to see Della?"

"We're not certain he's the villain in all of this. A guy in Fort Walton bought it from Reuben Foster and gave it to April Adams. The Adams family never knew where the jewelry box came from."

A long pause followed. "Now you *have* to meet us for dinner. We want to hear all about this. So it's likely…" Her voice trailed off, and Christy knew she was putting it all together.

Christy didn't detail the rest of the story, that Reuben said he got it somewhere else. Nothing was for sure at this point, but this bit of information might encourage Ellen; perhaps now she would be glad the detectives had been relentless. Christy didn't plan to reveal that she, not the detectives, had found Tex.

Christy felt bone-tired and hadn't spent quality time with Dan in days. Nevertheless, she couldn't pass up an opportunity to observe Ellen, Vince, and Wayne Crocker over dinner. After all, these were people on her suspect list, even if Reuben currently loomed at the top. It was possible he had lied to Tex about where he got the jewelry box. In retrospect, of course he would say he got it somewhere else when his boss surprised him by noticing it. And he'd already have emptied the contents if he'd stolen it.

"Where did you have in mind for dinner?" Christy asked.

Ellen named the place. "It's been a favorite of ours ever since we lived in Lynn Haven. Is seven too early? With the boys, it's hard to keep a babysitter late."

"That's fine. I'll go ahead and commit, then if Dan has made other plans when I talk with him, I'll call. Otherwise, we'll see you tonight."

"Wonderful." Ellen sounded better than she had since Christy delivered the jewelry box. If the robbery and murder could be pinned to Reuben, it would be a relief to get the entire thing solved and move on.

They said good-bye and hung up, and Christy collapsed back on the sofa.

"Honey, I'm home," Dan called, as he opened the door. "I hate that silly phrase, don't you?"

Christy sat up. "Not when you say it."

He checked the alarm system, giving her a thumbs-up on handling it properly, then came over and settled in beside her. "It was hard saying good-bye to Zeffie, but I believe she'll be back. If you look closely, she does bear a resemblance to R.J."

Christy had told him everything on their drive home from the hospital.

She lifted her hand to caress his cheek. "I hope you're right. And before I forget, I just obligated us for dinner tonight. If you really don't want to go, just say no."

"It sounds like you want to go."

Christy nodded. She explained Ellen's call and who would be there. "I know we won't have to stay long, because Ellen mentioned getting back to Deerfield to let the baby-sitter go home before it got too late."

Dan nodded slowly. "If that's what you want to do. You look exhausted, and I didn't sleep well. So we can call it an early night after dinner, if you're agreeable to that."

"Completely agreeable," she said, leaning forward to kiss him.

∽

Dan went home to unpack and clean up for the evening ahead, and Christy drifted off to sleep on the sofa. She couldn't have slept more than half an hour, but she bolted up, staring wide-eyed at the clock. She had forty-five minutes to get ready before Dan arrived to pick her up.

It was a cool evening, just right for a black pantsuit and a black and white, striped silk blouse. She brushed her hair out, twirled it around her shoulders, and added gold hoop earrings and the gold bracelet Dan had given her. She turned back to her closet, her gaze moving to her extravagant purchase for the month—or the next three months. Red, sling-back patent leather heels and a matching red handbag. Perfect.

As she transferred the essentials from her big shoulder bag to the smaller purse, she lined up the questions in her head that she wanted to slip into the conversation.

Dan's headlights swept the driveway, flashing across her bedroom window just as she closed the handbag. She hurried through the house and met him at the back door, setting the alarm. He wore a tan cashmere sport coat with a brown turtleneck and tan pants, and Christy exaggerated a swoon.

"Aren't I the lucky girl!"

He chuckled at her dramatics. "And I'm the lucky guy."

His dark hair still gleamed from a shower, and the fresh nick on his cheekbone testified to a hurried shave.

Christy glanced over her shoulder. She'd left lights on so she wouldn't return to a dark house. As they walked out, Dan took her key and locked the back door. Once they were inside the car, he handed her a small gift-wrapped box.

"A souvenir from Montana."

"Thanks, Dan." She untied the string and opened the box. Nestled in a fancy holder, a beautiful candle labeled Mountain Air gave off the scent of fresh pine. "Makes me want to go there," she said, watching him carefully as he backed out the drive, then turned the car east.

"I hope so," he said.

She waited for more, but he concentrated on navigating the evening traffic. A love song from a CD floated through the car. As the pleasant aroma of the candle filled the front seat, Christy turned to look at him.

"We haven't had an opportunity to talk about your trip. Tell me about Mr. Parker's property. When you called, you said you were impressed with the project."

"Very impressed. I advised him to grab the land and get busy as soon as the snow melts."

"So the project won't start until spring?"

"Probably sooner. There's a lot of preliminary paperwork to be done. Permits, that sort of thing."

She waited. "And…are you involved?" she asked quietly.

"Haven't made up my mind." He stole a quick look at her face.

"You'd do a wonderful job," she said, proud of his success.

"Why, thank you." He grinned.

They were passing the local animal shelter, and Christy thought of something.

"I saw in the newspaper that Bay Animal Control is gearing up for their annual fee-free adoption day. While you were gone, I was really lonely, and now I miss Zeffie, so I thought I might get an animal. Maybe a cat."

"Why not a dog?"

She sighed. "When I was in high school, I had this wonderful little mixed-breed dog named Fluffy. He died of old age when I went away to college, and it was like I had lost a family member. I decided not to get another dog."

"It might have made you feel better. You know, Christy, just because you lose someone or something you love, you can't let that stop you from being afraid to have those feelings again." He reached for her hand. "We learned that this past year, didn't we?"

She squeezed his hand and looked at him. "Yes, we did." She looked back at the city lights. "There's a picture in today's paper of a beautiful white cat. Maybe I'll go by the shelter and take a look when I get the chance."

They reached the restaurant and parked. Christy picked up her handbag as Dan came around to open the door. Inside, a host asked their names and then led them to a corner where Ellen and Vince sat opposite Wayne Crocker. In contrast to the pleasant smiles Christy had expected, they wore grim expressions.

"Oh, hi," Ellen said, as they approached. The men stood.

"I'd like to introduce my boyfriend," Christy said to Vince and Ellen, "Dan Brockman."

"Nice to meet you." Vince extended his big hand, and Christy noticed he looked much nicer than the day she had seen him in work clothes and a baseball cap. His dark red hair gleamed beneath the light, and he looked like a distinguished counterpart for Ellen, who wore a gray pantsuit with a pink shell.

"My pleasure," Dan said. "And I know Wayne from the marina."

"Hey, Dan." As always, Wayne had that ruggedly handsome appeal, and tonight he looked especially charming.

As soon as they settled into their seats, Ellen broke some startling news. "As we were driving into town, we heard on the radio that a man named Reuben Foster was shot behind a bar in Pensacola Friday night. They're searching for the shooter but haven't found him. The man who came to our house drunk to see Della was named Reuben Foster."

"Probably not the same one," Vince said, unwrapping a pack of crackers.

"This man's in critical condition in a Pensacola hospital," Ellen continued. "The announcer quoted a doctor who said he was in a coma."

Christy sank back in her chair, her thoughts swirling. If Foster died, he would take with him their last link to the jewelry box.

"When did this happen?" Dan asked casually.

"Late Friday night," Ellen answered. "The announcer said it was behind a bar—let's see—the Happen Chance Bar. I thought it was a funny name."

Wayne looked up at the group. "I've heard of that place. It's in the seediest part of Pensacola."

"How do you know about it?" Christy asked.

"Years ago, when I was selling cars, I delivered a used one to a guy in that area of Pensacola. The buyer, whose name I don't remember, said he lived two blocks east of the Happen Chance Bar and gave the address."

Wayne shook his head, reaching for his water glass. "Another salesman followed me to take me back to the car lot. When we got to this guy's house, I hurried through the final paperwork and handed over the car keys as fast as I could. When I jumped into the car with my buddy, he said, 'Don't ask me to come here for you again.'" Wayne grinned. "I told him not to worry. I wouldn't be coming back either. But speaking of this Reuben Foster, I know something about a Reuben Foster."

All eyes turned to him, but just then the server approached their table, interrupting the conversation.

"We know what we want," Ellen said, taking charge. She and Vince ordered grilled flounder. Wayne followed with a steak, medium rare, and Christy stared at the menu, wondering what her nervous stomach could tolerate.

"I'll have the seafood platter," Dan said. "I just got back from Montana, and I've missed our fish."

"Did you go skiing?" Ellen asked.

"No, it was business."

Christy decided on grilled shrimp, something over which she could dawdle. They gave their side orders, asked for a round of iced teas, and the server rushed off.

Christy turned to Wayne, keeping her voice light. "So how did you know Reuben Foster?" She could feel Dan's hand slip into hers, squeezing lightly, his way of telling her to calm down. *Don't be so obvious.*

"You asked me about that name, remember? I wasn't sure if I'd heard Kirby mention him, but the more I thought about it, I realized I might have. That's why the name stuck in my mind. When the Andersons arrived to buy the boat, I showed them around the marina. We walked up a side block, past a small bait shop. I noticed a guy painting the side of the building. We walked on down to a restaurant and had lunch. When we passed again, another guy came outside and yelled, 'Phone call for Reuben Foster.' The painter climbed down from his ladder."

"What did he look like?" Ellen threw the question like a dart.

Wayne shrugged. "An older African American. Kinda shuffled along like he had a back problem."

"Maybe it's not the same Reuben Foster," Vince said. "When was this?"

"Just a couple days ago. About the time the Andersons arrived." He looked at Christy. "They loved the clock."

"What clock?" Dan asked.

Christy suppressed a grin. Dan never missed a word, either. "Wayne bought a clock from Aunt Bobbie," she explained. "A mariner's clock she got from a restaurant."

"Have you been in that shop?" Wayne asked Ellen. "That Bobbie Bodine is amazing." He glanced at Christy. "Not to exclude you."

His gaze swung back to Ellen. "Bobbie and I met up at the Williamsburg estate sale. I was hoping to pick up some things for the houseboat for the Andersons. Bobbie asked me what I was looking for, then persuaded me to come back to her shop. Said she'd find just what I needed. She took me over to show me that mariner's clock." He shrugged. "I thought it might be okay, even though it was dusty and plain. She bought it, shined it up, and painted a little boat on it. Turned out to be perfect for what we needed."

Christy could barely sit still through the extended conversation. She took a sip of water, spread the napkin over her lap, glanced around the crowded restaurant, and waited for him to finish. Then she jumped back into the topic that interested her.

"Did it look like Reuben Foster was finishing his paint job on that bait shop?" she asked. She knew she should have been more subtle, but her mind burned with curiosity.

Wayne looked at her, while the server placed a salad before him. "I didn't pay much attention, but it's a small building. I'd say he would have finished that day or the next."

"And when would that have been?" Ellen asked.

Wayne speared a leaf of his salad. "Friday."

Christy glanced at Ellen, who was staring at Wayne. "The announcer said this guy was shot Friday night in Pensacola."

Christy picked up her fork and pretended an interest in her salad.

"I think that's a long shot, Ellen," Vince said. "That's over an hour away from where he was working. Why would he go to a bar over there when he could go to one here?"

Everyone fell silent. Christy glanced at Dan. They both knew there was an APB out on Reuben Foster. Dan had learned from Bob that Tex identified a mug shot of Reuben Foster as the man who painted his bar and sold him the jewelry box.

Christy looked at Vince, recalling what he'd said about Wayne making money so quickly, which hadn't seemed odd to Christy. He'd also thrown suspicion toward Willie Pitt. Now he seemed to be casting about for some reason to deny Reuben Foster's identity. She found herself liking him less and less.

"Vince, you're right," Wayne said. "Could just be a coincidence. The guy I saw looked like he'd be traveling on foot."

"I know he'd been in jail for a DUI," Ellen supplied.

Christy decided to let them talk it out while she listened, all instincts alert to pick up anything that didn't sound right.

"Then he probably didn't have a vehicle," Vince said.

"Maybe he rode over there with a buddy," Dan suggested.

Christy looked at him, amused. Obviously, he'd decided to play the game.

"Well, we can't let him spoil our evening together," Wayne said, turning to Dan. "Did you get your boat repaired? He and I both keep our boats at R.J.'s marina," he explained to Vince and Ellen.

"Yeah, R.J. left a message that it was back at the marina," Dan responded.

Then everyone fell silent, as though someone had turned on a television set and they were all watching the same channel.

R.J. and the marina. A block from the bait shop Foster was painting. Christy decided her next trip would be to the bait shop to ask who recommended their painter.

Wayne cleared his throat, as though trying to break the tension. "I'll be pulling out later this week for Key West, so I'm glad we got an opportunity to see each other again." He looked at Ellen. "When Vince and I ran into each other, I thought of Kirby. And you. I wanted to see you again. I miss those days at Deerfield."

Ellen nodded, pushing her salad aside. "I do too." She stared at the tablecloth.

"I rarely play golf on Sunday afternoon," Vince said, "but Ellen and the boys had committed to a birthday party, and I was bored. Decided to get out my clubs. When I ran into Wayne, we agreed not to discuss Saturday's football game."

Everyone laughed, aware that the Florida State Seminoles and the Florida Gators were big rivals. Wayne and Christy had attended FSU at different times, while Ellen and Vince attended the University of Florida. The Seminoles had won the big game, and Christy agreed it was a good idea to stay off that subject.

"Of all the golf courses in this part of the state, it's quite a coincidence you two chose the same one," Christy said, prodding them. She wasn't about to let this coincidence slide by.

"We all lived in Lynn Haven at one time," Vince explained, "and there's a good golf course near there."

"Yeah, I hadn't played that course in years," Wayne replied, "but the ones closest to the marina were either packed or had golfers lined up and waiting, so I decided to drive over here."

"Well, however you two got together, I'm glad you did." Ellen seemed to have come out of her speculation enough to reenter the conversation.

Their entrees were placed before them, and everyone dug in. Everyone but Christy. She surveyed her shrimp, trying to appear enthusiastic. "Looks great," she said.

"Dan, what line of work are you in?" Wayne asked.

Dan launched into an explanation of his building projects, naming some homes he had built.

"Hey, I might want you to do something for me," Wayne said. "Whenever I come up here, I stay on my boat. It'd be nice to have a little place."

"I'll bet with the commissions you make on these boat sales, you could afford one," Vince said, reaching for his tea.

Christy's mind leaped back to her conversation with Ellen, and Vince's not-so-subtle hint that Wayne had quickly escalated from car salesman to boat broker. She reminded herself that fifteen years was enough time to build a solid sales career, particularly when one was as smooth and charming as Wayne.

Thinking back over the dinner conversation so far, Christy realized she might have been a bit obvious with her questions. Everyone would think she and Dan had joined them just so she could snoop into their lives. She decided to be more sociable.

"How are the boys?" she asked, turning to Ellen.

"Rowdy as ever," Vince answered, a grin tugging at his big face. His gray eyes lit up at the mention of his sons.

Christy turned to Dan. "They both have red hair and are cute as can be. They're also well mannered," she added. "You two have done a good job."

"Thanks," Ellen said, her eyes lighting up just as Vince's had. "My blond hair and Vince's dark red somehow combined to give us two fiery little boys. But we do adore them, and both of them are stars on their soccer teams."

Wayne ate heartily, as though bored with the conversation topic. Christy noticed he kept glancing around the restaurant, probably on the prowl for a woman. She chewed on her shrimp, wondering what other information she could pull from him. She decided to sneak in by way of Deerfield.

"Dan," she said, turning to him, "you should see Deerfield. It's a beautiful place. Seth and I had so many good times when we went up to Granny's farm and ventured over to Deerfield where the fun was."

Ellen sighed. "Everyone came to Deerfield. And Kirby had so many friends."

Wayne looked at Ellen. "Yeah, he was that kind of guy."

"Christy said you guys had a winning football team," Dan said to Wayne.

"We did." Wayne nodded. "Kirby was quarterback, I was a running back. We had a good thing going."

"He always got that ball to you," Ellen said.

Wayne grinned. "That's because we had a good system."

"Not to change the subject, but talking about those early days at Deerfield reminded me of something," Ellen said. "Today when I was pruning the shrubs around the patio, I found that old house key, still wired to the wrought iron gate next to the brick column. Kirby was always forgetting his house key, so Mother suggested hiding one out back. Remember how you guys would sneak home when Mother was away and do…whatever you did?" Ellen finished with as much humor as she could manage, which was saying a lot for Ellen.

The bite of shrimp seemed to swell like a balloon in Christy's mouth as she stared from Ellen to Wayne and back. She swallowed. "Are you saying that everyone who knew Kirby well also knew about the house key?"

Suddenly, everyone seemed to lock on the same channel again.

"I suppose so," Ellen replied, looking thoughtful. "I know what you're thinking, but that old key didn't look like it had been touched in years." She looked at Vince. "Still, we should call the detectives and see about the fingerprints on it."

"Which would probably be ancient," Vince replied. "But I will call." He reached into his pocket for his cell phone.

Ellen stopped him. "It's not that important. You can wait until we get home. Honestly, I don't think it had been touched."

"Well, guys," Wayne said, laying his steak knife across his empty plate, "I hate to run out on you, but I had already made a commitment for later this evening." He looked at his gold wristwatch.

Ellen nodded. "I'm not surprised. Kirby joked that you always got the girl."

But he didn't get Julie, Christy thought, watching Wayne grab the ticket for their meal.

"Wayne, don't do that," Vince said, reaching across the table. Wayne stepped back, shaking his head as Dan tried to persuade him to allow everyone to pay for their own meal.

"Like Vince said, I got a nice little commission on that houseboat. Hey, it's been a pleasure seeing you two again." He looked at Ellen and Vince, then turned to Dan and Christy. "And maybe since your boat's repaired, I'll see you two at the marina before I pull out."

Dan stood to shake his hand. "I hope so."

Wayne looked at Christy. "It's always a pleasure to see you, Christy."

"Thanks," she replied lightly. He wasn't going to charm her, no matter how he affected other women.

Vince yawned and checked his watch. "We'd better think about leaving too."

Ellen nodded, still looking at Christy. "What do you think? About this Reuben Foster, I mean. I can tell your mind is always clicking."

Christy shrugged, reaching for her handbag. "I really don't know, Ellen. Maybe he did it. I'm sure the detectives will piece it all together."

She could feel Dan's eyes on her. She didn't really think that way, and he knew it, but Ellen didn't, and Christy wanted to keep it that way for now.

As they stood and said their good-byes, Ellen promised to stop by the shop the following week. The Browns headed for the side door while Christy and Dan left through the front.

"Thanks," she said, once they had settled into the car.

"For what?"

She laughed. "You know for what. It was as though you were reading my mind with your questions."

Dan grinned at her as he started the car. "I was. Remember, I told you I wanted to help you with this investigation. I didn't realize when I made that statement that part of my role would be as body-guard."

She smiled. "Thanks."

He reached for her hand, and she placed her head on his shoulder. It was so good to be with Dan again. She didn't want to talk about Montana or anything else that might spoil their evening together.

26

Monday

C hristy shivered in her robe as she filled her coffee mug and stared at the Sunday paper, still unread.

Yawning, she picked it up, remembering Reuben Foster. She sat down at the barstool and thumbed through the paper for an account of the shooting. She looked through several pages before she found the article.

> At 11:05 Friday evening, Reuben Foster, 69, was shot in the
> back as he attempted to get in his truck in the alley behind
> a bar in Pensacola. There were no witnesses to the shooting.
> The bartender reported that he heard a shot, then about ten
> seconds later, another shot. When he ran to the back door to
> investigate, he saw Foster lying in the alley beside his truck.
> The case is under investigation.

Christy placed the newspaper on the counter and sipped her coffee. Shot in the back. Foster had probably told Tex the truth—that he'd cleaned out a garage and was supposed to haul the contents to the Dumpster. He'd kept a gym bag and found the jewelry box inside.

She glanced at the sunshine beyond her kitchen window. Reuben Foster was in a coma. She felt certain police were swarming like mosquitoes around the hospital. Someone had tried to kill him for a reason. Even if he had not seen who shot him, if Foster lived, he could incriminate someone.

She dug her bare heels into the rung on the barstool and swung her body back and forth. What to do?

She grabbed the phone directory, turned to the yellow pages, and studied all the bait shops listed. She spotted one on the side street that led from the marina and quickly dialed the number. A gruff voice yelled the name of the shop in greeting.

"Excuse me," she began, "but you had a painter there last week."

"What about him?"

"I need a painter. Did he do a good job?"

"Yeah, suited us okay."

"Do you mind saying who recommended him?"

"Nobody. We just felt sorry for him. He'd been sleeping on that bench down at the marina."

Christy caught her breath. Would he sleep there without R.J.'s permission?

"Anyway, it won't do you no good to try and find him. He got shot Friday night behind a bar over in Pensacola."

"Oh no. Did they catch the person who shot him?"

"Nah, probably won't, either. They don't pay a lot of attention to old alcoholics. You could smell him a mile away. Don't know how he did such a good job painting."

"Well, thanks." She hung up. R.J. must have seen Foster sleeping there. Maybe he'd given him permission. *Maybe he owed him a favor.*

What if… She lined up her facts. R.J. knew the area well, and the bait shop was a block away. Granny had suspected him, having seen his sports car on the road that day when he had no reason to be there. R.J. had moved to this area to be near Julie; after Kirby's death, he finally persuaded her to marry him. From their conversations, she could tell his family had money, and thus R.J. had access to money. Had he hired someone to kill Kirby and make it look like a robbery? Someone like Reuben Foster?

What if the paternity test proved R.J. was Zeffie's father?

Christy's heart sank to her feet. What should she do? R.J. and Julie might provide a better home for Zeffie, and Julie obviously adored her. But if the investigation led back to him, what would happen?

Taking a deep breath to strengthen her resolve, Christy glanced at Julie's home phone number, written on a pad near the phone, and began to dial. The answering machine picked up, and she felt like a fool. Just because she was looking at a Sunday paper didn't mean today was Sunday. It was Monday, and of course they'd be at work.

Maybe she should persuade Dan to call R.J. It would seem less obvious if he asked about Reuben. No, she had to bide her time. After all, R.J. had not proven he was Zeffie's father.

Her thoughts returned to Reuben. She had a Pensacola phone directory in the bottom drawer beneath the cabinet. She reached down and yanked the drawer open, shuffling past a couple other directories until she found Pensacola. Flipping pages, she located the number for the hospital and dialed.

When an operator answered and directed her to Information on Patients, she was told that Reuben Foster was in critical condition but doctors felt there was slight progress, since he was awake for short periods of time. No visitors other than family were allowed.

Family? Did he have family? Della and her husband had been his closest friends for years. How strange that Reuben would be shot on Friday night, and Molly Adams had died on Sunday.

Thinking of Molly, her eyes automatically moved to the answering machine, where Sally Carver had left a message while she was out last night. A graveside service would be held for Molly on Wednesday. Christy closed her eyes, wanting to hug Zeffie, yet dreading to see her unhappy face.

She grabbed the phone and dialed her aunt at home. Bobbie answered with a sleepy hello. "I'm sorry to wake you, but something has come up, and I can't get to the shop until later on. If at all. Would you mind terribly?"

She could hear Bobbie yawning. "No, hon. I know Dan's back. You two have a good day. It'll be slow, so don't worry about coming in."

Christy hesitated. "Thanks."

Dan had told her he had a lot to catch up on at work, and she wasn't expecting to hear from him. Bobbie didn't need to know that, however.

She raced to her bedroom and started grabbing clothes.

～

An hour later, she pulled into Sunset Manor. Although it was only ten minutes past nine, she could see people—with walkers, in wheelchairs, or shuffling along on their own—leaving the dining hall. She paused, searching the group for Della. She was the last one to be wheeled up the hallway, and Christy paused, trying to decide how to greet her. She looked at the small bouquet in her hand. This time she'd brought flowers.

Della recognized her immediately and smiled. "You came back."

"Of course I did," Christy responded cheerfully.

"Follow us down to the room, then."

The nurse pushing Della glanced at the flowers and smiled at Christy. "Della doesn't get many visitors," she said. "You'll be a welcome guest."

When they entered the room, Christy noticed the bed beside the door was neatly made up.

"Lorraine passed," Della called over her shoulder.

Christy grimaced. There was too much "passing" going on, in her opinion. Was any of it connected? She shook the absurd thought from her head and waited as the nurse wheeled Della around to face her.

"Do you need anything else, Mrs. Young?" the nurse asked.

"No, thank you. Christy, pull up a chair."

"First, where shall I put the flowers?" Christy asked.

The nurse overheard as she was leaving and turned back. "I'll go get a vase."

"That's awfully sweet of you," Della said, gazing at the bouquet of assorted flowers. Already, the colorful array seemed to brighten the plain room.

When Christy handed the bouquet to Della, she lifted it to her nose and closed her eyes, as though savoring the smell. "Been a long time since anyone gave me flowers. I reckon the last person who did was Kirby." She looked at Christy. "It was my birthday, and he remembered." She sighed. "That's the kind of person he was."

The nurse returned with a vase and offered to put the flowers in water. Della reluctantly handed them over.

"Della, speaking of Kirby," Christy said slowly, "something has happened that I want to discuss with you."

"About Reuben?" Della asked. "A friend called me yesterday. Saw it in the paper."

Christy scooted her chair closer as the nurse left the room. "Della, a man identified him as the one who passed along the jewelry box. He said Reuben had the jewelry box in the back of his truck as payment for cleaning out a garage for someone."

Della stared at her. "You mean…" Her watery eyes drifted from Christy, staring into space.

"Before the detectives could locate him to question him," Christy explained, "I think the person who gave Reuben that jewelry box tried to kill him to keep him from identifying the owner of the garage. This would link the murderer directly to the jewelry box."

Della stared at Christy. "What can we do?"

Christy's hopes lifted. She had planned to ask Della's help, but the older woman was already volunteering it. "I called the hospital.

He's still critical, in and out of a coma. They said only family members—"

"I'm the closest to family Reuben has. They oughta let me in. I'd like to see him." Della reached for a Kleenex. "After all, he saved my Sam's life. Sam's quality of life was poor, but at least I had him with me for another year. I can thank Reuben for that."

She wiped the tears from her face. "I doubt they'll let me leave here without a nurse." She waved to someone in the hall. The nurse who had brought the vase reappeared.

When Della spoke, her voice brooked no argument. "I need to go to the hospital to see a friend who may be dying. I'll need permission."

"The doctor will have to be called and—"

"Then call him now. I want to go."

Another nurse entered the room, looking very serious. Della introduced her as Milly Jordan. "She's our boss here at Sunset Manor."

Milly looked at Christy. "I wouldn't advise taking Mrs. Young out."

"I didn't ask for advice, Milly," Della snapped. "A friend of mine is dying, and I'm going to the hospital to see him. You don't make a lot of money off me, but I haven't asked for a favor in all the years I've been here. And you'd have to agree I don't cause anybody any trouble."

Milly's round face softened. "I agree with you. I'm just concerned what the shock might do for your heart. And it's a cooler morning—"

"I'll wear a coat if I have to. As for my heart, it's gonna break if I don't get to say good-bye to my friend."

Christy could see Milly relenting.

"All right. If the doctor agrees, I'll sign the papers. I insist on a nurse accompanying you and…" She hesitated, looking at Christy.

"I'm Christy Castleman."

"You and Miss Castleman," Milly finished.

"And how long will that take?" Della demanded. "You know mornings are my best time, and this young lady has taken off from work to help me."

Milly nodded, obviously outdone in the fight. "I'll page the doctor and explain."

"We'll take good care of her. And she won't be gone long," Christy added, knowing if they got into the ICU, it would be a very short visit.

∽

The nurse who had been sent along with them sat quietly in the backseat while Christy drove Della to the hospital. Della didn't seem to want conversation, so Christy put on a soothing CD.

The same boldness that had resulted in Della being allowed to leave Sunset Manor surfaced again as she faced the nursing station outside the ICU.

"I am family," Della snapped at the woman behind the desk. "I'm the only family he's got."

Christy held her breath, her eyes darting around the waiting room. She didn't recognize any familiar faces, but she spotted a policeman in uniform reading a newspaper. She decided to be forthright while they waited the fifteen minutes before they could be admitted to the ICU.

Christy approached him. "Excuse me."

He laid the paper aside and stood.

"Are you here in regard to Reuben Foster?" she asked.

"I'm here to see that no one but family gets through that door to him," he stated firmly.

"Well, I'm not family, but she's the closest to family he has." She turned to indicate Della, who sat in her wheelchair, the nurse standing beside her.

The policeman's face softened. He lifted a clipboard from the chair beside him. "What's her name?"

"Della Young. Mr. Foster and her husband were in business together. Mr. Foster saved her husband's life years ago."

The police glanced at her again, then wrote her name on the legal pad attached to the clipboard. Christy peered at the page, trying to read the other two names. She recognized Captain Davis's name, but the other name was unfamiliar. She felt certain he was in law enforcement.

The policeman looked up at her. "If he tells her anything, do I have your word you'll pass it along?"

"Oh, yes sir. We want the man who shot him caught."

He nodded. "He hasn't been able to talk. He's barely alive."

She thanked him and returned to Della, quickly whispering

what they needed to find out. "Where did he get that jewelry box he sold to Tex when he was painting Tex's bar in Fort Walton around the Fourth of July in 1998? He cleaned out a garage for someone. The jewelry box was in a gym bag. We believe whoever owned those is the person who shot him. Della, try to make him understand."

Della nodded firmly.

Christy looked at the nurse. "May I take her in? If there's a problem, I'll come right out for you."

"Well…" The young nurse hesitated. "All right."

Christy grabbed the handles of the wheelchair as the doors swung open and family members began to file into the unit. Christy had been told Reuben was in the last cubicle on the right for his protection. That would be the hardest one to reach without being noticed.

As she pushed Della through the ICU, Christy glanced down at her gray hair, neatly combed. She had put on a red, long-sleeved sweater and black pants. She'd insisted on dressing up if she was going to visit Reuben.

Christy slowed at the last room and guided the wheelchair carefully up to the bed.

If possible, more monitors, cables and IVs were hooked up to Reuben Foster than she had seen with Molly. But then Molly had had no chance of recovery. This man did.

He lay still, his eyes closed. She thought he looked older than the age given in the paper. He could have been in his late seventies, but he'd lived a hard life, and heavy drinking had aged his frail body.

Della reached over to squeeze his hand. "Reuben! Reuben, it's me, Della. Wake up."

Slowly, the thin lashes fluttered and opened. His eyes looked hazy, and Christy wondered if he could even see.

Della looked up at Christy. "He squeezed my hand a little." She leaned toward him. "Reuben, there's something we've gotta know. You have to think hard. Think back to the summer of 1998, around the Fourth of July or before. You were painting a bar in Fort Walton and had cleaned out a garage for someone about that time."

He stared at her.

"From that garage you got a gym bag with a jewelry box inside it. You gave the man at the bar the jewelry box. The man you cleaned out the garage for stole that jewelry box, and it was full of valuables. That man shot you to keep you from giving his name."

Reuben stared hard at Della, and Christy wondered if anything Della said had registered with him.

His eyes moved slowly down to her red sweater then back to her face. He tried to move his lips, but there was no sound. He stared at her red sweater, his thin lashes batting furiously.

"Do you remember who that man was? Where did you go that day you cleaned out the garage?"

Again, his eyes drifted down to her red sweater, back to her face, back to the sweater. His eyelashes fluttered, then closed again.

"Reuben, stay awake," Della pleaded, but his eyes remained closed. She kept squeezing his hand and talking to him, but there was no further response. "I don't think he understood. But he knew

I came." Della removed a Kleenex from her pocket. "I'm sure he knew it was me."

Christy patted her shoulder. To her, he didn't appear to know anything, but she wanted Della to believe he knew her, even if he couldn't name his killer.

A nurse appeared, motioning to them it was time to leave. She checked his blood pressure and looked up at the monitor.

"Is he...?" Christy fumbled for words.

"Still alive," the nurse whispered. "Just out again. He drifts in and out like that constantly. When the police officers were here to talk to him, he opened his eyes but didn't seem to understand what they wanted."

Christy nodded and wheeled Della back to the waiting area where the policeman waited.

"He didn't respond," Christy said.

The policeman looked down at Della, who wiped tears from her cheeks.

The nurse from Sunset Manor quickly took control. "Are you all right?"

Della nodded. "Thank you for bringing me. We can go home now."

The ride back to Sunset Manor was a quiet one. The nurse tried to make appropriate remarks about the weather, the fact that the mall was already playing Christmas music, and that the nursing home planned to put up Christmas decorations on the weekend, but none of it seemed to matter to Della, who stared straight ahead, her expression grim. Christy wondered if it had been a mistake to take her to the hospital.

She parked in a handicapped space in front of the nursing home and hit the button for the trunk. The nurse hopped out to get the wheelchair, and Christy reached over to squeeze Della's cold hand.

"I'm sorry."

"Don't be," Della said. "I'm glad I got to see him one last time. He knew me, and he knew what I was saying. I know he did. I just don't know why he kept staring at my sweater." She paused, looking down at her simple red cardigan. "I need to think on this and do some praying." She looked at Christy with the same determination she had displayed all morning. "I just got this feeling he was trying to tell me something."

She looked at her sweater again.

"Well, you did your best. If you should think of anything, call me," Christy said as the nurse opened the passenger door to help Della into the wheelchair. "And I'll come back to see you again. Do you like chocolates?"

A tiny smile touched Della's lips. "I love chocolate, but I'm diabetic."

"Oh," Christy said, thinking this woman had been deprived of some of life's best gifts. She planned to put her on the shut-in list at church. That would insure Della a few visitors, some prayers, and a Christmas gift or two.

"I'll see you soon," she called, as the nurse settled Della into the chair. "I gave you my phone number, didn't I?"

Della nodded. "It's on the nightstand beside my Bible."

Christy smiled. "Get some rest now." She looked at the nurse. "Thanks for your help."

The nurse nodded and draped a shawl around Della before pushing her up the sidewalk to the entrance.

Christy sighed and backed out of the parking space. At least she had given Della and Reuben the satisfaction of seeing each other one last time. A strange sort of good-bye, but she supposed it helped both of them make peace with each other. If Reuben had recognized her. Della claimed he squeezed her hand, that he knew she was there, but Christy hadn't seen any emotion in his face. Did Della just want to believe?

Her cell phone rang, and she yanked it out of her purse, reading Dan's number.

"Hey, what are you up to? I just called the shop."

"I'll tell you later."

He sighed. "Later will have to be tomorrow. I called to tell you that after work I'm going to pick up a hamburger, then go home and fall in bed. I can hardly stay awake today. I didn't rest that well in Montana. Guess I was missing you."

"I guess you were. Get your rest. I'll probably go over to my parents' house tonight, anyway. They know Mrs. Adams died, but I haven't had a chance to tell them anything about Zeffie, and they want to know."

She could hear Dan trying to stifle a yawn. "See you tomorrow night," he said. "Until then, you keep out of trouble."

"Don't worry. I've managed to behave myself quite well."

He laughed and they hung up.

She thought she *had* behaved herself quite well. She'd resisted the urge to grab Reuben and shake a name from him.

As she turned down the main street of shops, Joy, one of the Red Hatters, waved her over. Christy pulled over to the curb. Joy jumped out of her green Jeep Wrangler and hurried to Christy's window. She was a cute, vivacious blonde who could light up a room with her presence.

"Christy, I just heard about poor little Zeffie. She and I had fun picking out sequins for my purse the other day at the shop. Anyway, I've called the girls—the Red Hatters, that is—and we're sending flowers and going up for the funeral. When is it?"

"On Wednesday at two o'clock. I'll have to e-mail you the address."

"That's fine. Since we made her our little princess, we'd like to do something special for her later, after things have settled down. The Christmas parade is coming up, and she's been asked to ride on a float. I was thinking after the parade it would be fun for all of us to take her to the Destin Outlets and present her with gift cards for the shops she likes."

Christy reached out to squeeze Joy's hand. "That's so kind of you. I know she'd love that. This will give her something to look forward to. And she needs that."

A horn beeped and Joy turned. "I'd better get out of the street. Talk to you later. Send me the address where the service will be held. We're taking two or three carloads of ladies."

"That's wonderful," Christy called as Joy darted back to her Jeep.

Everyone here loved Zeffie and wanted her back. If R.J. turned out to be the father, she'd be back soon. The Carvers probably wouldn't put up a fuss to keep her. Christy got the impression they regarded Zeffie as an obligation rather than a blessing.

She started her car and drove toward the shop, pulling in at the curb. As she entered, she saw Jack propped on a stool in front of the counter, his hands cupping his chin. Bobbie had folded her arms on the counter and was smiling and talking softly with him.

"Ah, you have a prosperous-looking customer," Christy said upon entering.

Jack shook his head. "Your timing stinks. I was whispering sweet nothings in your aunt's ear."

"Looked more like she was the one whispering sweet nothings," Christy replied. All three laughed.

"I thought you were taking off with Dan," Bobbie said, scolding her with her eyes. "He just called the shop looking for you."

"Well, he found me. No, actually I went to the nursing home to visit a friend who isn't doing well."

Both stared blankly at her, as though trying to make a connection.

"Why don't you two get going?" She looked at the wall clock. "You've got just enough time to make it to the Hickory Pitt before the dinner crowd hits."

Jack made a face. "No point going if I can't give Willie a hard time."

"Why can't you do that?"

"I drove down there yesterday to pick up some food for Bobbie and me. They said he had to go out of town for a while."

Out of town. As in Pensacola? No. Tex had identified Reuben Foster. But...

"You don't need to twist my arm to get out of here," Bobbie said, grabbing her silver handbag. "Jack, let's go over to that thrift shop I've been telling you about. If it's as nice on the inside as it looks on the outside, no telling what we might find."

"We get to stop for fried chicken," he bargained.

"Okay. You get fried, I'll get grilled."

"Jack, when did Willie move from Panama City?" Christy asked bluntly.

Jack stared at her. "Where have you been today?"

"I told you, to visit a friend. Do you remember when Willie left Panama City?" she repeated in a tone that indicated she needed an answer.

He frowned, pursed his lips, and stared at the floor. "Sometime in the summer of '98. I know it was a few months after the Strickland murder. He found that place at Mexico Beach and worked on it a month or so before opening. I believe it opened sometime in August. Why're you asking?"

"I just wondered how long he'd been in business."

"Oh, Christy," Bobbie spoke up, "before I forget, Julie Wentworth called for you. She said it wasn't important, that she'd call you back."

Christy absorbed that bit of information and wondered why Julie'd called. The paternity test?

"And don't forget we're having a birthday dinner for Bobbie tomorrow night," Jack called over his shoulder. "Your momma is making her famous lasagna."

"So I'd better start counting calories," Bobbie added as they walked out the door.

Christy stared after them. She had completely forgotten about Bobbie's birthday in all the confusion of the past few days. Even Dan had remembered—or at least, Christy supposed he meant the party when he'd said, 'See you tomorrow night.' At least she already had a gift for her aunt.

She plopped down on the stool Jack had occupied and let her mind wander over the facts of the case in light of what she'd just learned from Jack.

Willie had been a suspect in Kirby's murder, and he'd moved out of the Panama City area about the time Reuben cleaned out a garage.

She needed caffeine. Crossing to their coffee station, she poured herself a cup and picked up a doughnut. She refused to feel guilty about the doughnut; she hadn't eaten all day. She wrapped a napkin around it and, with coffee in hand, wandered over to a comfortable chair and sank down.

Where had Willie been this weekend? How could she find out? If she learned it was the Pensacola area, his name would move to the top of her suspect list. She wanted to believe R.J. was not involved, so she tried to build a case against Willie.

It would take money to start up a new business, even if it were a small one. And no doubt he had a stack of medical bills from Lou's illness plus the expense of a funeral. But then, maybe they had life insurance.

What if… She took another sip of coffee, her thoughts picking up. What if he was the only person who could confirm Kirby paid him in the office? He'd mentioned his workers, but maybe they'd already left or were cleaning up after the barbecue, not paying attention to Willie's whereabouts. Maybe Kirby paid him in cash in the kitchen or out on the patio.

Naturally, Willie knew there were valuables in the house, and someone had told her that everyone knew Kirby had to leave at five. Willie knew the house would be empty. He probably noticed the laundry window was open, or maybe he purposely unlocked the back door as he left.

The authorities maintained that Kirby surprised someone who panicked and shot him. The who and why comprised the mystery that grew colder with each year. If Willie's fingerprints were on the back of a chair and on the desk, was he already in the office when Kirby returned to pick up the list?

Kirby saw Willie and rushed to the cupboard for the gun. Willie reacted, then fled. As for no one's DNA matching up, what was there to match it to? All the DNA taken that day had proven nothing, except that the intruder must have worn gloves, perhaps even a ski mask to prevent hair and saliva from being left at the scene.

There was still Willie's "air-tight alibi" to be considered.

Having finished the coffee and doughnut, Christy walked to the phone, focused on one question now. She dialed Deputy Arnold's office, and his assistant, Sara, told her he was in Walton County. Christy thanked her and hung up.

The business card for Captain Davis was tucked among the other cards in their shop Rolodex. Bolstering her nerve, she dialed his number. To her surprise, he answered.

"Captain Davis, this is Christy Castleman."

"Hello, Miss Castleman. What can I do for you?"

"Well, this might sound like an odd question, and one you aren't at liberty to answer, but I was wondering if in your files you have the name of the preacher's wife—well, I guess it's the husband's name I need. I'm referring to Willie Pitt's preacher."

"Why are you asking me? Why not call Willie Pitt?"

She decided to be truthful. "Do you believe his alibi?"

"We've checked and double checked. Willie's neighbors saw the preacher's car parked at his house, and the preacher's neighbors verified the time he returned from Willie's house. Also, a couple of eyewitnesses back up his story. Why? Do you know something I should know?"

"Not really. I'm just curious. And while I'm asking, how's Reuben Foster? I heard he was shot in the back on Friday night."

There was a moment's pause. "I'm not sure."

He probably thought she was overstepping her bounds, so she tried to explain her motivation.

"Captain Davis, I can't recall if I told you, but Kirby Strickland saved me from drowning when I was eleven years old. I want his killer caught."

"So do we, Miss Castleman. Bob Arnold has already told me about your solving two crimes in the area, so it's not that I don't respect your instincts. We just can't discuss this case. Believe me, we want it solved too." He paused. "I understand there was a break-in at your house. Has anything developed yet?"

"No, but I now have a good security system, and there have been no other attempts."

"That's good to hear."

"Any idea who might have shot Foster?" she pressed, even though he'd just told her he couldn't discuss the case.

"We're working on a couple leads. I assume you know something about Willie Pitt?"

"I know he's gone out of town," she stated bluntly.

The momentary silence made Christy wonder if this was news to Captain Davis. "As I told you, I can't say anything more."

"Okay. Thanks for your time." She hung up. She'd just thrown Willie Pitt's name back into the ring of suspects, if indeed he had been anywhere near Pensacola. She placed Captain Davis's business card in her purse. It would be no use to her in the shop Rolodex if she needed to get in touch with him when she was at home or in her car.

She noticed the pink slip by the phone where Bobbie had written Julie's number. She wasn't in the mood to talk to Julie, unsure as she was about R.J., but Julie might have some information. With a sigh, Christy reached for the phone and dialed her number.

"Hello, Julie. Aunt Bobbie told me you called."

"Our hearts are breaking for little Zeffie. R.J. called the lab

today. They're backed up with lab work because one of their techni-
cians is on vacation."

"Julie, do you want to be Zeffie's mother if R.J. turns out to be
her father?" It might sound like an odd question, but she had to
know for sure.

"Oh, Christy. Nothing in the world would make me happier. I
fell in love with that little girl the first time I laid eyes on her."

"I understand. Everyone does. Are you going up for the funeral
tomorrow?"

"Yes, of course. That's why we were hoping to know something
by then."

Christy nodded. Maybe everything was working out for the
best. After all, it was the detectives' job to prove who killed Kirby.
Like Julie, Christy loved Zeffie and wanted her to be happy.

"Well, good luck," Christy said. "Dan and I are driving up too,
so we'll see you there. If you hear anything in the meantime, let me
know."

"You'll be the first one I call."

A customer entered the shop, and Christy forced herself to get
her mind on her business.

When finally the hands on the clock turned to five, Christy
locked up and turned out the lights, then did exactly as Dan had
planned to do: she picked up a hamburger, went straight home, and
curled up on the couch.

The phone rang, and she picked up the handset. As soon as she
answered, Zeffie's small voice came over the wire.

"Christy, before I left Aunt Julie gave me a cell phone with a hundred and twenty minutes on it. I'm in the bedroom that is supposed to be mine with the door closed."

"Oh, Zeffie. I'm so glad to hear from you, darling. How are you?"

"Terrible. I hate it here. I wish you'd come get me."

Christy sighed. "Honey, I can't do that. Dan and I are driving up for your grandma's funeral. We'll talk then."

Zeffie sounded so disappointed when she said good-bye and hung up that a new wave of sadness washed over Christy. She hoped that any suspicions against R.J. concerning Kirby would be dispelled, and that the real killer would be caught. As Zeffie's sad little face filled her memory, she began to pray that R.J. would be Zeffie's father after all.

27

A car edged into the back row of the parking lot at the Pensacola hospital. Again, the stranger wore the associate pastor tag, hoping to make himself respectable.

He had waited until nine in the evening to sneak in. He knew it was too late for a visit, but not too late to get to Foster, if necessary.

He made his way up to the third floor, where a policeman guarded Foster's room. The stranger turned quickly away, approaching an attractive young nurse.

"Good evening," he said softly. "I'm here to check on Mr. Reuben Foster. A friend of his attends our church and is really concerned about him."

The nurse paused, shifting the tray she carried to the other hand. Her blond hair was pinned back from her face, showing off her large blue eyes, which filled with compassion at his words.

"That's very nice of you. Mr. Foster could use some prayers, but you'll have to check with that policeman over there."

"Yes, I will. I just don't want to bother anyone."

"No bother. But you really should pray for him. At his age, and with the amount of blood he lost, I just don't know."

"I see. Is he able to talk or understand if I speak with him?"

Her blue eyes saddened. "I'm really not sure."

But she had told him what he needed to know. Foster was dying.

"Well, thank you very much. God bless you," he said, as he turned and hurried off.

The policeman was staring at him now, a clipboard in his lap. His name would not be on the list of people permitted to see Foster.

The stranger smiled and nodded at the policeman, then casually pushed the elevator button.

The next time he came, he'd wear a police uniform.

28

Tuesday

C hristy's phone rang at 7:00 a.m. and she frowned. She hadn't slept well, and she resented phone calls before eight. Her family knew that, and Dan knew that, so it had to be someone else.

She answered, not in her most pleasant tone of voice.

"Christy, this is Della. I'm sorry to call so early, but I've thought of something that might be helpful."

Christy sat up, reaching behind her to adjust the pillows. "Della, it's good to hear from you. What did you think of?"

"I don't suppose you could drive over to see me today."

"Of course I could. What time?"

"Well, as I said before, mornings are best for me."

"I'll be over in an hour," Christy said. "What can I bring you?"

Della hesitated. "Since you've been so kind to me, I feel bold enough to ask you for some sugar-free cookies. I think you can get them at the grocery store."

"I'll be happy to do that. See you soon."

Christy made a mental note to stop at the market as she peered through the drapes. The sun was shining, and it was a beautiful day. She noticed the kids next door racing to their mother's car, lunchboxes in hand, wearing sweaters and jackets. Apparently it was a cool morning despite the sunshine.

She walked to her closet and selected a pair of jeans and a white knit turtleneck. Hurrying into the bathroom, she began to freshen up for her trip to Sunset Manor.

∽

When she arrived, holding a sack with two different flavors of sugar-free cookies inside, the nurse who had accompanied them to the hospital greeted her warmly. "She told me you were coming. It's so nice that you always bring her something. No one ever visits her."

Christy hurried down the hall, remembering Della and her late husband had never had children. Did she have no other relatives?

She found Della seated in her wheelchair by the window, looking fresh in a green and white checked housedress. Her dark eyes gleamed. Because of the cookies or excitement over what she had to tell Christy?

Then she noticed Della was staring at the sack.

"I hope these suit you," she said.

Della peered into the sack and grinned. "My favorites. Sit down. We have to talk."

Christy settled into the vacant chair. It was clear that the excited expression on Della's face had nothing to do with the cookies. She placed them on a table and fidgeted in her wheelchair, as though she couldn't wait to talk.

"What did you want to tell me?" Christy asked.

"I may have figured something out," Della said. "It's been weighing on my mind how Reuben kept looking from me to my sweater and back. I knew in my soul that he was sending me a message; I just couldn't figure it out. Then last night, when the nurse was in my closet getting out a fresh gown, I spotted that red sweater, and suddenly I knew what he was trying to tell me."

Christy blinked, wondering where this was going.

"Reuben gave me that red sweater a long time ago. Please, bring it here." Della pointed.

Christy went to the closet and carefully removed it from the hanger. It was a cashmere cardigan with a name-brand label. Someone had paid a lot of money for this sweater. Holding it, she returned to the chair and sat down.

"One afternoon years ago—I've thought about it and prayed about it, and I believe it was in the summer of 1998. It was before I had the stroke in July of '98 and had to come to the nursing home to live."

Christy sat riveted to the chair. Maybe Della had something, after all.

"Anyway, Reuben came to see me and brought the sweater late one summer afternoon. Said it was a small payment on the money he owed me. He admitted the sweater was in some stuff that he was supposed to throw away. Two buttons were missing, but I replaced them. Can you imagine anyone throwing a nice sweater away just because two buttons were missing?"

Christy's mind shot to Julie, then Ellen.

"He didn't say what else he got, but I know he cleaned out a garage in one of those condos near Bailey Bridge at Lynn Haven. Said he saw people catching fish down around North Bay. He was going home to get his fishing pole and then heading back where the fish were biting."

Della paused to catch her breath. "When he kept looking at my red sweater, I believe he was trying to remind me of that day. That way, I'd remember him bringing it to me and telling me about the garage he cleaned out. He said there was a special little box he wanted to bring me, but a guy paid him ten dollars for it and he needed the money. I believe in my soul he was trying to make me remember that day. Does that sound crazy?"

Christy thought about it. Maybe this meant nothing, but she knew Vince and Ellen had lived in Lynn Haven. The Browns moved out to the farm after Kirby's death. Wayne Crocker had lived there for a while as well. As for R.J., he could have rented a place in Lynn Haven, which was closer to Deerfield. That way he could make his runs back and forth, checking on Julie and Kirby. Maybe he'd kept a condo there before moving to the beach.

"You're awfully quiet," Della said. "You must be thinking hard."

Christy nodded. "Did you ever know a Willie Pitt? I can't remember if I asked you that."

"I believe my husband knew him. Used to buy barbecue from a little stand Willie had before he opened a restaurant." She frowned. "No, there was something else about him." Della stared into space for a moment. "I know what it was. He recommended my husband for a paint job, because Willie moonlighted as a painter. It was a day job, and he couldn't do it."

Christy nodded, wondering again where Willie had gone. And where was he now?

"Maybe I'll take a drive over to the North Bay area and look around," Christy said. "Thanks, Della. We may be onto something."

"I hope so. Reuben had his faults, but he didn't deserve to be shot in the back. Nobody does." Tears filled her eyes, and Christy reached for her hand.

"You're doing the best you can to help us find out who shot him."

Della dabbed a handkerchief to her eyes. "I sure do hope this helps."

Christy smiled at her, not sure how much of what Della had told her would help, but she was determined to pursue it.

She thanked Della and hurried out. Lynn Haven was only fifteen minutes from the nursing home, so Christy turned her SUV in that direction. Spotting a card shop along the way, she remembered Bobbie's birthday party and whipped into a parking space. She found a funny card that seemed appropriate and returned to her car. Now she'd be ready for the party. She could devote the rest of the day to her search.

She thought about Captains Davis and Kramer and then Big Bob. Perhaps she should call one of them, but what would she say? *Reuben Foster stared at Della Young's sweater, and we believe he was trying to convey a message about a red sweater.*

Christy sighed. Reuben had not responded to anyone, so it was unlikely this would seem like a hot clue. And maybe it wasn't, but Christy felt that even the tiniest hope had to be explored. Besides, she had promised Della she would.

She slowed as she crossed the bridge, studying the progress that had overtaken Lynn Haven in the past years. How on earth would she find the right condos when there appeared to be so many around? *But not at the bridge,* she reminded herself hopefully.

Spotting a dry cleaner that looked as though it dated back to the eighties, she parked and got out.

An older woman was writing up an order for a young mother bouncing a crying baby on her hip. Christy waited her turn, and the woman looked up at her with an expression that seemed too weary for such an early hour.

"Excuse me for bothering you," Christy said, "but I'm trying to locate some condos that were here in 1998."

The woman looked at her as though she had lost her mind. "I'm not the one to ask. I just moved here a month ago after my divorce. Started working here last week. The owner might know."

When she offered nothing more, Christy asked, "Could I speak with him?"

The look again. "He's gone to Mobile to see his new grand-child."

Christy sighed, realizing she was wasting the woman's time as well as her own.

"Okay, thanks."

She got in her car and drove to the closest convenience store. The young man at the cash register looked as though he would have been in high school in 1998, but she asked about the condos anyway.

He shook his head. "I don't know. My dad got transferred here two years ago. Mr. Hunt, the owner, might know. He's been here a long time."

"Could I speak with him?"

The young man shook head. "Sorry. This is his day off."

Christy could recognize defeat when it hit her squarely in the face. She needed to go home and do some research on the Internet, rather than blindly striking out.

Halfway back to Summer Breeze, her cell phone rang. She read her mother's number and answered.

"Hi, dear. I'm cleaning house for Bobbie's birthday party. Dinner is at six, and I was wondering if you're busy later. I need some items picked up from the bakery, and I could use a hand in the kitchen."

"Sure," Christy said, trying to sound cheerful. She glanced at the little white sack on the passenger seat that held Bobbie's birthday card. "What time do you want me to come to the house?"

"Is three o'clock this afternoon too early?"

Yes, it is. "No, I'll be there at three."

She had to notify Dan about the change of plans, so she dialed his cell phone. His voice mail picked up, and she left a message telling him she'd meet him at her parents' house and that she was looking forward to seeing him. The thought of the party and Dan lifted her spirits, and she smiled and drove faster.

When she arrived home, she parked her car in the driveway and grabbed the sack that held the birthday card, then glanced back toward the mailbox. She might as well check. She walked down the driveway and opened her mailbox, removing a small stack of envelopes and the usual sale circulars. She thumbed through the obvious bills. At the bottom of the stack, she spotted a small pink envelope with her name and address written in cursive. She noted the return address in Montgomery.

She hurried through the back door, then sat at the eating bar, placing the other mail on the counter. She opened the pink envelope and unfolded the plain sheet of notebook paper.

> Christy,
>   I miss you so much. Every night I pray to come back to Summer Breeze. Are you coming up on Wednesday? Can I go back with you?
>   Love,
>   Zeffie

The carefully written words brought a rush of tenderness, then sadness. Christy hated the thought of Zeffie homesick and unhappy. Maybe she'd call her tonight. No, there was the party tonight. And they'd be driving up tomorrow for the funeral.

All she could do was pray for Zeffie. Christy's father had placed her on the prayer list at church, and the Red Hatters and half of Summer Breeze were praying too. Surely something positive would happen, since so many prayers were going up on behalf of the little angel of Summer Breeze.

❧

Bobbie's birthday was a festive occasion. Christy brought some colorful balloons and strung pink streamers from the chandelier over the dining room table. Pink was Bobbie's favorite color, so the cake was white trimmed in pink, and an arrangement of pink roses graced the table.

Beth's lasagna had been superb as always, and the cake and ice cream added the perfect final touch. Seth had called earlier to wish Bobbie a happy birthday and had spoken to everyone in the family. Even Dan.

"You are all too good to me," Bobbie said, looking around the table as they finished dinner. Jack sat beside her at the long dining table. Dan and Christy sat opposite them, and Beth and Grant flanked the ends.

"We love you," Beth said. "You deserve a special birthday. Now open your gifts."

Bobbie made her wish and blew out the ten candles on her cake, which was all she said she wanted.

"Maybe you'll get your wish," Grant said, a wide smile on his face.

Christy went to the sideboard for the wicker basket that held the gifts and placed it on the table beside Bobbie, who had been trying all evening not to cry.

"I can't remember the last time I had a birthday party," she said. "As for gifts—well, I haven't had this many since I was sixteen, Beth."

"A friend gave her a surprise party," Beth explained.

Bobbie began to open gift bags and untie boxes, profuse with her thanks and appreciation. Grant and Beth gave her a gift card for the Destin Outlets.

"Wow!" she said, reading the amount. "Jack, we can shop for a whole day."

Jack pretended to dread the idea, but everyone at the table could see the glow in his eyes when he looked at Bobbie. They loved being with each other.

Bobbie gushed over the crystal brooch Christy gave her, holding it to the lapel of her pink jacket.

"It came from Julie's boutique," Christy said.

Bobbie's eyes widened. "Oh honey, you shouldn't have spent that kind of money."

"She gave me a real deal."

Seth had sent a silly card with a rumpled ten-dollar bill tucked inside. "That sweet boy can't afford to be sending me money," Bobbie said, smoothing the bill on the tablecloth. "I know he's on a strict budget with all his college expenses."

"Seth doesn't do anything he doesn't want to do," Grant said.

"He'll be home in a couple days for Thanksgiving. He can save money by filling up on Beth's delicious free meals."

"Speaking of Thanksgiving," Bobbie said, "I want everyone at my place. I know it's small, but we can put a card table in the living room. Besides"—she looked at Jack—"I want to cook some of the things Momma cooked for Beth and me."

"Will you let me help?" Beth offered.

"You can bring your pumpkin cheesecake, if it's not too much trouble."

"I was going to make it anyway. I already have the ingredients."

"Will I be allowed to carve the turkey?" Jack asked. "I plan to provide one."

"Of course," Bobbie said, then laughed. "I guess I'm just home-sick for the smells, Beth. Remember how we had to chop celery and onions for Momma's stuffing?"

"And the ground cranberries for the salad," Beth replied wist-fully.

"I have her recipes for everything." Bobbie looked around the table. "Don't worry. I've done Thanksgiving dinner on a few occa-sions, and everything turned out okay."

"What should I bring?" Christy asked.

"Dan." Bobbie winked.

"Oh, I'll do that. Are we having lunch or dinner?" Christy asked.

"Midday meal," Bobbie replied. "That gives us time to stuff our-selves, take naps, then stuff ourselves again."

Jack put his arm around Bobbie. "My birthday gift to Bobbie

will come later. Which brings me to an announcement we want to make."

Bobbie fidgeted in her chair, her blue eyes radiant as they moved over the faces around the table.

"I've asked Bobbie to marry me," Jack said, his voice filled with tenderness, "and she's accepted."

Suddenly everyone was on their feet, hugging the couple and offering their congratulations.

"I told Jack I don't want a diamond. Diamonds never brought happiness or marital success to me in the past. We're going to have matching gold bands," Bobbie announced with pride.

Jack turned to Grant. "And we'd be grateful if you would marry us in a quiet little ceremony sometime over the Christmas holidays."

Grant extended a hand of congratulations to Jack. "I'd be honored."

The tears Bobbie had been holding back now flooded down her face. "I wish you knew how happy we are."

"We can tell," Dan said, looking from Bobbie to Jack. "And we're very happy for both of you."

Beth and Christy were sniffing, and even Dan and Grant's faces reflected love and tenderness. Jack and Bobbie hugged each other, and Beth slipped out of her chair to grab a calendar. The discussion of a wedding date began, and Grant suggested coffee in the living room. Dan glanced at Christy, and she got the message.

"Well," she said, "Dan and I have spent very little time alone since he returned, so would anyone mind if we slip out early?"

"I have a disk from my camera that I wanted to show Christy on Montana," Dan added.

"By all means, don't hang around here with us old folks," Bobbie said, always one to appreciate quality time with her man.

Christy kissed Bobbie and then her mother, congratulating her on a job well done. She hugged her dad, who then turned to clamp a hand on Dan's shoulder.

"Glad to have you back," he said.

"Thank you," Dan replied. He turned to Beth. "It was a great meal."

"By the way," Christy remembered, "we're going up to Montgomery tomorrow for Mrs. Adams's funeral at 2:00. Julie and R.J. are going as well, and Joy told me all the Red Hatters are attending."

"Do you think we should go?" Grant asked.

"Not if you weren't asked to speak. I imagine Mr. and Ms. Carver will use their minister. No, I don't think Zeffie would expect you to be there."

Bobbie frowned, glancing at Jack. "I should go."

Christy shook her head. "No. Stay here and run the shop. Zeffie will understand."

"Please give her my love," Bobbie said, her eyes sad for the first time all evening.

"I will. Now go on with your fun. Zeffie will be happy to know that you and Jack are engaged."

With that, they all said good night and Christy and Dan hurried out to Dan's car.

"I'm happy for them," Christy said as they drove back to her house. "It seems like such a miracle. At this point in their lives, at their ages, they've found true love."

Dan reached for her hand. "True love can come at any age. Do you think we've found it, Christy?"

She turned in her seat and studied his face. "I have, Dan. What about you?"

He nodded. "I'm sure I have. When I was in Montana, I thought about us a lot. I think it's time to talk about a commitment."

Christy didn't know how to respond as they turned into her driveway.

"Remember our little discussion the other night?" Dan said, cutting the lights. "Well, I'll show you what I mean." He moved around the car to open her door.

They had discussed many things that night, but when she stepped inside the screen door, Christy realized what he meant. A small wooden container with a tiny wire-mesh door sat on the floor. She could see a white face peering out at her.

"Oh, Dan! How sweet of you."

"You'd better reserve your judgment till we get her out of the carrier. I also brought litter and cat food."

They flipped on the light, and Dan knelt and opened the carrier door. The white cat strolled out and surveyed its surroundings. Christy dropped to the floor, gathered the cat in her arms, and stroked its soft white fur. The cat purred in contentment.

She looked up at Dan. "This is one of the most thoughtful things you've ever done."

He sat down beside her. "I wanted to reinforce our discussion of not being afraid to lose your heart again—to a person or an animal."

She nodded. "You're right."

"Let's call our new friend here a precommitment gift. Maybe there'll be something better coming your way soon."

She gazed at him, her eyes full of love. "God knew what he was doing when he saved you for me."

29

Wednesday

Dan and Christy drove back from Montgomery, their mood as somber as the clouds filling the sky. The funeral service had been brief, family and friends departing before Molly was laid to rest. Zeffie had clung first to Christy and Dan, then to Julie and R.J. Watching the touching scene, Christy decided she couldn't possibly say or do anything to incriminate R.J., unless the detectives came up with positive proof against him. Then everyone would have to face facts. Julie had whispered that they would know something soon. Until then, Christy wasn't about to do anything to hurt Zeffie.

The Red Hatters were in full attendance, and Miz B's rendition of "Amazing Grace" brought chills to all. After the minister's verses of comfort and prayer, people filed out of their chairs and left the tent. Zeffie lingered, placing a single rose on her grandmother's grave. A red rose that came from the arrangement the Red Hatters brought.

Sally Carver looked stricken, and Bailey was very quiet and thoughtful. They thanked everyone who made the long trip, then turned to wait for Zeffie.

Christy couldn't bear to stay longer, and she slipped her hand into the crook of Dan's arm and suggested they leave. Once they reached the car, she burst into tears and cried for the next half hour. She didn't feel like stopping to eat. All she wanted to do was go home and grieve privately.

In her driveway, Dan kissed her good-bye. He needed to get back to the office to check on his employees, and he promised to call her later.

She stepped out into the gloomy afternoon, grateful the sun had at least come out during Molly's funeral. As she entered her kitchen, her new friend waited patiently. She reached down to stroke her soft fur.

"We have to give you a name," she said. "But I want it to be right, so let me think about it."

Hearing the cat purr as she held it, Christy suddenly recalled her father's sermon on grief and walking through the valley. She had gone through her own valley of shadows and thought she had conquered her fear of being hurt again. But another valley had followed. As she hugged her new pet, she realized she would always be vulnerable where loss and grief were concerned. But who wasn't? At least she had learned not to cast blame or fall prey to useless "if only" arguments.

"Let me change clothes, and I'll see about your food and milk," she said, placing the cat on the floor and standing up. As she walked back to her room and changed into sweats and a T-shirt, the cat followed.

"I wish Zeffie could see you. But she will when she comes to visit," Christy said, recalling the look of desperation on Zeffie's face when they said good-bye.

As she returned to the kitchen, she had to pray and believe that Zeffie's world would get better. Many people were trying to help her. Especially Julie and R.J. If, in fact, R.J. was her father, Zeffie's world was about to change. A change which, in the beginning, would make Zeffie feel like Cinderella.

The phone rang, and she saw Dan's number on the caller ID. "Hello, you sweet man," she greeted him.

"That's a nice way to start a conversation," he said and chuckled.

"I love my little friend. What do you think of the name Snowflake? She looks like a little snowball, but I like Snowflake better. It makes me think of snow falling in Montana."

"Nice. I like that." He paused for a moment. "Listen, with tomorrow being Thanksgiving and family meals, what about something different on Friday?"

"That sounds good to me. What did you have in mind?"

"If I tell, it won't be a surprise."

"I know I'm different, but I'm skittish about surprises. However, I did like the ones I got last night. Snowflake is wonderful, and I've been thinking about something else, a sentence that had the word *commitment* in it."

"Mmm. We'll discuss that later. Are you feeling better?"

"I am. Thanks for checking."

As she tidied up the counter, she came upon her Lynn Haven city map. She made a quick decision not to mention her condo search to Dan yet. Reuben staring at a red sweater meant something to Della, but connecting a time and place to his stare would seem like a stretch to some. Yet Della had seemed so sure… Christy was operating on her own radar now, and she heard a beep. Not loud, but definitely a beep.

"Get a good night's rest," she said, not wanting to hang up. "We have a busy day tomorrow—Thanksgiving."

"You too." He hesitated. "I'll be glad when we don't have to say good night like this."

A feeling of joy soared through her. If that wasn't a hint about marriage, she'd never heard one. "So will I," she admitted. "Good night."

She ended the conversation so she could thrust an arm in the air and shout, "YES!"

Snowflake jumped, cream dribbling from her chin.

"I'm sorry." Christy picked her up and pressed her check against the soft white fur. She checked the doors to be sure they were locked, double checked the security system, turned out the kitchen light, and sauntered back to her bedroom. She had set up Snowflake's litter box in the master bathroom, so while she removed her makeup and changed into her pajamas, Snowflake did her own preparations for the evening. Christy placed a big, soft pillow on the floor at the foot of her bed for Snowflake to sleep on.

"Time to go to napper's house," she said, recalling the phrase her father had often used when telling her and Seth good night.

Christy turned the covers back, crawled under the comforter, and glanced at the clock. Ten minutes till 9. An early hour for going to sleep, but she felt exhausted. She picked up her pen and her prayer journal and made a notation of the day's events. Her thoughts lingered on Zeffie and all the heartache she had suffered. She closed the journal and placed it on the bed with her pen. Then she began to pray for Zeffie.

Just before she turned out the light, she felt a weight on the foot of her bed and faced the green eyes of her cat. "Good night," she said, feeling her spirits lift.

She smiled and turned off the light, wondering if this would become a habit.

30

Thursday

I t was a beautiful day, sunny and warm, a perfect day for giving
thanks for one's blessings. As Christy dressed in a white pantsuit
with a blue shell top, she wondered what kind of Thanksgiving
Zeffie would have with the Carvers.

That thought led to an eagerness to talk to her other lonely
friend, Della Young. She picked up the telephone. After several unan-
swered rings, she hung up. Tomorrow she would visit her.

When Dan arrived to pick up her up, he was holding a small
brown sack in his hand.

"Pickles?" she teased, knowing he had offered to bring something for the Thanksgiving meal. Bobbie had told him just to bring
himself and Christy.

"How'd you guess? Actually, I brought something that will keep
me from worrying about you when I can't play bodyguard." He
entered her kitchen and placed the sack on the counter.

"Really? I'm intrigued."

He pulled out a slender black can, about six inches tall, and for
a moment she thought it was some kind of hairspray. As she studied
it more carefully, she realized it was a different kind of spray.

"Mace?" she asked.

"Red pepper spray. I want you to keep it with you until this Kirby Strickland case is solved. Let me show you how to use it—I don't want you spraying yourself."

"I'm not a dunce," she retaliated, watching as he pointed to the can's red top.

"It's locked now, but if you need to use it, you simply swivel this little spout at the top and press down on it like hairspray. Aim it at the face of your attacker—if, God forbid, there ever is one. Be sure you get the eyes. It will blind someone temporarily so you can get away."

"It scares me just to think about a situation like that, but thanks, Dan. I could have used it on a couple other occasions."

"That's why I got it for you."

"Shall I take it with us today?" she asked with mock seriousness, then leaned forward and kissed him. "Sorry. I don't mean to make light of a very thoughtful act. I really appreciate it."

"We'll leave it here on the counter." He hesitated. "Can Snowflake jump that high? On second thought, I'll put it on the ledge over here on the wall where you keep your car keys."

"Great. Now let's go have fun."

∽

When Bobbie opened her front door and gave each of them a hug, the aromas of Thanksgiving—onions, celery, and cinnamon—

enveloped Christy. He petite aunt wore a white cotton bib apron over a pair of hot pink pants and a matching short-sleeved shirt. Christy enjoyed her aunt's flamboyant nature.

"Dan, you've never been here," Bobbie said as they entered the foyer. "It's small but it's home." The little house reflected Bobbie's flair for color and style. French country furnishings dominated the house.

"I like your place," Dan said, looking around.

Voices drew them toward the small den, where Seth and his parents laughed and talked.

Seth stood as they approached, and Christy thought he seemed even taller and older than when she'd seen him a week and a half ago. She crossed the room to hug him, glancing at his khakis and blue button-down shirt. "You look great," she said.

Seth waved the compliment aside and turned to shake Dan's hand. "You're still putting up with her?" He indicated Christy with a jerk of his head.

"Well, you know how it is," Dan replied. "When somebody steals your heart, there's not much you can do."

Christy turned to him, pleased to hear his open admission.

Her dad spoke up. "One of these days, if Seth's lucky, it'll happen to him." Grant shook Dan's hand and waved him to the sofa.

"Okay, Christy, we need you in the kitchen," Bobbie called, opening a drawer and pulling out a red apron.

"What can I do?" Christy glanced around the kitchen. A huge brown turkey rested on a platter, flanked by casseroles and salads.

"Keep an eye on the bread." Bobbie pointed toward the oven. "This is going to be buffet style."

Jack emerged from the garage, holding a knife sharpener and a stainless steel carving knife.

Christy threw up her hands. "I surrender."

Jack chuckled. "Your aunt's knives aren't sharp enough to cut butter."

"Darlin', that's why I need you." Bobbie swept by, pausing to give him a peck on the cheek, which brought a glow to his blue eyes.

Christy stood at the sink, washing her hands. Jack sidled up to her and whispered in her ear, "Willie went to Birmingham to attend his sister's funeral. He's back now."

Christy glanced at him, feeling slightly embarrassed by her suspicions. She nodded and smiled. This put Willie out of the running as a suspect.

She remembered the bread and rushed over just in time. After pulling out the long pan, she placed the fluffy dinner rolls in the breadbasket, noting the delicate butter dish and knife already on the counter.

"Okay." She looked at her aunt. "Bread's ready."

"All right, everyone." Bobbie clapped her hands. "Two tables are set up with silverware and napkins. Come get your plate, and then choose your seat."

Beyond the counter, the sliding glass door stood ajar, offering fresh air and a view of the Gulf. Bobbie had sacrificed square footage in order to have a view.

"The meal looks wonderful," Grant said. "Shall I offer a blessing?"

Everyone joined hands as Grant named their blessings. At the end, he included the upcoming marriage of Bobbie and Jack.

After the prayer, Seth looked at Bobbie. "Do I get to give the bride away?"

"Honey, I'm a little old to be given away. It'll just be all of us, and maybe my dear friend Betty and her husband. Or if Jack wants to invite J.T. and Cora Lee."

Jack chuckled. "J.T.'s not comfortable at weddings, and Cora Lee can't fit into her Sunday dress anymore."

Everyone tried not to laugh while Bobbie swatted his shoulder. "Grant just offered a prayer. You be nice."

Seth was the first to grab a plate, and everyone followed suit, finding their places at the linen-covered tables. Jack and Bobbie joined Beth and Grant, and Seth hunkered down with Christy and Dan.

"So what's up?" Seth asked Christy. "You solved any murders lately?"

Christy frowned at him, thinking of Kirby and then Reuben Foster. This was a day for giving thanks, not worrying about crimes. "Can we keep the topic pleasant?"

Seth shrugged and turned to Dan. "I hear you've been to Montana to scout out a project for some dude."

"Right."

As Dan explained the details, Christy listened with interest to his description of the land Mr. Parker had purchased. Dan went over his plans for the best use of the land, and Christy studied him with pride. He was so good at his work.

She took a sip of tea and thought about her reluctance to leave Summer Breeze. She liked the comfort and predictability; life, however, was not predictable. Being with Dan was the important thing. She'd stepped out of her last fear by agreeing to love another pet. If Dan wanted her to go to Montana, she would not cheat him or her out of time together.

"So..." Seth looked from Dan to Christy and back. "Can I come visit in Montana?"

Dan glanced at Christy. "I haven't decided for certain if I'll take on the project."

Christy touched his hand. "I think you should, if that's what you want to do."

A look of surprise preceded a happy glow in his blue eyes.

"Well," Seth said, chewing his food, "I'm just teasing about a visit. I'm trying to work out something exciting for my summer."

"Like what?" Christy asked, curious about his plans.

"I'd like to go down to Sarasota and work in the marine laboratory. One of my professors knows a guy down there who works with manatees. We've been talking about it, and I think I could get a job."

"Are you interested in marine biology as a career?" Dan asked.

"That's why I want to go down and work in the marine laboratory."

Dan nodded. "Sounds like a great idea. Can your professor recommend you for a job?"

"He said he would. I kept my grades up this year, and I *haven't missed classes,*" Seth emphasized, looking at Christy.

Bobbie came around to refill their glasses. Beth's pumpkin cheesecake was sliced and waiting.

They enjoyed a wonderful meal together, and there was no more mention of the Strickland case. It seemed as though everyone had a made a silent vow to focus on blessings rather than heartaches.

31

Friday

C hristy was tidying up the kitchen when her cell phone rang. Finding it odd that someone wasn't calling her home phone, she unplugged her cell phone from its charger on the counter and answered. She recognized Della's voice in the polite greeting.

"Hi, Della. Did you have a nice Thanksgiving?"

"It was all right. The folks here knocked themselves out preparing a good meal for us. Even gave us little ceramic turkeys to take to our rooms."

"I called you around ten yesterday to wish you a happy Thanksgiving, but you didn't answer."

"That was sweet of you. They came after us early, took us down to the party room for some silly games. But I have news. A nurse just called me to say Reuben is out of the coma and starting to mumble. He's not making much sense yet, but they're optimistic."

"Della, that's great."

"Did you find any condos with garages around Bailey Bridge?" Della asked.

"Well, that area has changed a lot over the years, but I intend to continue my search today." Christy glanced at the Lynn Haven map, on which she'd circled a few areas in red.

"I know Reuben was trying to tell me something the other day, Christy. I just know it has to do with some condos near Bailey Bridge."

"Well, I'll do my best to find them, Della."

They said their good-byes and hung up. Christy laid her cell phone on the counter and glanced at the clock. Ten minutes after twelve. She and Bobbie had agreed to close the shop on the day after Thanksgiving so they could have a day of relaxation.

"Jack's dying for us to go pick out wedding bands," Bobbie had said. "It's bugging him that he hasn't given me a ring. I agreed to go and select our bands so I could at least show mine, when asked. Since this is a holiday weekend, let's just close the shop."

The idea had appealed to Christy. Dan would be tied up in meetings today, and she had decided to catch up on projects at home. She had planned to check on Della as well.

She stared out the kitchen window at the cloudy day, replaying Della's words in her mind.

What if Della only imagined Reuben had looked from her red sweater to her face, trying to relay a message? But what if she hadn't imagined it? What if that had been his helpless way of trying to catch the person who shot him?

"A promise is a promise," she said to Snowflake. "And I promised Della."

She glanced down at her clothes, khakis with a brown V-neck sweater. Fine for a day of snooping. Researching, she preferred to call it.

Her attention returned to the Lynn Haven map. She grabbed

the map and her car keys, then hesitated. On the ledge, the can of red pepper spray stared back at her.

"Okay." She grabbed it and shoved it into her oversized purse with the map.

The heavy clouds hinted of rain, making the day dreary. The weather had not hampered the shoppers, however. When she hit the highway, she saw local and out-of-state cars riding bumper to bumper, heading to the Destin Outlets. It took over an hour to get to Lynn Haven after she stopped to fill up her car with gas.

She located the first condominium complex with attached garages. When she went into the office to speak with the manager, she was told that these units had been sold and renovated in 2000. The previous owners had taken their records with them when they moved to Fort Myers.

"After six years and a major move, I don't know if they still have the records," the man replied. He seemed eager to finish up with her, grabbing the office phone on the first ring. "I haven't heard from them in years," he said, then entered into a lengthy conversation with his caller.

Nevertheless, Christy wrote down the previous owners' names, along with the words "Fort Myers." She'd call the previous owners as a last resort if she didn't turn up anything at the other locations.

She drove two miles to the next unit, only to stare blankly at an office complex. She checked the map and the address she had written down. This was the right address.

Christy got out of her car and walked into the office complex.

She paced and looked around the lobby, waiting for the receptionist to finish speaking with the handyman about a water leak.

After a long wait, Christy was rewarded with a friendly greeting.

"Sorry to keep you waiting," the young woman said. "We do our best to keep our tenants happy, and just this morning…" She rattled on about a scenario that held no interest to Christy. She'd already wasted fifteen minutes.

When finally the young woman took a breath, Christy jumped in.

"I think I'm lost," she said, looking around. "A friend of mine lived at this address years ago, but it doesn't look the same."

"This entire block was filled with condos," the receptionist explained, "but they were old and needed repairs. A development company bought them, leveled them, and built this new office complex."

"Oh," Christy said, facing another disappointment. "Do you think anyone would know how to get in touch with the owners of those condos?"

"No. The man died in 2001. The woman developed cancer and was glad to sell the following year. She moved up north to live with her daughter. Sorry I can't help you."

"Well, thanks anyway." Christy pushed through the revolving doors that led out to the parking area. The condos replaced by this office complex were torn down because they were in bad shape. She couldn't imagine any of the people on her suspect list living in condos that were about to fall down.

The day seemed even more dreary. She glanced up at the sky. Why hadn't there been a cloudburst on such a gray day?

Now what? she asked herself as she got in the car. *Three strikes and you're out.* She had swung twice.

One condo complex remained near the bridge, and it looked as though it had been built in the last ten years. All the units had garages.

Encouraged, Christy hopped out and hurried up to the office. When she entered, she saw a tall woman whose blond hair needed a touch-up at the roots. She was polishing her long red nails. She looked to be in her midforties.

The woman gave Christy a long, curious look. "What can I do for you?"

"Hi. I'm Christy Castleman. I wanted to inquire about someone who may have lived here."

The woman capped the nail polish, then replied, "I can't give out personal information."

Christy reached into her purse for Captain Davis's business card and handed it to the woman. "I'm connected with Deputy Bob Arnold and FDLE in Tallahassee."

The woman picked up the card, studied it, then handed it back to Christy, her expression a bit more cooperative.

"FDLE has reopened a cold case," Christy explained. "I'm tracking down some leads. I hope we can cut this short. I'm looking for someone who lived here in 1998 and—"

"In 1998?" The woman looked astounded.

"I know it seems like a long time ago, but we need to go back in your files to late spring, early summer of 1998."

"You're asking a lot." The woman's blond brows hiked a half an inch higher as she looked Christy over. "All those filing cabinets are locked up in the back room. I wouldn't even know where to look."

"I don't expect you to. It's a lousy thing to ask of anyone. I'll go back and look through the files, if you'll just show me where they are."

"It would take hours. What's the name of this person you're looking for?"

Christy hesitated, going back to her list of suspects. "I'm not sure. It could have been R. J. Wentworth, Vince and Ellen Brown, or Wayne Crocker."

Christy thought she saw a brief flash of recognition in the woman's eyes before she looked down at the phone. "I've worked here for ten years," she said, looking up at Christy, "and I pride myself on remembering names. None of those names means anything to me."

And you're lying, thought Christy, more determined than ever to find those files.

"Speaking of names," Christy said, "what's yours?"

"Marion Volkin."

"Nice to meet you," Christy said. "It's amazing that you have such a remarkable memory."

Marion made no response.

"Okay, Marion, I'll be straight with you. If I go back to my people and tell them I wasn't permitted to look through the files, someone will come back with a search warrant. And I can promise you, they'll go through more than the files. They'll examine tax records or whatever they think might be pertinent to our search. It's a matter of you letting me look through the files or subjecting yourself to the bloodhounds."

"Okay." Marion stood up. "You've made your point." She opened the center drawer of her desk and removed a set of keys. "Follow me."

Christy followed her down a hallway to the third door. Marion turned the key in the lock, opened the door, and hit a light switch. "I'll warn you if you have allergies, it's musty and dirty in here."

"I'll manage," Christy said, ignoring Marion's attempt to discourage her.

Marion looked at the five filing cabinets lining the walls. Some held labels of past years, some did not. She walked to the third one, opened the top drawer, and peered inside. "This drawer is stuffed full, but it should hold all the occupants of 1998. Good luck," she said in a tone that indicated she thought Christy was on a hopeless pursuit.

"Thanks." Christy laid her purse on top of the filing cabinet and began to flip through the files, yellow with age. Halfway back, she opened a file out of curiosity and noticed the date was 1997. She opened another one. It, too, was 1997.

Was sweet Marion mistaken, or had she deliberately misled her? Christy closed that drawer and opened the second drawer. The first file was dated 1998.

There must have been three or four dozen files stuffed in the drawer, and she knew she had a long and tedious search ahead of her. If not for promising Della and the negative signal from Marion, she would have been tempted to turn back.

The room was hot and stuffy, despite the cool morning. Christy riffled through the files, breaking a nail in the process, until one of the names she sought leaped at her. She wiggled it loose from the others and flipped it open. Move-out date: July 1, 1998.

She read on, checking the date of birth and occupation, and she knew she had the right person.

She heard Marion moving around near the door, so Christy yanked the file from the drawer, closed it, then grabbed her purse.

"Did you find what you were looking for?" Marion asked as she strode out.

Christy tucked the folder under her arm, hoping to hide the name. "Thanks. I'll be in touch."

She hurried to her car, jumped behind the wheel, and twisted the key in the ignition, her thoughts spinning. She merged into the flow of traffic, her thoughts as tangled as the Christmas lights boxed in her closet. Then slowly she began to line up the facts, and they pieced together to form the puzzle picture no one had been able to see.

As soon as Christy was out of sight, Marion rushed back to the filing cabinet, checked the files, then picked up the telephone and dialed a number.

"Hey, cuz. A little blonde named Christy Castleman was here, said she was with the FDLE. She asked me about some people who might have lived here in 1998. Your name was one she mentioned. I took her to the filing cabinet for another year, but she was too smart. She found the right drawer, grabbed a file, and left—it was yours." She hesitated, listening, then added, more firmly, "I know it was because you were the only one of the people she mentioned who lived here, and now your file is gone." Another pause. "She just left. And even if you are my cousin, I could use a little cash."

~

Once Christy was a comfortable distance from the condos, she reached for her purse. Digging into the pocket where she kept her cell phone, she felt only empty space. She frowned and searched through the main compartment of her purse. No cell phone.

Trying to keep one eye on the lane of traffic, she scanned the area around the car seat. She must have dropped it somewhere, and she needed it now more than ever.

A horn beeped as her SUV almost strayed into the wrong lane. She straightened the wheel, took a deep breath, and tried to organize her thoughts.

This morning Della had called her cell phone, and she'd removed it from the charger. When she finished the conversation, she'd laid it on the counter. Then she'd gotten sidetracked by the cat. She'd never even thought of her phone when she locked up and left. Why did she have to leave things and lose things?

She turned down side streets, trying to avoid traffic. She spotted a pay phone on the corner near a convenience store and turned in, screeching to a halt. Reaching over to the glove compartment, she pulled out a Ziploc bag of quarters saved for newspapers and drink machines, then jumped out of the car.

She dialed Seth's cell phone and lifted her eyes upward in a thank-you prayer when he answered.

"Where are you?" she asked.

"At Mom and Dad's. You sound like you've been running."

"Seth, I need a quick favor. There's a spare key to my house in the top drawer of the counter next to the fridge. It has my name on it. I need you to go to my house, grab my cell phone off the counter, and meet me at Coram's Coffee Shop on Back Beach Road. I'm thirty or forty minutes away. It's important, or I wouldn't ask." She remembered her new alarm system and gave him the code.

"Okay," he replied, picking up on her urgency. "I'll meet you there with your phone."

She grabbed more quarters and dialed Big Bob's cell phone. All she got was his voice mail, so she rushed through her dilemma. "Bob, this is urgent. Meet me at West Marina. It's ten till five and I should be there in an hour, depending on traffic. I know who killed Kirby and who tried to kill Reuben. Please call me right away."

Frustrated, she called his office, but it was closed. Either Sara had shut down early because of the holiday, or the office had been closed all day.

She deposited more quarters and dialed Bob's home phone number. Rob Jr. answered and informed her that his parents had gone to look at cars but would be back soon. "Phil has to be driven to football practice."

"Rob, as soon as your dad comes home, tell him this is urgent. He's to meet me at West Marina *now.*"

"Yes, ma'am. I'll tell him."

∽

It seemed to take forever to get to the coffee shop through the heavy traffic. Vacationers had flocked to the beach, and local residents had family and friends visiting, all adding to the swarm of cars along the highway. Christy had lost a couple of hours in Lynn Haven trying to find the right condos, then getting the file, and another hour getting back across the bridge.

Now she was in the bumper-to-bumper traffic of late afternoon.

She heaved a sigh of relief when after almost an hour, she spotted Seth's red El Camino parked at an angle in the coffee shop lot. She pulled to a halt next to him, rolled down her window, and stuck out her arm. He got out of the car and handed her the cell phone.

"Are you chasing a fire truck, or is one chasing you?" he asked.

"Neither. I'll explain later. Thanks for bringing the phone. I owe you."

"You bet you do. I'll take a hamburger and a malt for dinner. That'll be soon," he called as she put her car in gear.

In her rearview mirror, she could see him staring after her, hands on hips, slowly shaking his head.

"Sorry, Seth," she mumbled, opening up her cell phone. She had messages and pressed the number to retrieve them. The first was from Big Bob.

"Christy, I'm on my way. About twenty minutes from the marina."

The other message was from Della.

"Christy, I just wanted to tell you Reuben is now able to get out a word here and there. There are several police with him, and a couple detectives. A nurse just called me and put him on the phone. He said Crock or Crockett, something like that. Hope that helps."

Christy nodded. She had the right man. It all made sense to her now.

Wayne Crocker knew where the house key was hidden, he knew Kirby was leaving, and he thought he could sneak in and grab enough valuables to set himself up with a nice boat. He liked nice clothes and nice cars, and he worked hard, yet it was Kirby who was in the limelight, moving up the ladder of success, making more money, and getting engaged to Julie. Did Wayne feel he was the one who should get all the glory? Had he cared for Julie more than he admitted?

She tried Bob's cell phone again, and he answered immediately.

"Wayne Crocker is the killer and I have proof," she said. "Furthermore, Reuben Foster is starting to talk, and he's trying to name Crocker as the shooter. I know Wayne planned to leave this week, if he hasn't already. I'm only five minutes from the marina."

"Stall him if you can, but don't do anything foolish," Bob warned. "I'm about fifteen minutes away and I have my siren on. I'll turn it off before I get to the marina."

Christy hung up and a few minutes later swung into the marina parking lot, disappointed to see only a few unoccupied cars. Her eyes riveted on the dark office. R.J. had already left, if in fact he had worked today. The gloomy day was bringing an early darkness, which descended slowly over the scene.

Toward the back of the parking lot, she heard a tailgate slam, and then a figure moved down the steps to the boat dock. She drove slowly through the lot, steering her car into an empty space a few feet away from Wayne's H2.

She peered through the misty lights surrounding the marina. Wayne was nowhere in sight. She gripped her purse, wondering if she should call Bob again. He should be here any minute.

Glancing over her shoulder at the empty highway, a wave of fear rolled over her when she spotted only an occasional passerby. She was on her own. Slowly, she opened her car door and got out, closing it quietly behind her. There was an eerie quiet to the night. No voices rang out from the walkway below; there was no music or laughter, so typical of nightlife at the marina.

She crept toward the Hummer and peered through the half-open windows. The muted outer lights lining the walkway shone dimly into the back of the truck. She could see a pair of duffle bags and a set of golf clubs. A briefcase lay at an angle on the passenger seat.

Footsteps sounded on the pavement, and she whirled to see Wayne approaching. He held a shaving kit in one hand and balanced an armload of clothes in the other. On top of the pile, she spotted a policeman's uniform, which puzzled her.

"What are you up to, Christy?" He reached her side and glared down at her.

Her heart rate had tripled, but she tried to keep her voice casual as she looked up at him, pretending not to notice the obvious anger riding his features.

"Hey, Wayne," she said, trying to push a smile onto her stiff lips. Suddenly all she could think about was how dangerous he was, and she instinctively began to back away. "Have you seen Dan? He's supposed to meet me here any minute."

He opened the back door of his Hummer and tossed his load carelessly inside. "Sure he is," Wayne growled, slamming the door. He leaned down, the features of his face hard and mean as he looked her in the eye. "You get your kicks off sneaking around playing detective, don't you?" His hand shot out and gripped her arm. His fingers bit into her skin. "This time you picked the wrong guy to jerk around."

The sound of a woman's laughter broke the tension, and Christy jumped. A couple walked up from the dock, arm in arm.

Wayne's grip tightened as he walked Christy around the front of his car toward the passenger seat. He withdrew something dark from his pants pocket, and a split second after she realized it was a gun, the barrel jabbed her in the ribs.

"Get in the front seat," he said in a low voice, underlined with anger. "If you open your mouth or try to get out of the car, you and that couple back there will get hurt."

Christy caught her breath, never once doubting him. She reached out and opened the car door, darting a glance toward the distant couple, who seemed unaware of anyone else in their world.

Wayne shoved her into the passenger seat, and the sharp edge of his briefcase bruised her backside. She stifled a moan as he yanked the briefcase from under her and thrust it onto the floorboard. The gun aimed steadily at her chest as he moved catlike in and out, pressing the lock on her door. The dark threat in his eyes pinned her against the seat. He covered the gun with his hand, jogged around the front of the Hummer, and opened the door on the driver's side. She felt the car sink beneath his weight.

She had experienced close calls in the past, filled with pain and fear. None equaled this.

32

Wayne inserted the key in the ignition, turning it with his left hand while his right hand aimed the gun at her.

She took a ragged breath, knowing she was trapped if Bob didn't show up. Then, as she gripped her purse, she felt the outline of the pepper spray tucked inside. She glanced at Wayne as he watched the couple crossing the lot to the convertible parked opposite them.

"I'll do what you say," she said, gently sliding the zipper back on her purse. "I know how dangerous you are."

"No." He gave her a glance, then looked back at the couple. "You *don't* know how dangerous I am, and you don't want to know. So just sit tight till these idiots get out of my way."

While he spoke, she worked the zipper all the way back on her purse. Covering one hand with the other, she reached inside for her only weapon. Could she spray him before he shot her? It didn't seem likely.

God, help me!

The plea became a mantra. Her hand locked onto the bottom of the spray just as the convertible's bright lights flashed straight into Wayne's face. Loud music erupted from the car where two heads huddled close. Wayne muttered a curse and turned on his headlights, shooting a bright beam back at the other car. The convertible swung into motion, and the young guy behind the wheel laughed as he swerved close to their fender, teasing them.

As Wayne turned to glare at the giggling couple, Christy knew this was her best chance. Maybe her only chance.

She pulled out the spray can as the convertible backed up and shot across the parking lot. Swiveling the top of the can, she aimed for Wayne's face just as he turned to look at her. The hot pepper spray shot through the air and nailed him in the eyes. He howled in pain.

Her hands flew to the door, unlocking it, shoving it open. Hard pavement smacked the side of her face and neck, and pain shot down her leg.

A *ping* echoed as a bullet struck metal somewhere along the dashboard. A hoarse shout and a spasm of coughing followed the gunshot.

Christy struggled to get to her knees, looking wildly around as the decorative lights along the boardwalk blurred and danced before her. She had inhaled enough spray to tighten her throat and affect her vision. She tried to crawl away from the truck, blinking, struggling to regain her balance.

Headlights blazed into the parking lot as Big Bob's SUV roared toward the Hummer and screeched to a halt.

"Bob, he's got a gun," she yelled.

"So do I," Bob's deep voice rumbled back as a door slammed. "Get out with your hands up, Crocker!"

Christy backed away from the truck, watching Bob yank the door open while Wayne coughed and struggled to wipe his eyes.

"Okay, Mr. Crocker," Bob yelled, pulling Wayne from the car. "We'll clean the pepper spray off when we get you to headquarters." He glanced at Christy. "Are you hurt?"

Christy leaned against the back of the SUV, trying to calm her nerves. "No. You got here just in time." She stared at Wayne, who lay spread-eagle across the hood of his truck while Bob searched him and read him his rights.

Wayne muttered something about a lawyer, and Bob snorted. "Yeah, you're gonna need one."

A patrol car zoomed across the parking lot, siren wailing. Christy smoothed her hair back from her face, trying to calm her nerves as two officers took control of Wayne.

Bob had holstered his weapon and walked over to envelop Christy in a bear hug. "Reckon I'm gonna have to deputize you after all."

"No." She shook her head. "No more detective work for me. I want a life with Dan, and this time I came too close to not having one."

She tilted her head back and looked up at a silver patchwork of stars. "Kirby, may you rest in peace now."

Sunday, December 3

Christmas decorations filled the home of R.J. and Julie Wentworth in Rosemary Beach, and an afternoon Christmas party was under way. The front door held a blue spruce wreath with tiny crystal angels and a white velvet bow. Christy glanced at the long plate-glass window beside the door, noting that the wreath mimicked the Christmas tree—a huge blue spruce decorated with more crystal angels, lots of crystal ornaments, and crystal icicles that glistened like water frozen in the act of motion. White lights twinkled everywhere.

The sound of laughter and music filled the air, and a mood of happiness seemed to float on the Gulf breeze. The Christmas season had officially begun the day before with the annual Christmas parade. Santa had come to town on a big red fire truck, and various floats followed, along with marching bands from the schools. As Deputy Arnold had promised, Zeffie had been the mascot for the Summer Breeze float. Everyone had a wonderful time, and the Wentworths had decided to continue the celebration at their home.

Activity swirled throughout the house. Out on the patio, despite a cool breeze, Willie was barbecuing ribs while teasing Miz B about which one of her pies tasted best. She responded with a wide smile. She wore a red dress sparkling with rhinestones, and her hairdo complimented an obviously happy face.

"I think you'd like my pecan pie," she said, peering at the sauce he was brushing onto the ribs. "I like to watch you barbecue," she added. "When can I get a tiny sample?"

Inside the kitchen, Vince, Ellen, and the boys were slicing freshly baked bread from everyone's favorite bakery. From the living room, the soft notes of a baby grand piano drifted through the house, mellow and inviting. Julie sat on the piano bench, her small fingers trailing over the piano keys.

"Go ahead," she said, smiling up at Bobbie, who stood beside the piano.

"Silver bells…" Bobbie's rich voice filled the room. R.J. and Jack stood by the piano, staring at the women they loved, completely absorbed by their music.

Behind the closed door of the study, Dan and Christy sat on a soft leather sofa beside Zeffie, who wore a red velvet dress with a lace collar. Her blond hair had been styled in soft waves about her face.

"How do you feel about R.J. being your father?" Christy asked gently, taking Zeffie's hand in hers.

"I'm *really* happy about it. I wanted him to be my father ever since we took that DNA test. And Julie is the best mom in the whole world."

Christy didn't mention the Carvers. She'd already been told they were happy for Zeffie and relieved she was going to a good home.

They had reluctantly admitted they felt a bit old to take on a child her age.

A knock sounded on the door, and Christy called, "Come in."

The two redheads, Luke and Parker, said, "Excuse me," in unison. Parker spoke up. "We were wondering if Zeffie'd like to come outside and kick the soccer ball around."

Zeffie jumped up, eager to play with her new friends. "Sure." She looked back at Christy and Dan. "You're staying for dinner, aren't you?"

"You bet," Dan answered.

Zeffie's green eyes lit up, and she raced out the door, closing it softly behind her.

"What a wonderful day," Christy said, snuggling against Dan.

"Yes, it's perfect." He reached down and tilted her chin back, looking directly into her eyes. "So what do you think?"

"About you going to Montana for six months?"

"About *us* going to Montana for six months. I realize your father will not allow this without a wedding, but we haven't exchanged Christmas presents yet, have we?"

She grinned at him. "No, we haven't."

"I know some people like to make a big deal about surprises in little velvet boxes," he said, "but I'm not comfortable with that. I'd like you to be in on selecting your ring."

"I'm so glad you said that. I'm not great with surprises either. And it will be so much fun if we pick out my ring together."

He pulled her close and kissed her, and she thought of something.

"I've always hoped for a spring wedding with lots of fresh flowers. There's such a nice feel to spring, full of hope and promise." She looked at Dan. "A great time to start a life together."

"That would be wonderful. We'll take a trip up to Montana over the Christmas holiday so you can see the area. Maybe we'll go snowmobiling." Dan smiled. "It's snowing there now."

"Mmm." Christy put her arms around his neck. "I love snow."

Acknowledgments

I wish to thank the following people for their advice and contributions to this novel:

Lori O'Callaghan at Junk Warehouse in Lake Barrington, Illinois. Her expertise in tools and their many uses inspire a novice like me. Thanks again to Carmie and Dianna at Unique Pieces Décor in Polson, Montana. Your demonstrations and advice have proved invaluable in this series. Thanks to Denise Upchurch for educating me in period furniture. Captain Dan Bates, Investigations, in the Panama City Police Department patiently explained the procedures involved in a professional investigation, particularly a cold case. Any mistakes in this area are mine. Finally, thanks to Judith Masters in Lynn Haven for keeping me updated on activities in and around the Florida panhandle when I wasn't there.

Thanks to Joyce Holland who is always willing to help other writers and does so graciously. A hug of appreciation to Sammie Barstow for opening her home and fantastic library to me, then utilizing her skill as a writer and editor to help me when I was stuck on a plot point. Thanks to Lori Barstow, author, for her input on two important scenes.

A tip of my red hat to the Frankly Scarlets in Seattle who hosted the best-ever high tea and to my wonderful friends in A Lotta Dazzling Divas, along with their leader and my great friend, Judy. Fond memories and a hug to my snowbird friends in Destin, with whom I shared good coffee and amazing friendships.

I'd be remiss not to thank my encouraging friends at Rocky Mountain Chapel. I'll always treasure the special book signings and inspirational gatherings.

Once again, I'm indebted to all the staff at WaterBrook, especially Shannon, Jessica, Judy, Ginia, Steve, Dudley, and Kristopher, who make writing and publishing a pleasure.

A huge thank-you to my readers and all who stock my books. Where would any writer be without you?

And many thanks to my family for your love and encouragement, and a big hug to Gus, the newest member of our family.

Last but certainly not least, I'd like to thank my husband Landon, who has provided suggestions, encouragement, and a steadfast love that has guided me through every writing project from day one. I could never have done it without you.

About the Author

I have been writing off and on for twenty-three years while raising a family and living in different parts of the United States. Writing is my passion, and nothing is more fun for me than stepping into a brand-new world, filling it with characters, and planning a life for these characters. I've written romances, historicals, romantic suspense, and mystery. The cozy mystery is, by far, my favorite, because this genre allows the reader to participate in solving the mystery.

My faith has been a fundamental part of my life, and I thank God for being richly blessed. One of the greatest blessings is the opportunity to write. I hope to show in my writing how God works in miraculous ways through the lives of the people. I want my stories to portray themes of hope and forgiveness through his love.

My husband and I have reached a point in our lives when we can now pursue the dream of spending our summers in the Colorado Rockies and our winters near the Florida seashore. I draw inspiration from both places. I love hearing from my readers, so please stop by my Web page, www.PeggyDarty.com.

Since my readers are my friends, I'll end this little note with a favorite Irish blessing: May the road rise to meet you, may the wind be always at your back, may the sun shine warm upon your face, may the rain fall soft upon your fields, and until we meet again, may the Lord hold you in the palm of his hand.

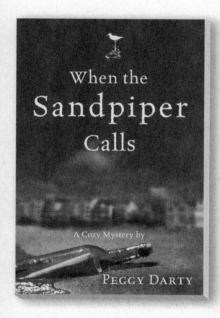
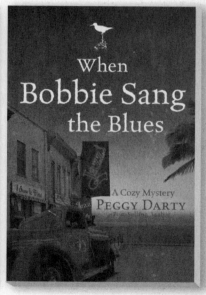